WHERE THE RIVER RUNS

RICHARD S. WHEELER

AN AUTHORS GUILD BACKINPRINT.COM EDITION

Where the River Runs

AN AUTHORS GUILD BACKINPRINT.COM EDITION

Published by iUniverse, Inc.

For information address:

iUniverse, Inc.

2021 Pine Lake Road, Suite 100

Lincoln, NE 68512

www.iuniverse.com

Originally published by M. Evans

ISBN: 0-595-32888-1

Printed in the United States of America

For Lenore Carroll

Chapter One

His nose had stopped hurting, and that was always the danger sign. He touched a leather mitten to it and felt nothing; inside the doubled mittens, his fingers also felt nothing. He thought of Weasel Tail's camp, and the warmth of a lodge fire, and pressed on. A half hour of lavender daylight remained. If he didn't hit the Marias River and the Piegan camp before dark, he faced another bitter winter night.

Every winter in the mountains, Jean Gallant regretted that he was so thin. If only he had a little lard to fend off the brutal cold, a little padding. But God had fashioned him as thin as a toothpick, so that his ribs hung like washboards down his chest and his waist pinched narrower than a girl's.

Each winter Jean Gallant also regretted that he lacked hair, good thick black hair to temper the icy winds and trap warmth around his skinny chest and skull. Now cold air probed up under his beaver-pelt hat, making him ice-brained. In the summers he enjoyed being bald. He fancied

1

that it was a sign of virility, a thing to give the ladies. He jammed the beaver-pelt hat down over his skull, hoping the forlorn remnants of black hair over his ears would trap the eddying air, so his addled brain might warm. He punched and rubbed his nose, feeling nothing. He owned a fine sharp narrow nose, as keen as a Green River knife, set between saturnine brown eyes that he considered soulful.

He felt frozen into his saddle and wondered if he should dismount and stomp his moccasins. But he feared he could not clamber up again, so he kicked them out of the stirrups and pumped them out and down and up, pumped life into limbs and toes he no longer felt. The pony took it for a signal to stop, and Jean Gallant kicked the dun mustang furiously.

It was only midafternoon by the tick of clocks, but already the light failed, from slate gray to lavender to indigo. At least the winter had been open so far, and the frozen dun bunchgrass could feed his pony and packhorse. His practiced eye surveyed the desolate sweep of open prairie, naked of even the slightest shelter. He wouldn't make the village tonight; Weasel Tail would do without esteemed company. But unless he found shelter soon, the whole world might do without his company, evermore.

Ah, the pain of it! Give Jean Gallant a mad errand and he'd set out like a baying hound, for the sheer novelty of it. He bayed at the bitter dusk and heard a wolf baying back, sad songs, when the mercury hung far below what that lunatic Swiss Fahrenheit thought was absolute zero. Mad Jean Gallant bayed into the bitter northwind and kicked his pony to the right, to the east. The icy fingers crept under his four-point blanket capote from a new angle. He'd freeze tenderloin for a while instead of nose and chest.

There remained in Jean Gallant's bag of tricks the ultimate weapon. Twice it had saved his life, and now he would call upon it once again, as any worldly man must. It would not be quite as successful this time, because he had no wife in Weasel Tail's village, but no matter. Maybe Weasel Tail would lend him one. Jean Gallant had married, actually, more wives than he knew what to do with. Not all at once, of course, but over the years. His main one, Owl Song Woman, waited comfortably in the warmth of Fort Union, near the confluence of the Missouri and the Yellowstone. But he would not think of her. This mortal danger required someone younger, more voluptuous, crazy as a loon in the robes.

But there were so many! He could scarcely choose among them. In the village of Running Fox he had tall, lusty Civet Musk, who was Running Fox's own daughter. He thought of Civet Musk for a little, Civet Musk awaiting him in a warm lodge, awaiting him eagerly under the heavy buffalo robes. He had given two flintlocks for her and had enjoyed her for a month, until he grew annoyed because she whinnied like a mare. He promised her he would return. Her image started his cold heart thumping a bit, and that felt good. A faint warmth spread through him. But then his thoughts turned to mad, abandoned Maria Two Moccasins, half French herself but living with her mother in Bull Medicine Shield's band of Piegans, somewhere around the Teton River.

The thought of her sent a stab of warmth through his numb body. Maria Two Moccasins Gallant! He had brought the bride price last summer: three horses, ten twists of tobacco, an old Nor'Wester fusil, powder and ball. Ah, *mon Dieu!* What nights! Mad, insatiable, laughing and weeping, golden and silky. There was a memory to save his life! Jean Gallant forced the brutal cold out of his mind, forced his vision to peer inward, into the vaults of memory, inward upon the golden flesh of his new bride, Maria Two Moccasins. And soon enough his heart pumped and a new heat, generated from deep within Jean Gallant's loins, radiated outward into his numb limbs, giving life and painful, tingling sensation to flesh gone dead.

Thus he occupied himself for a quarter of an hour, and just as slate gray slid toward black, he steered his ponies into a sheltered creek bottom thick with naked cottonwood, black brush, and an overhanging cliff of stratified dun sandstone. The image of the naked Maria in his arms had saved him, just as the images of Beaded Quiver Woman of the Crows and the gorgeous Fawn Antelope of the Gros Ventres had rescued him in winters past.

Firewood here, and the calm protected air he would need to kindle it. Ah, these mad errands! But what would life be without risk? He slid lamely off the shaggy amber pony and fell in a heap. Apparently his thoughts of Maria Two Moccasins had not yet penetrated to his calves and ankles. Either that, or Maria was not as exciting as he remembered.

He stumbled to his feet and made his legs work, dancing up and down and around until his toes prickled, his breath forming clouds in the icy air. Warmth wouldn't come, but pain did, biting at him viciously. A wolf howled, and Jean Gallant howled back. He would not be outdone by a mere wolf. His pony snorted and tugged back upon the reins.

Shaking, Jean Gallant gathered dry snapping sticks in the lingering light, just a few for the moment. He could not delay kindling a fire. From a small leather sack at his side he withdrew his striker and flint and plucked up a tiny ball of cottony tinder. He could not feel the instruments of salvation in his hands, but his eyes told him he was holding them. In the lee of the cliff, he dashed sparks into the tinder until it smouldered. He blew softly into it, until finally it flared. Swiftly he built a pyramid of tiny twigs, bits and pieces of wood. It burned unsteadily but gave no heat. He needed heat, desperately now. He was beyond the help of visions of Maria and needed fire. But the smothering cold air curbed the tiny flame, baffled it, almost blew it out, until finally it gusted into a true blaze, and some faint warmth reached his numb hands.

An hour later Jean Gallant, the American Fur Company's legendary scout, diplomat of the prairies and veteran man of the mountains, felt almost warm. A hot fierce fire, as hot and fierce as Maria Two Moccasins herself, warmed him from two sides, radiating off the sandstone wall behind him. It offered comfort, and heaven knew Jean Gallant liked his comforts. He rubbed his nose ruefully, aware of sharp pain throbbing through it, and his ears, fingers, and toes. The warmth of Jean Gallant's loins had not spread far enough to save him from frostbite.

Ah, he thought. My life is the triumph of bigamy over wilderness! Bigamy has rescued me again! I have more wives than those peculiar Mormon Yankees who have flowed to the Great Salt Lake these past two years. I am American Fur's diplomat by marriage! Wherever a village roams, there is my wife! If I lack a wife in any village, that's an oversight to be corrected. I'm related by wedlock to every tribe on the plains. Who among their warriors would attack a relative? I have wives I can't remember! I've married into two bands of Piegans, one band of Bloods, three of the Assiniboin, one of the Gros Ventres, the River and Mountain Crows, one band of Bannocks, one of Flathead, one of Pend d'Oreille, two bands of Snakes, Hunkpapa and Sans Arc Sioux, and have ladies among the Arapaho and Northern Cheyenne, thought I haven't heard from them in years and can't remember their names.

Some accomplishment, he thought. Heroic wedlock. For American Fur, he'd do anything, even cement alliances by marriage. Keeping all his lovelies happy had been another matter, though. It made him tired, trying to remember them all. Once in a while it had been a source of vast embarrassment—uncounted children, forgotten *amours*, jealous darlings, angry fathers, mad chiefs and always payments: rifles, powder, ball, blankets, kettles. But American Fur didn't mind. What other engagé had made himself welcome in every band of every tribe? What other engagé could the great fur company send anywhere, on any delicate or difficult mission, such as this one? Let him ride into any village and some half forgotten bride would welcome him joyously and prepare him a great feast. From there it was but a simple step for the likes of Jean Gallant to treat with chiefs and headmen, form alliances, set warriors upon enemies, and foster buffalo robe trade with the company.

Warmed at last, he pulled the packs off his restless ponies, set them to cropping in the sheltered brush, pulled heaps of dry wood out of the bitter night, and boiled up some parched corn.

Today he'd stared death in the face and won. Maybe some day he wouldn't win. Forty years had he survived in these wilds; maybe his forty-first would never come. Maybe next time images of delightful young brides might not warm him. A man grew old . . . A man deserved to pick and choose among the requests that came to him. He made the sign of the cross and tackled his gruel.

He found Weasel Tail's village the next day, when the pale sun had risen its highest in the distant southern sky. The band was wintering on a crescent-shaped flat on the north bank of the Marias, sheltered by steep bluffs. Abundant firewood, cottonwood bark for the ponies, shelter from wind, ever-flowing water under the ice of the river. He eased his rawboned pony out onto the ice, which looked as thick as rock. But the pony wouldn't budge until Jean put the switch to the animal, and then it minced delicately across the creaking cap. On the far shore only two blanketed Piegans watched, so shrouded by hoods and skins and high, thick, fur-lined moccasins that he could not even tell their sex, which was always regrettable. From each lodge a plume of blue smoke drifted southward over the river. The black cottonwoods to either side seemed alive with life, and he realized the village herd roamed through the brush, gnawing twigs and bark and stray gray grasses. No village guards or town crier greeted him. Not on a day beyond the imagination of that mad Fahrenheit. Leave it to the Swiss to bungle the mercury, he thought. Zero—the absolute, the ultimate, the negation of all heat—should be fifty degrees lower. Any French Canadian could have told him that.

He would warm with Weasel Tail. He turned the cadaverous pony toward the largest lodge with the smoke-stained flaps and peak and the lemon yellow medicine weasels painted gaudily around its circumference, the work of a warm summer's day. Now at last a few heads peered from door flaps, and vanished back into the warmth within. Such a lazy people, he thought. They could all be massacred by the fierce Assiniboin or the crafty Crow. But they had sealed themselves in their lodges, doing the only thing that northern Plains Indians could do all winter. In nine months there would be lots of little new Piegans. He dismounted, and his legs failed him again. He hadn't realized that they'd gone lifeless on him. The earth was frozen hard as a skillet, and he banged his cold shoulder. While he thus floundered upon the bitter ground the flap parted an inch and an elderly squaw peered out.

He could speak their tongue fluently; he knew all the tongues, learning them in the buffalo robes of his wives, word by word. Some words he learned eagerly and practiced regularly, while some interested him little.

"I've come from American Fur Company and have urgent business with Weasel Tail," he said. The flap snapped shut and then opened. The squaw nodded, and he clambered into the lodge, smacked by heat and darkness as he fumbled to close the cover behind him.

Weasel Tail stood in the place of honor, directly back of the fire pit. The old man was bundled in fur-decked skins and wore a blanket capote, for not even a lodge like this, with its high inner lining pinned down by rocks around the perimeter, kept out all the bone-numbing cold of December. Beside him stood his sits-beside-him squaw, equally old. Each of them had woven their gray hair into two braids. Lying on thick buffalo robe couches to either side were his other wives, young and succulent, bedecked with furs. Jean Gallant eyed them with professional interest.

"Welcome to my lodge," said Weasel Tail, reaching for the medicine calumet that hung from a lodgepole in a soft skin sheath. "What brings my friend Gallant to our village on a day when the Cold Maker roars? We will have the smoke now, and then you will tell me."

At the beckoning of the leathery and seamed chief, Gallant settled himself in the place of honored guests and opened his capote to the radiance of the small hot fire. His fine beak of a nose pained him again. Deliberately, for this was winter and any diversion was stretched to its limits, Weasel Tail tamped tobacco into the bowl and lit it with a brand from the fire, sucking slowly, filling the lodge with the acrid fragrance. Then at last he turned solemn, saluted the cardinal directions, the Earth Mother and Napi, One Above, as well as Sun. He began to hand the pipe to Jean, but a scratching on the door flap waylaid him. Moments later the war chief and headman Pretty Fox settled beside the chief, invited to counsel with the scout. When the ritual was at last done and the chief had tapped the dottle into the fire pit, the powerful Blackfeet readied themselves to listen to the best scout working for American Fur Company.

Jean Gallant sighed, feeling the prickle of life deep within his moccasins at last. This winter's errand had not originated with the company or the great Chouteau family of St. Louis, or even the *bourgeois* Alec Culbertson down at Fort Benton. No, he'd come in behalf of the soldiers of the United States. Toward these blue-coated English-speaking gentlemen he felt no allegiance at all; neither did he feel the slightest allegiance to the red-coated English-speakers north of the invisible line. The latter had stolen French Canada; the former had just finished stealing Oregon from the British, and Mexican possessions south and west, calling it Manifest Destiny. Jean concluded from all this that he had been destined into the republic, but he would never permit the republic to destine him. And there it had stood, until the company sent him here.

He felt enormously hungry now that he'd baked his frontal half, but that could wait. "I am sent not by American Fur, exactly, but by the Americans, the blue-coated army."

Talk of armies, any army, caught their attention always. They listened patiently.

"Last spring, in what they call the year eighteen forty-nine," he began, "the American fathers sent a peace commission up here to befriend the northern tribes, discover their wishes, bring gifts, and begin talks to give each tribe a home so that wars might end. These ambassadors from Washington City . . . three of them in all, were joined at a place far down the Big River called Fort Leavenworth by a few soldiers. Two ambassadors and their clerk—one who made the records—one captain, or subchief of the army, a guide and translator, and the rest blue-coated men. Twelve in all.

"These twelve, laden with good gifts for the Piegans, Bloods, Blackfeet . . . and other tribes, left the white men's fort when the grass turned green and the river ran high with ice floes. They took the American Fur Company steamboat, the *Wyandotte,* up the long river to Fort Union, where you have been many times. There they unloaded their horses and supplies and rode to Fort Benton, to the trading post of the one we all know, Alec Culbertson. That happened in the moon they call June, when the summer was young and the air filled with the scents of flowers, and all the maidens of the tribes hunted for husbands."

Weasel-Tail nodded solemnly. Jean Gallant pulled his thawed legs back from the corona of the fire.

"On the eleventh day of July, as the whites reckon it, this small party of soldiers and ambassadors to your tribes rode out from Alec Culbertson's post on the Big River and were never seen again."

"Ah!" exclaimed Weasel Tail. "Were they killed in war?"

"No one knows. They rode out: the commissioners, the officer, the guide, the soldiers, the pack train. They would treat with the Blackfeet confederation first, they told Monsieur Culbertson. Then the Gros Ventres. Then Flatheads, Pend d'Oreilles, Assiniboin, the northernmost Sioux. The next moon passed, and the two after that, and no one heard from them. No runners from them arrived at the fur company posts. They were to return to Fort Union in September and go down river in a keelboat. But at Fort Union we waited in vain. In the moon of falling leaves, my company sent messages down the Missouri by boat and horse. Grim news. No one had returned. The ambassadors from the great chief of the Americans had vanished without a trace!"

"There is a story!" muttered Weasel Tail. "These white men missing, and they must think we have killed them. Are you telling us war has come?"

"No. No one of the whites blames you. No one knows. From Fort Leavenworth runners were sent back up the great river bringing messages to the fur company: please send out searchers to the villages, even in the middle of winter. Send your best men. Send out engagés such as"—he smiled—"Jean Gallant. So the *bourgeois* called me out of my winter bed, away from the warmth of my beloved wife, and asked if I would go from village to village, seeking news—any news. Life, death.

Accident. Captivity. News of the American treaty makers and soldiers."

"And so you have braved the anger of the Cold Maker and have come," said Weasel Tail. "We know of no such party. No word ever came to us of these white men. If we had found them in distress, we would have helped. They came peaceably, and with good gifts."

Pretty Fox nodded solemnly.

Gallant waited patiently, gauging the moment. "I would like to ask the headmen and warriors," he said. "Can it be arranged?"

Weasel Tail responded sharply. "Every man here is bound to tell me of such things if they know of them. My word to you is that no one in the village has heard of this."

"Ah, Chief Weasel Tail, I don't question your word," replied Gallant hastily. "I only wish to find some last scrap of news, the bit of gossip that eluded your ears."

"We are one hundred and ten lodges," the chief replied shortly. "And in this weather I will not ask them all into the bitter air."

"Perhaps you might send village criers from lodge to lodge. Then any Piegan with news might come here."

"I will think about it," replied the chief with an edge to his voice. "I will think what this may mean when spring comes and armies march. I will counsel with my headmen. I will ask the medicine men."

Gallant sat patiently, wishing for a chinook. With warmer air, he might address the whole village at once—and keep a sharp eye peeled for blue woolen tunics.

The ancient chief smiled suddenly, crinkling webbed flesh. "My wives prepare a broth of buffalo back fat and roots, and soon we shall eat," he said. "When the sun rises again, we shall see."

"You have the most beautiful wives of any chief," said Jean Gallant. "I enjoy looking at such ravishing beauty."

Chapter Two

She remembered how he had proposed to her that Sunday in March, which had broken warm and stayed warm all day before winter closed down again.

"Miss St. George," he said, "it is a day for a buggy ride."

"Captain Owen," she replied, her gaze raking him and the buggy and trotter, "I accept. I will tell my father."

She had bundled herself in azure wool, afraid the weather might turn, and for good measure he tucked a buffalo robe about her, and they drove out upon a rolling prairie of dun winter-quiet grass, the jingles on the gray trotter's harness the only noise in a vast empty sea.

"You rescued me, Jed. Sabbath afternoons are too quiet, and I grow weary."

"This will not be a dull afternoon," he said, flashing a quick smile. "Today we'll put aside the cold."

Well west of Fort Leavenworth, where the umber prairie stretched limitlessly toward the wilds of an unexplored land, he tugged gently on the reins and the mare halted, steaming slightly in the brass sun.

Before he stopped, she knew. Intuitively she knew.

He did not waste words. "I love you, Susannah."

She smiled, and their eyes locked. His were gray and as distant as the horizons, hers a soft brown, very like the fine hair coiled into a bun at the nape of her neck. He saw things distant; she saw things close.

"I love you, Jed Owen," she replied softly, catching the firmness of his jaw and enjoying the feel of his big gloved hand in her own. She knew what she would say when he asked. But here he faltered a bit and couldn't bring himself easily to the question. So she thought to help him.

"Love is a bond that grows, I think. It changes and becomes many things over time. But especially friendship," she said.

"I was thinking the same thing," he replied hoarsely. "Yes, I was thinking how it endures."

She chuckled. Jed Owen was having a time of it. She thought to help him further. "Ask what you will, and I'll say yes."

He grinned. "Am I an idiot?"

"Yes!"

Merriment seeped from him. "Are you frivolous?"

"Yes!"

"Will you marry me and be my lover forever?"

"Yes. Oh, Jed, *yes.*"

They turned silent, suddenly shy. Gravely he kissed her, and the taste of his lips on hers felt new and right. He held her closer and her heart tripped. She wanted the unfathomed things, the unexperienced things, and she slipped her hands up upon his head and held it, ruffling his coarse hair.

"Soon," he said with a great severity in his face.

She teased. "Not now?"

He said nothing but drew her tightly until her breasts pressed against his hard chest, through their thick coats. She knew he'd reached a line and would not cross it, and felt glad. She had chosen him for this very thing. In Jedediah Owen, Captain United States Army, lay something stainless and strong that separated him from the many men she'd known while growing up in military camps. West Point had molded him, but it wasn't West Point that had attracted her. The Mexican War had seasoned him in his long march with Stephen Watts Kearny and Alexander Doniphan, but it wasn't his genius or courage in battle that had touched her soul.

The other thing, the thing so rare in men of arms—and, she supposed, civilians as well—had drawn her to the strong rough man to whom she'd said yes. She had no words for it, so she called it honor. He did not pay lip service to ideals but tried always to live by the things he cared about. One of those things was not staining her virtue, and now she hugged him, knowing how this joyous moment would end. In his arms, she giggled softly.

"What?" he asked gently.

"I am wishing for something and glad that you refuse."

He laughed affectionately. Whenever she said something direct, saucy and bold, his face lit up and his gentle gray eyes turned from vast horizons to her own soft brown ones.

"I'm all army and half lady," she said to make her point. "Thank God, only half!" With her gloved hand, she brushed bunched hair away from his forehead.

He released her, and immediately she felt separated and alone. The experience of being held, of holding, had touched some tender point within her. Would that be marriage, holding and becoming one, joined in soul as well as flesh, only to endure long separations, feeling halved by life, halved again by the eternal army?

"I've received orders," he said abruptly in a voice curiously different.

She waited, pressing her hands snugly into his.

"I am to command a treaty and exploring party. Two Indian commissioners from Washington City, an interpreter or two, scouts who know the country, and several dragoons I'm to pick."

He was saying the army would take him away for a while, she knew. Any woman of the corps knew. Her mother knew, and now she knew.

"Where, Jed? How long?"

"To the far northwest. Up the Missouri to its headwaters at the three forks. President Taylor chose me personally. He remembered me from the war. My first full command! What an honor, Susannah! We're to treat with the Blackfeet, Crow, Flatheads, Gros Ventre, and if possible, the Sioux. Leaving on the American Fur Company steamer when the river's up enough, coming down in the fall, by keelboat supplied us by the fur company."

"That's longer than I can bear."

"Will you wait for me?"

"I would wait forever for you, Jed Owen."

Not knowing seemed worse than knowing. When the leaves fell from the elms she watched the river, watched the silent chocolate stream flowing quietly past her moist window. When frost formed on puddles and on the birdbath, she knew he had been delayed. Still she watched. She arranged her chores so that she might watch. She darned Nathan St. George's black hose before the window, her soft eye upon the silver curve of the river, scarcely attending to the stocking pulled over her darning egg. She had two skeins of yarn sent from St. Louis and knit blue mittens to match Jed's blue tunic, and a white scarf, a warm scarf, for her captain of dragoons. Then she ran out of yarn.

That's the lot of the army's women, she told herself. Born to wait. And worry, too. The Blackfeet tribes were extremely dangerous, she remembered. But so were the others. How many trappers in the beaver days had lost their lives to the Blackfeet?

"Remember this when I'm gone," he had said at the levee. "I'll be upon this great river. Even when we visit the farthest tribes, I'll be near the headwaters of the Missouri. The water that will flow past you has first flowed past me. Where the river runs, there will I be, my darling."

The days grew short and the nights harsh, and she watched the autumn gray river flow silently by. On November 30 a mackinaw from upriver docked, bearing bales of buffalo robes and news. The treaty party had not returned, wrote Culbertson, the man in charge of upper river operations. The American Fur Company would begin inquiries. News usually drifted from tribe to tribe. And more: the American Fur Company had dispatched its best man, Jean Gallant, to inquire from band to band, village to village, braving the northern winter.

The message had been sent to Patrick McGonigle, commanding officer, who called in Colonel Nathan St. George, quartermaster for the western command, and read him the brief report. A few minutes later Colonel St. George stepped into numbing damp air beneath a chalky sky, angled across the parade to Officers Row, found Susannah at her window, where she spun away her days now, and told her as gently as he could.

Vanished.

Quietly she set down *Mansfield Park* without placing a bookmark where she had stopped. Below her window rough bearded men in fringed buckskins and blue blanket capotes poled the mackinaw out into the wind-frothed current, and the messengers from the high country disappeared down the gray belly of the river. That night ice formed along its banks, and only the greasy gray main channel remained open.

She wrapped Jed's scarf and mittens in scarlet paper she had carefully saved from last Christmas, freshly pressed, and added the bundle to the growing mound of Christmas gifts on the waxed sideboard. She fashioned an Advent wreath from emerald holly and lit one of its four candles. She carried baskets of sugar cookies to Suds Row, where the laundress wives of corporals Donegal and Hoch, the two married men with Jed, received her uncomfortably. She entertained at tea, baked Christmas scones, contributed pies and preserves to the enlisted men's ball in the mess, and never looked at the ice-clad river.

Nathan St. George fretted about his silent, taut, tall youngest child Susannah. Too much sentiment burned in that fragile vessel. The casual observer might have found her poised and serene, but his practiced eye spotted the torsion of doubt that slowly twisted her soul.

Years earlier he'd offered her a life in the east: finishing school, living with her mother in the Shenandoah Valley, whatever she wanted. Fort Leavenworth seemed a poor place for a motherless young woman to blossom, her brothers grown and gone, her father buried in the thing he loved: supply, logistics, purchases; two tons of flour in hundred-pound cotton bags at Laramie on the seventeenth instant, twelve gross of canvas gloves, medium.

She'd refused. The rough life appealed to her, she said. Not to mention the privileges of the stable and the fun of being a belle where women were scarce. Besides, she added, who would care for him?

That touched upon the very point that troubled Nathan St. George. The last thing he desired for himself or her was to shape her into a dutiful, dull daughter whiling her bright young life away, caring for her father, a surrogate for the woman who couldn't bear the frontier. Belle had vacationed for longer and longer periods at her family's tobacco plantation near Norfolk, until she no longer came back. Nathan had a comfortable purse. He could well afford a batman or servants and any sort of bachelor quarters he might choose. But Susannah had smiled and stayed and made a life. He in turn, being a man who saw beyond his own needs, encouraged each of her beaux, rejoicing when his favorite of all, rough, fusty, dark Jed Owen, won the race.

The young man kindled admiration in Colonel St. George. Those things Owen learned at West Point, duty, honor, country, had become something larger in him. Nathan St. George had spent a decade wrestling with mountebanks, crooked suppliers who filled the bottom half of flour bags with clay, sold the army wormy beef, and slipped galled horses with dyed hair to the Remount Service.

"Susannah," he said on Christmas Eve. "Let's talk about Jed."

"I'd like that," she replied. "Perhaps we can conjure him here."

She'd dressed for the evening in a green sateen party gown with an ivory cameo at her throat. Her brown hair, fine as mist and red-tinted by lantern light, glowed softly, matching the softness of her lustrous brown eyes. She was uncommonly attractive, he thought proudly. Not exactly a beauty, but tall and well shaped and stamped with the long face of his own Virginia people. He'd dressed too, in new-blacked boots and brushed blues with epaulets of gold cord.

"We're a handsome pair!" he exclaimed.

She smiled, and he felt he'd gotten off on the wrong track, after bringing up Jed.

"You've never come asking. I'd expected you to ask. Please send out rescue parties. Send word to Laramie. Send a force into the winter out there."

"The army did what it could. Any officer's daughter would know that. Any post laundress would know it too."

"But you might have begged me, just for the record."

She smiled softly again. "You'd have told me that Jed is three or four hundred miles from any post. That if he's well and safe, he'll return; if not . . ." Her composure cracked the fleetest moment, and Colonel St. George caught it, and his heart melted for this brave daughter who, like her mother, was doomed to wait.

"Have you considered the—the 'if not,' Susannah?"

"No. Not seriously. That'd be faithless. Admitting defeat before any news. No, Colonel, he's trapped up the Missouri somewhere."

Usually she called him Pops. She'd turned military on him. "You're right, General," he replied.

A faint grin caught the corners of her wide mouth. "Jed wouldn't come in the winter, I think. He has men to care for. He'll come in spring, when there's pasture for horses and his privates and civilians can travel without catching the ague or pneumonia. I'll see him in the spring." She eyed her father intently. "In fact, I'm going up to meet him."

It took Nathan St. George a moment to register that. "But, how—"

"You and I'll be on the American Fur steamer next May, Colonel St. George. You as my chaperone; I as a lady in distress. Do you suppose there's a minister at that fur company post where the boat goes?"

She was teasing, he thought. "Not likely, Susannah. And I don't suppose a fur company steamer is a place for a lady."

"Neither is an army post," she retorted.

"You have me there, General," he replied. "But no. I can't permit it. It's unthinkable, and what's more, it won't really hasten the day when Jed returns. What if he comes back overland, via Fort Laramie and the California Trail?"

Her face softened in the amber lamplight. "Because he said he'd follow the river, he'd always be upon the river, or its tributaries. Because he said the waters that pass here would pass by him first."

"Pretty romantic, I'd say."

"Jed Owen is somewhere upon our river, Colonel St. George. So I thought to meet him upon it in the spring. Ship captains can marry. Let the river captain mumble the words, and you shall give me away. I know what I want, Colonel!"

"So you do, General, so you do. What's a liberal father to make of it?"

"A leave. You haven't taken one since . . ."

"Since your mother left," he replied quietly.

"Yes. A leave, and passage on the boat. On the *Wyandotte* or whatever. Cabins for two."

"Grub's rough on a fur boat. Mostly game they shoot on the banks, Susannah."

"I'm a child of the army."

"Have me there, General." He sighed. "I don't like this, though a boat trip seems safe enough—give or take a few hostiles on the banks, barbarous passengers, the boiler blowing, cholera morbus, snags, and the chance of ramming a herd of swimming buffalo. Not a good idea."

"Think on it. I'd like two passages for Christmas, Pops."

"Might be that McGonigle will send a search party on that boat. Washington City's pushing hard. They're upset. Two high muckety-mucks haven't been heard from. Commissioners, rough and Ready's appointees. Important men. It's not the soldiers' hides or Jed's they're howling about—army hides and scalps don't count, not even in Zach Taylor's administration. Yes, I'd bet my britches, there'll be a command on that steamer, maybe a dragoon company and horses."

"All the safer for me."

He eyed her sharply. "In some ways, Susannah, you've been lucky."

"I'm a colonel's daughter, but when it comes to living out my own life, I outrank you."

"Let's go caroling," he said hastily. "Warm enough night, and I hear them singing down along the row. And then chapel at midnight."

Fresh wet snow whitened the post, reflecting yellow light from glowing frosted windows. They stood quietly through tattoo. Then Susannah smiled at her father and turned down the wicks.

In March, one year after Jed Owen proposed holy matrimony, the river ice cleaved away from the banks, groaning and cannoning all day, and the wide Missouri shimmered blue from shore to shore. On that day, Susannah resumed her seat at the window, resumed reading *Mansfield Park*, and did every chore she could, even peeling potatoes, right there where she'd be the first to see the low prow of a rough mackinaw round the distant bend, or the wide curve of a keelboat from the high country.

Colonel St. George watched her uneasily, his restless mind spilling out love, admiration, pity, tenderness, trepidation, fear she'd do something rash, hope that she'd turn to some other beau if worse came to worse, dread of death upon her . . . She occupied his thoughts even more than five thousand infantry boots, twenty cast iron twelve-pounders from the Memphis foundries, one thousand model 1841 Harpers Ferry muskets, one hundred spare percussion locks, one hundred spare ramrods, and twenty tons of grass hay free of mold.

He knew the set of Susannah's stubborn jaw, and wondered what spring would bring.

Chapter Three

Scurvy. Jed Owen tasted the blood that leaked steadily from his gums to stain his parched lips and throat. Every tooth in his jaws wobbled loose in its socket. Blood caked brownly around his nose too, where red drops of it oozed out of his flesh with every sniff and breath. It seeped from under his fingernails and toenails, as if his whole body could no longer contain it.

He lay hollow-eyed, staring at the battered brown lodge cover wobbling above him, unable to focus on anything. He tried to lift his head and couldn't: no muscle responded. He felt cold and wanted to draw the ancient, vermin-ridden buffalo robe over him but lacked the energy for it. Not the fiercest willing of his young muscles yielded anything but feeble jerks.

Not long, he thought. Not long and he'd be the last one. He desperately wanted water, merely water, but no one came to give it to him. Scurvy, terror of the sailor, murdering a soldier in some unknown place. In 1841 he had listened to a wise, bluff, bearded colonel, a military historian, actually, lecturing upon it at West Point. His topic had been the health of armies, and he began with a summary of battles lost because of disease—cholera, scurvy, other disorders that he mentioned primly and with a ruddy blush creeping up his cheeks. Armies lost without a shot fired, for want of sanitation, clean camps, good water. That single lecture turned out to be all that West Point offered cadets on the subject of disease.

Jed Owen tried to remember what the man had said about scurvy. A problem of diet. The royal navy had conquered it with limes half a century earlier, taking some of the terror out of the seas. Sauerkraut had worked too. Potatoes. Cabbages. Tomatoes. Greens might help. Something in buffalo, too. Mountain men had lived long periods on buffalo alone without contracting scurvy. Especially those who devoured the liver.

Bitter air eddied into the lodge, reminding him that greens had long sinced vanished under layers of snow. Roots, then? If not potatoes, then some other kind? The camas root these people ate? He sighed, slipping back into the white haze that had enveloped him for a long time, just how long he didn't know. He drifted through the day—he knew it was day—until the woman came and stared down at him. He grew aware of her black eyes upon him, eyes as cold as his numb body. He'd be a sight, he knew: filthy black beard with lice crawling in it, gray eyes sunk in black hollows, flesh caked with dirt and dried blood. Body wastes caking his legs, rank and foul.

She had a moon face, all mashed in, wide nose jammed hard against massive cheekbones. Kootenai. He knew that much. A small tribe he'd never heard of before, fierce, vicious, enemies of everyone except the Flatheads. He'd learned that from Gabriel Charbonneau before the halfbreed died. The halfbreed son of the ancient interpreter for Lewis and Clark knew these endless prairies and mountain ranges, and all the dwellers upon them, better than anyone, better than any of the mountain men. He'd told that much to Jed before he died. When was that? A week, a month, a season ago? Jed couldn't remember. He and Gabriel had been the last.

Above him, the plain young woman stared, not the faintest expression illumining her blank face. Susannah, he thought. Oh, Susannah, if only it were you, not this ugly moon-faced creature who poured water into him and spooned some broth of boiled dog down him sometimes. He had no way of talking with her. When Gabriel died, the finger talk died too. Jed sighed. He couldn't even rise enough to draw stick pictures with charcoal, or point at what he wanted. The dour woman tugged the grimy robe off Jed, and he felt a new iciness insult his cold, pale flesh. She stared acidly at the length of him, but he felt too weak to care about it. Oh, God, how many more hours? Soon! Jed had, in his lucid moments, made his peace with God and surrendered his soul to whatever lay beyond. A world as sweet as the bosom of his Susannah, he prayed.

Before Gabriel Charbonneau died, he mumbled one last thing: these people didn't know what to do with their prisoners. Jed might be left to die; might be ritually tortured: might be nursed back to health by tribal healers and shamans. Kootenai hated the outside world, despised whites, defended themselves and their small valley by guarding the passes, and ventured out upon the plains only to kill the sacred buffalo. From the surrounding cobalt and black mountains they killed and tanned enough elk and deer to trade for white men's things at Rocky Mountain House, the Hudson's Bay Company post far north, on the upper Saskatchewan River.

So they still didn't know what to do with him, Jed thought. Too late. Death stalked him now, and he could measure his life in hours. Death had stalked all of them from the time they left Fort Benton, with the fur trader Alec Culbertson waving good-bye from his incomplete adobe fort on the Missouri. A bitter gust of icy air goose-pimpled his flesh, flapped the lodge cover angrily, and Jed pleaded with his eyes for cover. But she didn't cover him.

A small heatless fire wavered. Smoke gusted into the decrepit lodge, slow to whirl up to the hole on top. The flaps had been set wrong, and vicious blasts of wintry air plunged downward, driven by the channeling wind flaps. She had a small clay pot heating on the fire. From a bowl of water she spooned out some hard brown buds that had been ripped from some shrub. They looked like something from which a flower might blossom in the spring, he thought. After she had poured a handful of the soaked buds into a dish of hollowed stone, she mashed them with a bone tool, grinding steadily until they had been reduced to a pulp. This material she dumped into an earthen cup, adding warm water from the fire.

Now at last she smiled faintly and lifted his head with one rough hand, holding the mixture she had concocted to his lips with the other. He drank greedily, feeling the warmth and the bitterness of whatever plant buds she had ground up. It couldn't hurt, he thought, not when he breathed his last. He would die, of course, in this mountain-locked valley with the vast, long lake threading it and glacier-clad peaks to the north and east. Not upon the river, not upon the waters that would take him to Susannah. And Susannah would never know.

The woman washed him with a soft piece of elkhide, which she dipped frequently in the warm water. The warmth of the sopping hide felt good, but when the hot water cooled he felt colder than ever. Still, he endured, too weak to do anything other than endure, and unable to convey the slightest meaning to her. He wished for his ragged clothing, but they'd taken it away. He wished for the haversack with its precious cargo, but it had vanished too. If only the haversack might find its way back to any fur post, he could die happy. He searched the gloomy tepee once again and seeing no sign of it, fell into melancholia. How terribly important small things became in life's extremities, he thought. When they'd captured Luke Hawkins, Gabriel Charbonneau, and Jed, he'd clutched the blue haversack to himself fiercely until they'd ripped it away, ripped away the last things he would give his life to defend. He hadn't seen it since. Not the haversack, or his blue uniform and linens and his worn boots, not Charbonneau's buckskins or rifle, not Hawkins's uniform, carbine, and revolver. Not the panniers, saddles, and all the rest of the truck they'd tried to save, nor the horses. Now he lay naked, the possessor only of his body and soul, and barely even that.

Having fed him some primitive potion and washed him, the woman ladled a hot broth into him. This time it tasted better. His wobbly teeth mashed meat and something else, roots of some sort, and the warmth of it spread through his emaciated white body. She tugged the buffalo robe over him, threw some bits of pine upon the lazy fire, and stood. He peered up at the short moon-faced woman, still bundled in brown skins and gray wolf fur. She stared impassively.

"Thank you," he said. She nodded and crawled through the door hole, rearranging the flap behind her to slow the icy fingers of winter. He drifted into the white haze again, but something in the back of his mind whispered that soon he'd feel better. The magic potion.

A week later he felt able to sit up for brief periods against a woven reed backrest the woman provided. The bleeding from his gums had lessened, and his nose no longer bled at all. What was more, he had recovered his wits and no longer drifted through a confused fog hour after hour, barely aware of light and dark. They kept his blue woolen infantry britches and tunic from him but gave him a grimy two-point Hudson's Bay blanket, red with black bands, in addition to his moth-eaten robe.

The potion had its effect on him, and he drank it eagerly, more and more curious about it. The woman sensed his curiosity and one day brought him a long stem, thin and flexible, with thick thorns upon it. At its head was the teardrop-shaped bud she used in her potion. Very like a rose, he thought. A wild rose.

She smiled, an amiable humor lifting wide thick lips in a broad amber face. He tried talking: who knew what words and sounds and gestures she might fathom?

"I don't know your name," he said. "I'm Jedediah Owen, a captain—a chief—of the Americans, the Yankees. What is your name? I'd like to thank you, whoever you are. You've pulled me back from the brink of death."

He waited, wondering if she understood, but saw only curiosity, not understanding, in her alert opaque eyes.

He pointed a finger at his chest. "Jed Owen," he said. He pointed at her and waited. She said something incomprehensible, a name he couldn't even parrot.

"Where am I?" he babbled. "How far west of Fort Lewis? Or do you call it Fort Benton now? Culbertson told us he planned to rename the place, since everyone calls it Benton."

He thought he saw some faint recognition stir in her wide amber face at the mention of . . . Lewis? Benton? Culbertson?

"Where is my haversack? Of all the things I've lost, I want only that, and what's in it. My weapons, horses, saddles, blankets, mess gear—keep it all. But let me have the haversack please."

No response lit her eyes, but she listened.

"Miss, that bag is not just a material thing of canvas, with papers and such inside. It is promises, sacred promises, instructions from beyond the grave, and love. Yes, most of all, love. Miss, do you know much about love?"

She understood nothing. He'd grown weary. More words than he'd spoken for months, through a mouth that had barely stopped hemorrhaging. He felt the familiar fog returning, and his mind drifting toward phantasms and fragments of thought, meaningless. Only the haversack had meaning.

She picked up the empty bowls, threw bits of wood upon the smoky fire, and left. The air didn't slice at him now. He wiggled deeper into his robe and blanket and drifted into the white sleep again.

When she stepped through the lodge entrance the next evening, pushing the worn door skin aside, she had someone with her. The burly young man whose ebony hair hung in twin braids seemed familiar to him; the blue tunic he wore, with the captain's epaulets on it, certainly was. Jed peered up into the dim light of the lodge and recognized this one as his captor. A dozen of them had risen out of the grass on the other side of the mountains and had brought them here. Private Luke Hawkins hadn't survived the journey over the sawtoothed mountains. The scout and interpreter, Gabriel Charbonneau, made it, but only barely.

"You are better," said the man, staring intently.

"I didn't know you could speak English!"

"We did not want you to know."

Jed sighed, wondering what he and Gabriel had said before this unknown auditor. For the most part the guide had mumbled out his knowledge of the Kootenai between bouts of fever, with a desperation born of impending doom.

Through the smoke hole above, Jed glimpsed low iron-bellied clouds spitting snow. Flakes whirled into the flapping, chattering lodge. "How long have I been here?" he asked harshly.

"Long time."

"Why didn't she give me that potion sooner?"

"We waited to see. We talked in council. The elders, the medicine men and women. Chief Yew Wood Bow. I am the war chief."

Jed smiled dourly. "You are wearing a war chief's uniform—mine."

"Not yours. A slave of the People owns nothing."

Jed thought about that, sudden caution rising in him. "What's your name?" he asked.

"I don't have all the English words. Maybe it means Dawn Killer of Piegans."

"Well, Dawn Killer of Piegans, I've been sent by the great chief of the whites, far to the east, to make peace. Bring peace and good gifts to all the people here. Find out what your people want, what white men's goods, from the great chief. But sickness came to us."

"Yes, sickness and evil spirits. Bad medicine! We have kept you here, far outside of our village so you don't sicken the People!"

Jed grew silent for a moment. They knew he had scurvy; knew it wasn't contagious. But, yes, Gabriel . . . the fever. It had been a strange fever, first turning the ankles and wrists rosy-colored, and then the rose tint spread through all the flesh, even as the fever raged. Gabriel had escaped cholera, only to die of that strange fever. And now, at the last, scurvy.

"How long have I been here?" he asked again.

"Over two moons."

Late December, then. Maybe Christmas. A brutal winter still ahead. "Perhaps when I am able to travel, you will take me to Fort Benton, to the trader Alec Culbertson, on the great river. He'll give you good things in exchange for me."

Dawn Killer of Piegans shook his head. "That is the trading place of our enemies. We never go there."

"Where do you trade, then?"

"Hudson's Bay Company. Rocky Mountain House, far to the north. That's where I learned your words."

"I'd like my clothes back. Soon I'll be up, and I'll need my clothes to stay warm."

"Not yours anymore. If you don't have clothes, you don't go anywhere."

"I am your prisoner rather than guest," Jed said dourly.

Dawn Killer of Piegans nodded.

"I had a blue sack with white men's messages in it. Do you have it?"

"That is big medicine. I had to rip it away from you. It holds the white man's secrets. Like the black book of the blackrobes. It is worth much to a poor, small people. We will keep the medicine, and you will teach us the messages, and then the spirit helpers of the white men will bring us the rifles and metal pots and powder that flashes, and the soft ball metal and all of your things."

The bag was safe, and everything in it. They hadn't burned it. Gratefully, Jedediah Owen smiled. The letters of farewell, the confessions, the good-byes, the last wills and testaments. Maybe the locks of hair, the rings, the daguerreotypes too. Maybe the commissioners' journals, his own daily reports; his orders and papers. Maybe the four rosaries. Humble things, the last wishes and hopes of dying men, written in the throes of mortal cholera. Nothing earthshaking in the bag; nothing that would shatter nations, make new peace or transform a wilderness. Only men's dying words, often copied down by Jed himself for his illiterate soldiers as they lay fevered, dehydrated, sweating, trembling, minutes from their Maker. To each he'd made a sacred and inviolate promise: he would deliver these letters to spouses, priests, ministers, children, officials, parents; the loved ones of the high officials he escorted, the loved ones of the humble soldiers under his command. They'd died holding his hand, the fear in their eyes softened a bit by the knowledge that Captain Jedediah Owen would carry their words and effects back home and tell those loved ones in Washington City, or on Suds Row at Leavenworth or across the seas, the day, the hour, and the circumstances of their passing.

White men's magic indeed. No, not that. Something infinitely precious, which he was committed to deliver—and would do so, somehow, some way, no matter what the cost to himself.

"You will teach us what the black and white messages say?"

Jedediah thought quickly. "I will read each of them to you."

"You might lie!"

It angered Jed, but he felt too weak to argue. "You'll know if I do!" he retorted roughly. "Your medicine men will know."

Dawn Killer of Piegans nodded. "They will know. Tomorrow you will tell us."

He clambered through the door of the ragged lodge, letting snow whirl in. This lodge had no lining, and Jed had not felt warm for an endless time. The flat-nosed young woman fed him silently, pouring another dose of her rose potion down him, and then left, vanishing into the winter night.

For once he felt glad to see her leave. The talk had awakened memories, and he wanted to be alone with them. He adjusted the old buffalo robe and the thin blanket around him until he stopped shivering and let himself remember.

It had struck them four days west of Fort Benton, so swift, violent, shocking that he scarcely had time to gather his wits. He'd heard talk enough about cholera, but he had never before seen it. Private Aloysius

Harrison complained of fever first. Then he was running to the bushes, and finally vomiting. They were all on horseback, using pack mules for supplies. No wagons in that roadless land. No way to transport sick men. Leave them or take them along, sick, or stop the whole party. Captain Jed Owen stopped the party alongside a prairie creek with a few cottonwoods for firewood and shade against the July sun. Then Vincent Coppola, the cook. Then Corporal Conrad Hoch, the ferrier and muleteer and expert packer. Diarrhea, vomiting, raging fever, as fast as the racing scythe of the Grim Reaper. He poured water down them, but they couldn't hold it; he tried saline water, and it sickened them the more. Sun baked the high northern plains, roasting them by day, while the dying men shivered at night in their blue bedrolls.

Private Harrison called him first. Jed Owen knelt beside the sweating man, whose face looked ghastly and blue in the flickering firelight. It wouldn't be long, Owen knew.

"I'm afraid, Cap'n. Never been so . . . alone." Harrison's breath gusted irregularly now, and words seemed an effort.

Jed Owen grasped the private's hand in his own and held it.

"Cap'n. I can't write. I want—I want to say good-bye to my ma and pa. My sister Bridget. My big brother Tommy. If I tell you a few words, could you put 'em down? Words for them, words for my priest? Haven't a confessor . . ."

"I will, Aloysius. Let me get paper and my nib."

"*Hurry!*"

Captain Owen dug into his field desk and found his writing materials. By the flickering fire with its toying light, he wrote Aloysius Harrison's farewell. A humble thing: Bridget, I love you, and be good; Tommy, I love you, and Our Lord keep you from drink; Ma and Pa, I love you, and the cholera took me here in the Northwest, under Captain Owen, the fourteenth day of July, year of Our Lord 1849, a good Catholic to the last, and awaiting Paradise. . . .

"Do you have it, Cap'n?"

"Yes, all of it. But I need an address in Ireland."

Jed wrote down the address and accepted as well a tintype, a lock of blond hair, and a black-beaded rosary with a small silver crucifix.

"Cap'n, now I don't feel so alone," mumbled the private. "Promise me, oh, promise me—oh, God, *promise me* you'll get my last words, my last good-bye, safe to my family."

"I promise it," said Jed Owen, seeing peace steal across the face of the man.

Chapter Four

Jean Gallant nursed a dark mood. A chinook had blown the cold away and turned the air soft and seductive, but he refused to let his good fortune cheer him. It felt better to sulk and groan, and sigh inwardly, and lament a lost life. He'd grown old, and soon he'd lie beneath the cold earth, with no more young wives to delight him and fill the lodge nights with excitement.

The chinook had pummeled the last patches of snow on the vast prairie into puddles and turned the frozen earth soft, so that his gaunted ponies left an endless stream of hoofprints wending behind, mile after mile, day after day. But Jean Gallant scarcely noticed. He felt burdened with thoughts of his own mortality, and the life after death that would have to be suffered for all eternity without the pleasures of the body to enchant him. His notion of heaven conflicted sharply with the church's, and it irked him. If he had to spend eternity doing something or other, he knew exactly what it would be, provided of course that the supply of nubile angels was limitless.

For more days than he could remember, he'd pursued his melancholy errand for the company, for Pierre Chouteau *le cadet,* for Alec Culbertson, for James Kipp, for Malcolm Clarke, men who summoned him, sent him off on impossible missions, men whose beck and call he must obey. He regarded them sullenly, especially the rich Chouteau down in St. Louis, with all his slaves and carriages and wealth from peltries, gathered by cold hungry engagés here in the upper Missouri, by slaves and fools like himself, like old Jean Gallant.

He sniffed the soft west winds disdainfully, scorning his comforts. Let the weaklings and pork-eaters enjoy pleasant weather; he'd been made of sterner stuff. The day he welcomed a chinook would be the day he became an old man. He disliked that thought the moment he had it. The mild sunny day with the fresh breezes playing over the endless dun prairies threatened to turn him frolicsome.

From Weasel Tail's village he'd struck west along the Marias River, wrestling with bitter weather when the air itself turned blue and opaque with ice and haze and the ivory sun skimmed the south only to vanish and plunge the world into perpetual night. A pancake of distant blue smoke alerted him to another village, which turned out to be that of Six Eagles, a great chief of the Kainah, or Bloods, and a powerful leader of the whole Blackfoot confederation. There he had a wife, if only he could remember her name. Was it Falling Star? He'd wrestled with it as he rode in, but it turned out to be of no consequence. Whoever she was, she didn't show herself during his visit. A pity. His old bones needed a good warming. He'd given Six Eagles a twist of tobacco, and they'd smoked and he'd inquired about the missing bluecoats and had discovered nothing at all.

So he'd pushed on, through the most brutal weather of all, when he had to stop and build fires every hour or so to warm his frozen bones, on up the Marias, west and north, until the great sawtoothed front of the Rockies loomed in the distance, blinding white and cold, a massive barrier that blocked this prairie world from whatever lay beyond. Each night he found a sheltered spot, usually in cottonwoods, and carefully withdrew from his kit his most precious possession, a mercury thermometer calibrated to sixty degrees below zero. This he hung on its oiled leather thong from a cottonwood branch a suitable distance from his fire. Oh, he would show that stupid Swiss Fahrenheit a thing or two! Twice on those nights the mercury dropped to forty-seven degrees below what that ignoramus thought was absolute cold! . . . and one night it slid down to forty-nine below. It was the triumph of wilderness over science, he thought. Jean Gallant intended to prove some day that absolute zero was fifty below, but he had never seen the mercury slide that last degree, though he'd seen minus forty-nine three times. But when it happened, he'd be famous! *Oui!* The world would hear of Jean Gallant! Then he'd be famous and have slaves, like Chouteau, and women galore.

On Two Medicine Creek he found another village of Piegans, that of Mountain Ram, whose very own daughter was one or another Madame Gallant. Ah! The thought of it enchanted him as he rode in. Madame Gallant would make this miserable journey through almost absolute cold worthwhile! If he could remember her name, exactly. He reminded himself to listen and keep his mouth shut until her name came to him.

But Mountain Ram's warm lodge showed no sign of the young woman. He'd been coolly greeted by the old chief himself, and served by his sits-beside-him wife, Raven Wing, and sent on his way the next day with no news at all. Jean had ridden away irritably, feeling deprived of fair womanhood, full of self-pity having to brave the bitter weather without being warmed by the arms of his erstwhile wife.

Thus he rode in a dark mood even while the chinook blessed his journey. He ventured south, crossed the Sun River on thin and elastic ice, and pushed on southward toward the Missouri itself, which might pose great difficulties if its cap of ice had melted and he could not easily get to the far shore. When at last he reached the river valley he discovered open water and ice floes, a condition certain to discourage less stalwart men, but not the American Fur Company's greatest engagé. Shivering even in the chinook warmth, he stripped himself, bundled up his clothing with thongs, and draped the bundle over his shoulders. Then he remounted and coaxed his reluctant ponies into the gray ice water at a buffalo crossing, feeling the vicious river numb his feet and calves and thighs, and finally his *derrière*. When the arctic water crept over that portion of him he preferred to heat rather than freeze, he howled at the heavens, startling a doe, two antelope, and a coyote on the ivory bluffs. He bayed and howled and alarmed his ponies, which thrashed violently in the river and crow-hopped forward in powerful lunges until they scrambled out upon dry land. Anything for American Fur, he thought as he slid down to the ground, letting the crazed ponies flounder up the gravelly bank and shake themselves violently.

He was pulling up his britches when laughter—woman's laughter—greeted him. *Mon Dieu!* he thought, slowing down his efforts to tug the buckskins over his water-beaded thighs. He prided himself for that. Most men would have hastened the task, but not Jean Gallant. He squinted into the warm clear air and spotted a fair maiden some yards distant, Crow by the looks of her. And with her two children, a little boy and girl, probably twins. All of them out enjoying the splendid chinook. In all this he perceived a swift way to warm his chilled flesh.

"Gallant!" she cried, trotting forward. "Jean Gallant!"

"Ah!" he exclaimed, recognizing her: Owl Feather, one of his very own. "There's no one I'd rather see," he bellowed in Crow, feeling chinooky within himself at last. "My very own Owl Feather!"

His buckskin britches were still half up, but he let that enterprise languish and hugged her warmly, enchanted by his turn of fortune. Here in his arms was a Madame Gallant, and nearby would be her River Crow village wintering in some gray cottonwood forest beside the Missouri. He felt inclined to consummate his homecoming at once, but with the two little ones gaping nearby, his innate French delicacy forbade it. Owl Feather herself seemed at a loss, undecided whether to pull his greasy britches up or down. Finally, giggling, she opted for up.

"Ah, my own Gallant," she cried. "Meet your children!"

The news enchanted him. Save for his wives themselves, nothing delighted him more than the children of his loins. Ah, *vraiment*, what dear ones! Why, how they resembled him! He had made them, stamped them, bequeathed them to the Crows, his dear friends the Crows. Ah! Four-year-old twins!

"This one, Gallant, is called No Father," she said, pointing to the boy. "And this one, my girl, is called American Fur, in your honor."

"*Mon Dieu!* American Fur and No Father! How you honor me, Owl Feather!"

She frowned. "You have come home to me for all times, is it not so, Gallant?"

"My beautiful Owl Feather. Ah, only for a while, because the company has urgent work, *oui*, urgent tasks for your own Gallant. But let

31

us make merry. Have you your own lodge, warm and waiting for your loving husband?"

She sighed. "We are poor," she said softly. "No man hunts for us or protects us or shoots buffalo for us. But my brothers care for me, and I stay in the lodge of one. But now you've come home, Gallant!"

"*Oui!* Let us head for our nest! Have you a sister who will care for American Fur and No Father for a while?"

She frowned. "Why do we need that?"

"So we can make brothers and sisters for them, my Owl Feather!"

"We will wait until tonight," she said. "Absaroka children are very wise."

He groaned, and the chinook within him cooled slowly. Ah well, work before play. Anything for the American Fur Company. Was he not the company's finest scout and diplomat and engagé because of just such discipline and sacrifice? *Vraiment,* the company had no other the like of Gallant!

He plucked the wiggling, giggling children up and settled them on his packhorse, right on the packsaddle itself.

"Can he do that to the Absaroka?" asked No Father.

"He is your father, No Father," replied Owl Feather. "He can do anything he wants, because he is my man and one of the Absaroka."

Gallant mounted his pony and followed behind Owl Feather, who trotted on foot toward her village, downriver a mile or so. On the bluffs now Jean Gallant spotted some of the warriors whose task was to guard the Crow village and its horses night and day. Several of the mounted warriors watched with fascination as Owl Feather triumphantly led her reunited family into the village. The town crier spotted the visitor and made haste to sing the news, darting from lodge to lodge in the warm midday sun. Smiling Crows, many of them outside of their winter lodges, enjoying the chinook, beamed at the familiar fur trader as Owl Feather led him through a tumult of howling dogs and children and grinning adults. Then at last she paused before the great smoke-darkened lodge of the village chief, Coyote. The young chief stood in all dignity before his lodge, a powerful lean figure, wearing his ceremonial bonnet of eagle feathers, yellow leggings, aqua breechclout, high winter moccasins, and a tight blue infantry tunic.

They carried Jed to the great lodge of Chief Yew Wood Bow; he remained much too weak to walk. The moon-faced woman dressed him in his own tunic and britches first, and then a stocky Kootenai warrior lifted him easily into brilliant white light that dazzled and blinded him. The village lay in a vast mountain park with shimmering snowy mountains rising coldly on all sides except to the south, where a great lake stretched into white winter haze. He shivered in the bitter air.

Just as suddenly as he'd been exposed to the blinding light, he was plunged into blinding dark. But the great lodge contained warmth, and in its center a small intense fire crackled. He was carried to a place near the chief, eased down against a woven reed backrest, and covered with a fine buffalo robe, propped up and ready to face those within. As his disease-weakened eyes gradually adjusted, he discovered himself in the company of a dozen men, no doubt chiefs and headmen, elders and medicine men of the Kootenai. Among them he spotted Dawn Killer of Piegans, his translator, and in that warrior's lap rested the blue haversack, the magic bundle of all the whites.

So he would read, he thought. And live or die because of it. He thought of telling them nonsense, making magic out of the last messages of dying men. If he made magic he might live, and they'd come to him for mumbo jumbo, and he'd be a great man among them, revealing bit by bit the mysteries of the whites. But even as Jed had the thought he rejected it. He'd been as close to death as any man could be, had faced its terror and stared into Eternity, and somehow it didn't frighten him as it once had. No. He could only be true, come what may. He'd read what existed on those papers, and hope his translator could convey something of it to these chiefs. If fate decreed his death, then he could die honorably at least, in truth and beauty as he understood those things.

He found no kindness in any face. The young chief stared at Jed with hard intelligent eyes that seemed to see into Jed's soul, to read his private thoughts. They were all of a kind here, he thought, with moon faces and those squashed wide noses. They had not intermarried with other tribes, perhaps because of their isolation deep in these northern mountains. The chief did not withdraw his medicine pipe from its sack hanging from a lodgepole above him, surely a bad sign. And Jed discerned nothing resembling sympathy in the others either. They stared at their captive with cold curiosity, awaiting whatever would come.

He addressed Dawn Killer of Piegans. "Why have you carried me here?"

"You will share white men's medicine, show us the medicine in the blue medicine bag."

Jed sighed. "I will do that. But there's no medicine in it."

Dawn Killer of the Piegans snorted.

None of the others seemed to follow the exchange, Jed noted. They would depend entirely on the translation of the one among them who knew a few English words.

"My eyes are poor from sickness. I will read what I can if you will hand me my bag."

"No," said Dawn Killer of Piegans. "I will keep the bag and you will tell us what medicine is in it."

Jed already felt tired, though he'd been propped up for only a few minutes. "No medicine," he said wearily. "Messages of dying men to their families. And journals, a record of each day of our trip."

The translator explained Jed's words to the solemn assemblage, or at least Jed hoped so. He couldn't be certain. These Kootenai headmen seemed graven in stone.

"Tell us," said Dawn Killer of Piegans, "where iron comes from, and how to make the flashing powder, and how to be blackrobes. It is all here in the medicine bag."

Jed remained silent.

"We know about this bag. You held on to it even to death. Big medicine. All the medicine of the white men is inside. All the secrets of the long robes, the black book, the trappers with guns and steel knives. Tell us, or we will torture you."

"I will read whatever you hand me," Jed replied. "I must see it to read it, see the black marks to tell you what they say."

His translator returned to the soft tongue of the Kootenai again, and at last Chief Yew Wood Bow nodded. Dawn Killer of Piegans undid the buckle of the bag and reverently withdrew a crumpled sheet of foolscap and handed it to Jed, while the rest gazed warily, restless, as if afraid.

In the obscure light of a double-lined lodge it would be hard to read, Jed thought, and his eyes were half ruined. He squinted, turning the paper to catch the gray light of the smoke hole, and it was Clayton's last letter.

"You have given me a message from the chief, the Honorable Marcus Aurelius Clayton. Top man in the New Bureau of Indian Affairs. New this year. The army used to, ah, handle, ah . . . It is addressed to his

34

wife Eloise and says the things he wanted to say to her before he died."

He waited patiently for the Kootenai talk to stop, but Dawn Killer of Piegans had a question:

"Chief of what? Many warriors of the whites?"

"No, high commissioner of Indian affairs. . . . Ah, an ambassador, a messenger, the man who came to make friends with your people and other people and invite them to a meeting, a parley."

Jed listened, with utterly no idea whether he was being translated accurately. He doubted it, given Dawn Killer's limited grasp of English. No matter.

At last silence prevailed. They understood this was the message of a dying man, he thought, and their curiosity grew intense in the quiet of the lodge.

" 'My dearest Eloise—' "

"What is Eloise? That word I do not know."

"His wife."

"White men call wives Eloise?"

"No—her own name. Like you have a name of your own."

The translator nodded.

" 'I am stricken with cholera here on the far Northwest Plains and know that I am hours, perhaps minutes, from my Maker. I write with greatest difficulty but want only to see this through before I can no longer grasp my pencil. Captain Owen promises on his sacred honor to deliver this if breath is in him and he escapes this cursed disease. That is my sole hope of saying I love you and our children and hope to see each dear soul some time in Paradise.' "

Dawn Killer of Piegans wrestled with that a while, finding trouble with the Kootenai counterpart, but finally he subsided. Each of Jed's auditors stared at him with open curiosity. He read on.

" 'My hopes are dashed. I want only to see you before I close my eyes, but that is not possible. I will spare you a description of my torments, which are beyond imagining. I fear the government will not award you a proper pension and that you will suffer the indifference that is so commonplace in Washington City. My work is undone. I hoped I might lay the foundations of a great peace among all these far tribes of the northwest, and more, but I cannot write of that. Be strong, Eloise, and know that you will not be alone in the world, for our good captain promises me he will look after your every need, and above, our Great

Captain in heaven will weep for you and touch you with holy love.

"'Now the yawning grave awaits me, Eloise, my darling wife. Remember me kindly; remember our sweet embraces, and the springtimes of our days on earth. If I should be fortunate in my petitions before Almighty God, my spirit may hover beside thee as guardian and friend, even though I am beyond the veil of life.

"'My limbs grow numb and my hand falters. Blessed love to you for ever, as long as the mountains rise and rivers run. My deepest love for Benton and Lizette. All that I have I leave to you, and let that be my will and testament. Marcus Aurelius.'"

Jed set the letter down, and Dawn Killer of Piegans snatched it back. "I don't know all the words," he muttered. "How do I tell my people all that?"

"Tell them that this great chief of the whites sent love to his wife and children as he lay dying. Tell them that he hoped to see them in the other world. Tell them that he worried about his wife's future and feared she and the children would be very poor and would not get help from the—the great chiefs. And tell them that he died a little while after he gave this message to me, and I buried him on the other side of the mountains."

Dawn Killer of Piegans told them that, or seemed to; Jed couldn't be sure. They talked among themselves, back and forth, arguing, gesturing, polite and solemn.

"They say that is great medicine," said Dawn Killer of Piegans. "You are a medicine man that even your chiefs respect. We will hear more of white men's secrets."

But Jed had lapsed into sleep.

Chapter Five

Each afternoon they carried Jed Owen to the chief's lodge, where the Kootenai elders solemnly met in council. And each afternoon he read to them from the letters and journals in the blue canvas haversack until his strength ebbed. The potion of rose hips he greedily drank and chewed daily worked its magic on him, but it was a slow magic, and he remained weak, barely able to stand up. An hour of reading wearied him to the point of exhaustion, but he labored on, voice hoarse, censoring nothing, letting the words and ideas fall where they would, often upon stony faces.

The last letters and wills absorbed the elders and medicine men: they'd never heard such a thing, willing property to others, speaking from beyond the grave. They sat quietly in the subdued amber light of the cowhide lodge, lit more by the small blaze than by the low sun piercing translucently through leather, or by the smoke hole at the top.

Jed read the words of comfort he'd penned for Corporal Cletus Donegal, whose wife was a laundress at Leavenworth. The man had nothing to will to her except his love. He begged her to remarry swiftly, for the sake of their six children.

He read a letter from Private Vincent Coppola to his priest; Coppola had no relatives to write to. He wished to confess the sins of pride, using God's name in vain, and fornication. He asked for a mass for his soul.

His death had been slow and long, Jed remembered, twelve hours of dying. The cholera had felled the lucky ones in two or three hours. They'd buried Private Coppola in a shallow grave, rosary in his folded hands.

Slowly, Dawn Killer of Piegans translated, how well Jed couldn't guess. But the letter stirred something in the elders, and they argued gutterally among themselves, until at last the translator posed questions to Jed. What were sins? What was a mass? Could this confession affect the destiny of the ghostspirit, bring the mercy of the Great Spirit? Was this the medicine of the blackrobes?

That afternoon they wrestled with theology, wrestled with barriers of language and faith, for Jed knew little of Catholic belief. When he tired, they halted for that day, and he fell into a deep sleep after the moon-faced woman fed him a hot stew. He dreamed of Susannah, of sending his own last letter and will to her.

The next afternoon, a snowing and blustery one, he read the last letters of Corporal Conrad Hoch, ferrier and muleteer, to his wife and children at Leavenworth and to his parents in Wisconsin, and those of Private Luke Hawkins, muleteer and rifleman, to his surviving sisters in Tennessee. Hoch's parents spoke only German; the corporal had dictated the letter to Jed in broken English, trusting Jed to catch his meaning. Jed remembered it. Hoch was almost dead, gasping desperately, and Jed had strained to find meaning in the mumbling, finally inventing words and phrases, even as the corporal died in the midst of the writing, suddenly still and blue and lifeless, with the letter undone. Jed had added the time and date of death.

Hawkins had told him he couldn't read or cipher and neither could his sisters, but he wanted Jed to send them something anyway, date of death, time and place. Jed wrote it, read it back, and went on to the next dying man while Hawkins watched, dying slowly through that evening. The survivors buried him shallow.

The elders listened solemnly, and when he had finished they asked Jed why Hawkins made no mention of the Great Spirit.

"Hawkins wasn't a believer," Jed replied.

The answer astonished them. Not a believer? How could that be? Did he have none of the white men's medicine?

"Some white men believe; some don't," Jed muttered.

Why wasn't the unbeliever driven out of the village? asked Chief Yew Wood Bow through Dawn Killer of Piegans. Surely he brought evil to the soldiers and treaty chiefs.

Jed had no answer.

The winter days wasted by, and Jed found himself reading the last letters of Daniel Dance, the commissioners' clerk, who was half Delaware and half Mohawk and, it turned out, half married. He wrote his own letters, one to his wife in Washington City and two to mistresses in Baltimore and Richmond. Jed had not read the letters before, and they astonished him. But, come to think of it, Dance had shown all the signs of a rogue.

Letters written by an Indian! That intrigued the Kootenai elders. Could they learn this thing, the black signs? Jed spent the remainder of that afternoon teaching them the ABCs, using a charred stick to draw on rawhide, one medicine man glaring, hissing, and muttering at it all as he did so. That afternoon, Jed felt afraid when they carried him back to the ragged cold lodge. But he knew nothing; he couldn't fathom their language and barely understood their mood. The young woman fed him dourly that evening, as if he were a demon. That night he dreamed again of writing his own deathbed letter to Susannah, and the dream woke him in the blackness, while the smoke flaps shivered in the night wind.

But nothing happened, and the next day, amidst a chinook, he managed to walk to the chief's lodge, supported by Dawn Killer. That afternoon he read brief letters he'd written for Private Tiofilo Mendez of New Orleans, and Private Philippe Brasseau of St. Louis, both men without families, or so they said. He'd doubted that. Alone among the dying men, Mendez had sobbed. He lay on the dun grasses coughing, weeping, hating his fate, great tears oozing from his eyes, his dehydrated body spastic and convulsing. He'd dictated a letter to a woman, a Señora Olivera, and the address was a Carmelite convent. The letter was sparse: cause of death, time, place, and best wishes. A sister, Jed suspected, but he'd never know. Mendez died in a fit of terror and rage.

Mostly terror, Jed thought. He'd pitied Mendez; he still pitied him at the thought of that final terror. He remembered holding the man's hand as he slipped away, feeling Mendez's hand grip his, feeling him find comfort and succor at the last. By then there was scarcely anyone left to bury Mendez, but Jed had piled rocks up and hoped it would keep away the wolves.

Brasseau had died quietly, grinning and joking, willing his few possessions to, he claimed, ten wives. Jed had solemnly listed them all, somehow appreciating Brasseau's deathbed joke. It had been a good death, an unfought death. At the last, Brasseau had opened his eyes, told Jed he didn't fear the beyond, and comforted his captain. "You're the one got it hard, Cap'n," he whispered, and closed his eyes forever. Funny how men died, Jed thought as he read the letter to the assembled Kootenai, some in terror, some in peace. Some with humor, some with infinite sadness. Some scared, some desperate, some enraged. He droned out Brasseau's letter, Dawn Killer of Piegans translated, and the astonishment of the elders grew with the naming of each wife.

Could such a man, a lowly soldier, have more wives than even the greatest chief among the whites? asked Yew Wood Bow.

Jed smiled. "Perhaps it is so," he said. "Perhaps not."

There remained but one letter, a long one, penned by assistant Indian commissioner, the Honorable Sylvanus Quincy Elwood, written while he still felt well, but written just in case. And after the letters, Jed planned to read the journals, particularly Elwood's daily observations of the whole journey. He dreaded both: Elwood had shown no sympathy or sensitivity at all toward the Indians he would be treating with, and Jed expected the harshest and most patronizing sentiments to show up. He knew he'd read them as they were written; he couldn't help it. Jed Owen was not a man to manipulate or prevaricate, not a man to save his own life with lies. If a man believed in something such as Truth, let him live by his beliefs, he thought. But that didn't stop the fears that gripped him as he pulled Elwood's last letter to his family from its envelope.

"This letter is from the second chief," Jed explained. "He died two days after he wrote this. One of the last."

Word from a white chief. The Kootenai elders listened intently. Jed stared at them, suddenly aware that they trusted him to read truly now, to convey to them the man's actual thoughts and words.

"'My dear Sally,'" Jed read. "'I am well as I write this, but the cholera has stricken this command, and I am among the last. If I pass to the beyond, perhaps this letter will reach you. I am not sure of it but am forced to trust Captain Owen, which I do reluctantly.

"'He has stopped us here on a nameless creek, beside some cottonwoods, the only trees in a vast upland prairie. I opposed it because the air here is unhealthy and the miasmas from the creek bottoms are killing his command off even faster than otherwise. But what army captain ever listened to wise counsel? Here we are, with men dying like flies from miasma, and he goes about comforting them. I'd rather live than be comforted myself, so I am spending my time up above the bottoms in better air, and perhaps I will weather this folly.

"'Remember always, the army and the Indian Agency are opposed on the treaty matter. If the army runs the new agencies and distributes the treaty goods and annuities, our fortunes will diminish. Our hope of mending our fortunes with my appointment as an Indian agent will pass, and we will be forced to seek our fortune by other means. I am taking every step to prevent it, of course, by establishing a record.

"'At any rate, if the worst happens, put in at once for a large pension, as befits your station. We've entertained half the Congress, and now they can return the favor. And if the worst happens, make known at once that army incompetence was at the root of it, dwelling on Owen's deficiencies. Getting up a pension from Congress works easier when they think a public official has been cheated of life. You'll come out well enough if you go to Wiley, Parks, and Dillingham, who understand my views and are allied with us.

"'Actually, I expect to live. I'm safer here on the hilltop, give or take a few red brethren, and I plan to head east if this mission collapses, with a full report. There will be treaties soon enough, and new agencies, and I have ways and means of keeping the army out and putting ourselves in. A few years of that and we'll retire in splendor.

"'Meanwhile, my dear, let no opportunity pass, let no contact go unmade, let no man of influence escape your delightful charms. Your very own lover, Sylvanus.'"

The letter did not surprise, Jed. In fact, it struck him as a perfect reflection of the man's beliefs and approach to life. A way of life all too common in Washington City, he thought, where men climbed through politics and intrigue rather than merit. He would have preferred not to open that sealed envelope but he'd had little choice: the elders would have opened it for him and compelled him to read. The Kootenai elders seemed to grasp little of it. Neither did they understand the nature of the man who wrote it, a man whose ambition was hindered by no considerations of truth or honor. Elwood, like so many Indian Bureau agents before him, intended to enrich himself at the expense of those tribes who would become his charges, mostly by selling annuity goods rather than distributing them. But the Kootenai hadn't grasped that, and he was not inclined to tell them.

"White Wolf, our medicine man, says that this day you are not telling us everything," said Dawn Killer of Piegans.

"That's right," snapped Jed.

"You will tell us tomorrow."

He had not yet read to them from the Indian commissioners' official journal, kept by Elwood, or from the official government papers commissioning the treaty expedition and detailing its objectives. Those, Jed thought with some dread, might explode upon him when he began the readings the next day. Elwood's letter had given him a clue as to what he might expect.

"I'd like to take the blue bag with me to my lodge and read the rest of the things in it this evening," he said to Dawn Killer of Piegans.

The Kootenai eyed him suspiciously. "Why? Would you burn these medicine messages, or make lies?"

"I've pledged to deliver these messages, not burn them. My heart would lie on the ground, as you people put it, if these voices from the dead were lost."

"We will keep the bag."

"Two things remain, Dawn Killer of Piegans: messages from the fathers in Washington telling the treaty-makers what to seek, what my government wants, and a daily journal, a daily account of this journey for the official records. I want to read them so I may answer your elders wisely."

"Or twist the messages."

"Have I twisted any message? Have your elders and medicine men found untruth in my reading?"

The Kootenai glared. "I will talk with them," he said, and turned to the elders sitting quietly in the great gloomy lodge. The fire had almost perished, but no one replenished it or seemed to care. Jed had come to fathom a few words, but this debate he could not follow. He wanted to see the instructions to the commissioners, especially any portions involving the future of the Kootenai and their enemies in the Blackfoot confederation. He knew in general what Washington proposed: a vast reservation above the Missouri River, up to the forty-ninth parallel and British holdings, that would contain all the northwest Plains tribes—certainly the Assiniboin, Gros Ventres, Piegans, and Bloods, and some northern Sioux—and free the land below the river for settlement. But he had no idea where the Kootenai, a mountain tribe, and the other mountain tribes, such as the Flatheads, would fit in. But above all, he wanted to see what Elwood's journal would say about him. It was going to be a political document, intended to serve the purposes of the Bureau of Indian Affairs. It would probably be untrue, and the untruths would likely involve him, put him in grave trouble with these Kootenai as well as his army superiors.

The translator turned to him at last. "The medicine chiefs, our great Chief Yew Wood Bow, and the elders, have reached an agreement. If we give you the blue bag, you will no longer speak truly with us. We will not give it to you now. You must return to your lodge and eat well and be strong tomorrow, and then you will read us the exact true signs, and we will think about them."

Jed sagged, wondering if he'd live through another sunset.

She had her choice between the *Mary Blane* and the *El Paso*, with the *Mary Blane* scheduled to leave St. Louis first, in mid March. Nathan St. George had caved in, but not entirely.

"That first boat will be overcrowded and dangerous, and I won't permit it," he growled at Susannah. "The first ones up the river are always like that. Overbooked. Deck space only. Riffraff. Gamblers and fur men. No food, no, ah, conveniences for women."

"But the *El Paso* could be just as bad."

"No. We're booking an army inquiry party on it. Our friend Lieutenant Constable in command. They'll look after you, see you up and see you down the river."

One of her rejected suitors, she thought. Lieutenant Jay Constable. At her elbow every hour of every day on the *El Paso*. She sighed, knowing what to expect.

He grinned suddenly. "Gong to test your luck?" he asked, a faint taunting in his voice.

"No, Colonel. You've gone out of your way for me. I wish you'd take some leave and come."

"Quartermasters are glued to their depots. But I've pulled all the strings I could to keep you safe."

It was more than a young woman might expect, she knew. Her father had sensed the army steel in her and had gone further than any other father would. It had been an act of profound trust—and, she thought, an understanding of the condition of her heart.

"I'll be strong."

"Can't stand to see you pining. I pine too. You chose the right man, Susannah. That Jed Owen . . . that Owen . . ." A sudden quaver torsioned his voice. "You find him if he's alive. Marry him on the spot, with or without benefit of the—"

"Father!" She laughed, but uneasily.

Colonel St. George eyed her wryly. "I am not ignorant of the attraction between a handsome and valorous young man, and a beautiful and wise young woman."

She said nothing, feeling her cheeks redden.

"If cholera breaks out, Constable has orders to take his command—and you—off the *El Paso* at once. You'll be dumped on a wild shore, and that should be adventure enough for any daughter of mine."

"There's been so much of it," she said uneasily. The disease had rampaged up and down the great river, riding the boats. It had pierced out the California Trail, slaughtering thousands. It struck anywhere and everywhere people gathered, and death by cholera was horrible beyond description. Could it have struck Jed?

She twisted her thoughts away from that. There was no point in speculating about the unknowable. Cholera would be one of a hundred reasons Jed hadn't returned. Some instinct informed her that he lived, but some darker instinct hinted at bleaker things. She puzzled it: she wasn't used to conflicting intuitions. The one thing she understood clearly was her helplessness.

She resumed her station at the river window, feeling no heat from the late January sun. In only two months or so, the *El Paso* would pull free of the St. Louis levee and paddle west and then north, stopping as all riverboats did at Leavenworth for inspection. At that time she and her army contingent would board. If Jed was up the river, they'd find him. If not . . .

She frowned. She knew she ought to plan for that. The eternal secrets of the wilderness. Death or silence. But she couldn't, she couldn't form thoughts in her numbed mind. Jed dead? *No.* Only delayed by wilderness. He'd come down the river, sometime . . . . Could she stay at Fort Union and return on another packet later? Nathan St. George would be distressed, but no harm would be done. She'd need a patron there. She'd have to be a guest in the home of the factor. She knew their names. Everyone on the river knew of the American Fur Company's great leaders: Alec Culbertson. James Kipp. Malcolm Clarke. Surely the one at Fort Union would open his home to her. And she could wait out the summer there until Jed returned. Or didn't return . . . .

She stared out upon the empty gray river ice and the winter-locked river, and whispered threadbare words that were almost prayer. "I love you, Jed Owen," she repeated, as she had for almost three hundred days. "Come home to me. Where the river runs, there will you be."

Chapter Six

Jedediah Owen faced the next reading with foreboding. Through the long journey up the river he had fathomed something of the nature of the Honorable Sylvanus Quincy Elwood, second commissioner of Indian affairs. The man was one of those political animals who lived by images, caring endlessly about how he appeared to others, but scrupling not at all about the ways and means he employed to reach his goals. He'd been affable and smiling the whole trip, uncomplaining behind intelligent cold eyes. But Jed had sensed the other thing, the ruthlessness and cunning, and marked him as a dangerous man. Still, nothing had happened—until now.

Jed made his way unsupported to the council lodge that afternoon, under a threatening dark overcast that pushed damp air into his bearded face. He had not shaved because they'd taken his razor and strop. Neither had his hair been cut, and now it lay low on his neck, approaching his shoulders. This day Dawn Killer of Piegans motioned him to the place of honor beside Yew Wood Bow, a signal of new respect. He wondered if they'd respect him—and whites—at the end of this session. The elders awaited him patiently in the smoky lodge, plainly enjoying these councils that filled the afternoons of a long hard winter when there was so little to do. He knew them all now, the ones who scowled, the medicine man who snapped and crackled like a fire as he sat, the quiet phlegmatic chief, the amiable eyes of a friendly subchief . . .

They handed him the buckram-bound journal book from the blue haversack. It occurred to him that they knew exactly what had been read and what remained for their ears.

"Respected elders," he began. "This is a daily journal—a written record of each sun—begun by the subchief. His people, in the Indian Bureau . . ." He realized helplessly that these things could not be adequately translated, but he continued. "The Indian Bureau, and the army, each want to—deal with your nation and other Indian nations."

Dawn Killer of Piegans made a stab at that, but Jed saw only incomprehension in the faces of the elders.

He cleared his throat and turned to the first page. The entries were written in a clean copperplate that was easy to read, and the content ordinary. "'May the fifth, eighteen forty-nine,'" Jed began. "'*Wyandotte* made only twenty miles today. Caught on a bar. Stopped at half past noon to load wood cut by a ruffian on west bank. Captain paid him gold. Passed snags they call sawyers midafternoon. Rivermen dread them. Saw single bull buffalo, and several deer. Meal fare is very distasteful. Hard meat, gruel, muddy river water.'"

Jed read similar entries through the afternoon, detailing life aboard the packet as it fought its way up the great river, always starved for fuel and dependent on woodcutting gangs along the banks. Except that sometimes no woodhawks showed up and they had to stop and cut wood themselves, watching out for Indians.

Then at last, a reference to himself: "'June the first. We approach the fur company's Fort Union in a day or two, they tell us. From then on our fortunes will be in the hands of Captain Owen, who will take us by horse westward into wilderness save only for Fort Benton. He's West Point, I gather, with Mexican War service, which should comfort but doesn't. His soldiers seem cretinous if not moronic. I dread placing my life and safety in such hands. His views of our red brethren are typical army: kill them all.'"

Jed stopped, astonished. It was not his view and he'd never expressed such sentiments. He stared uneasily as Dawn Killer of Piegans translated, and instantly he felt the hardening of his hosts. He knew there'd be more. Elwood had casually and cleverly started to build a false record, a record intended to keep the army out of Indian affairs and keep the tribal agencies in the hands of Indian Bureau appointees. But how explain that? How explain to these Kootenai that records could lie, that the lies would ultimately allow men like Elwood to pillage the Indians in their care?

He could stop reading. He could invent entries. He could lie himself—to save his life. The Kootenai elders stirred and waited. He felt paralyzed for a moment, unable to breathe. He could plead illness, ask to read more tomorrow. He could try to explain that the writing, the black marks, could lie just as men lied with their tongues. He could defend himself. But in the darkness of the lodge he saw that the elders had already condemned him. A single sentence of Elwood's had sufficed.

"You must read," barked Dawn Killer of Piegans. "We will know. I can take the sign book to the Hudson's Bay post and have it read. We will know."

Jed felt his body stiffen and weaken, felt a curtain of gloom descend over him. He'd always believed in Truth, believed the biblical affirmation: You shall know the truth, and the truth shall make you free. But now, he thought, the truth would make him dead; the true reading of the lies. He cleared his throat, not wanting to continue, knowing Elwood's game now, knowing its effect on these people. Knowing that if he survived and took this report back east, it would ruin him with its lies.

Let it be death then. He had almost died a few days earlier, so why not now. He read. The next entries said nothing untoward: they had debarked at Fort Union, and met the chief trader, James Kipp, who did not impress Elwood. Met assorted Assiniboin and Cree chiefs and held their first treaty parleys, Kipp translating. Met also with northern Sioux chiefs, who proved to be suspicious and uncooperative.

Jed read through the entries with a harsh voice, relaxing a little when he found no further allusions to himself or the army. At Fort Union the army was barely present, and in fact Jed had spent his time outfitting. The Kootenai elders listened patiently, absorbed in the implications of reservations, lands reserved for their enemies, the Assiniboin and Cree.

Elwood kept exhaustive records, flattering to himself, dripping with praise for the splendid chiefs they dealt with, always making a record that would shine in Washington City, a record that had less to do with the present than the future. A record that could cheerfully be opened and read to a Senate committee by an Indian Bureau official.

Then the Fort Union negotiations ended and Elwood's record turned to the journey west, and suddenly the army and Captain Owen were back on its pages.

"'July the fourth, Independence Day. We are en route to Fort Benton now, all on horse, in Owen's hands. I do not see any great intelligence leading us. Owen tells his men and us we must stay alert for Blackfeet, the most vicious of all tribes. The order is to shoot on sight. I fail to fathom how we shall negotiate treaties with people we shoot on sight. But he tells us our safety depends on it, and the only remedy for Bug's Boys, as he quaintly calls them, Bug being an allusion to the Devil, is extermination, down to the last woman and child. Typical army thinking. His troops all agree and are whetted for it. I only hope they don't attempt it now, a dozen strong, but they have that attitude: a squad of soldiers can whip a whole village of Indians. It alarms me, and I fear for my life. Have they no pity and humanity? I fear the day that our red brethren, who need guidance toward civilized farming, are placed in the hands of such professional murderers.'"

Jed felt his voice turn to brass as he read, felt Dawn Killer of Piegans leer and translate fluidly, getting it exact, for this was something he understood, felt the eyes of his hosts upon him, felt them believe these recorded words, believe his truthful reading of a total lie. He was a fool, he thought. Only a fool would usher himself to his own grave by reading lies as they were written. Only a fool like himself would toss away sweet life, sweet breath in his lungs, the love of Susannah and the dream of her embrace, toss away his career, his future, the sunsets, reveille and taps, the proud blue line, the joy of life out upon an unsettled land, hawk free and eagle tamed . . . .

But a fool he was. The next two entries were routine, except that Elwood grumbled about comforts and Owen's camp discipline and food and hunting details who brought back unpalatable antelope instead of good venison or buffalo. He read on.

"'July the seventeenth. Owen's guide and scout, Charbonneau, spotted an Indian lurking in brush beside a creek where it flowed into the

Missouri, a steep bluff below us. At Owen's command his scout deployed down the slope and shot the poor wretch without so much as a question, setting his corpse adrift in the great river. I asked myself what the fate of all tribesmen must be, if this sort of thing represents our army? There were no witnesses other than myself, for the body of us had gone ahead. And that is the way our Captain Owen wanted it. I asked him privately about the matter later. It must be done, he said. They sneak in and steal food and weapons. I pondered it, and I felt the wrath of our Maker upon our party and its shameful conduct. Heaven pity our red brethren in the hands of our own blue savages.'"

Dawn Killer of Piegans translated all that amiably, enjoying himself, and Jed found himself staring into faces that concealed unfathomable thoughts. "Ah, Captain Owen, that is the right thing to do with Piegans," the translator said cheerily.

Jed nodded. Elwood's story had been an invention.

In the next entries the Honorable Sylvanus Elwood pulled out the organ stops, flooding his paper with complaints about the army, Owen, and Owen's views. Jed read them all, one by one, in a metallic voice, barking out his own death warrant in the quiet of the smoky lodge. His listeners believed every sentence as well as they might, experiencing the magic of written language for the first time. He read truthfully, never glossing a word, finally snapping out each phrase with a hoarse voice, snarling out the language of his own doom, feeling absurd, feeling his worship at the altar of Truth would be his end. Crazy, he thought. I'm crazy. Is truth and honor so important? Am I berserk, a willing accomplice of my own death? But there was more in him than that. At the back of his mind lay a fine hard pride, and beside it a contrasting humility. He would do his best, no matter the consequences, and if God willed, he'd yet live, and unashamed. He might well die, but he could go to his death knowing he had not been a lying coward.

Chief Yew Wood Bow muttered something.

"Captain Owen," Dawn Killer of Piegans translated, "you are tired from reading and will go to you lodge now and stay within it. We will hear more of this tomorrow. The elders and medicine men will stay here to talk of these things we have heard on this day."

Jed nodded. They would not kill him yet. Not until he finished reading everything. He might drag out his life a day or two by reading slowly. He might try to explain Elwood's purposes, and all the rest.

Futility flooded through him. These written words seemed as sacred to the Kootenai as the word of God. How could any mortal disbelieve the magic black marks? Wearily—he hadn't realized how exhausted he had become—he pulled himself through the door flap and stood in the harsh ice-needled air, feeling the fullest burden of winter.

Duty before pleasure, thought Gallant, as he dipped into the gloom of Coyote's great lodge. The young chief eyed him amiably and motioned him to the place of honor, while Coyote's wives scurried out the door.

"A small gift from the American Fur Company, and from me, my friend," said Gallant, handing the chief a twist of good tobacco.

Coyote nodded and began stuffing the tobacco in a large calumet with a red pipestone bowl.

It would take time, Gallant thought. Indians always took their time. He filled his mind with seductive images of Owl Feather while the chief lit the pipe, drew smoke, and then saluted the cardinal directions, Mother Earth, and One Above.

They smoked silently, Gallant's mind upon the forthcoming festivities with Owl Feather, Coyote smiling faintly. At last the charge of tobacco was burned and Coyote rapped the dottle into the lodge fire.

"What brings you to my village, my friend?" he asked. "The weather has been cold for travel until recently."

"Ah, *mon cher ami*, the American Fur Company has sent me on a mad mission. I must say, I alone could survive it. When they want something grand, they call upon Jean Gallant."

The chief nodded lazily.

"Have you seen a small party of soldiers—Yankee bluecoats? It is missing. Vanished many moons ago. I am prepared to pay you well for information."

Soldiers. Coyote paid attention now. "What has the fur company to do with soldiers?"

Gallant shrugged elaborately. "Nothing, *mon ami*. We've simply been asked to search."

"And what were bluecoats doing here? They've never come here before."

"They were sent by the American government to contact tribes here and make treaties. With them came two chiefs, headmen of the whites

51

in the east, coming to make boundaries for each tribe and keep them from warring with each other."

Coyote smiled wryly. "I'm familiar with white treaty makers," he said. "What they say they want and what they really want are two different things. Peace among the Peoples is not their real goal; herding us onto reservations is, taking land is. If these soldiers and treaty makers vanished, it is good, I think."

Gallant shrugged. "You have seen them. You wear a blue army tunic."

Coyote grinned, having anticipated that sally. Slowly he unbuttoned the tunic, revealing beneath a great bronze medal pendant from a leather thong around his neck. He pulled it into the light. On one side was the bas-relief image of James Polk. On the other side, an image of clasped hands, and the word PEACE.

"Ah." exclaimed Gallant. "It is so."

"Fort Laramie, one winter ago, Gallant, soon after the bluecoats took it over from the fur company. We were camping there, my village. The chief called us in and gave me this. He called it a Peace Medal. He gave me a paper too. The paper says that Coyote and his people are friends of the Americans and should be treated as friends. That's what it says, they tell me. Of course, they don't quite mean it. If they think we've stolen horses, then they are entitled to shoot us."

"Do you steal horses, Coyote?"

"Everywhere, and all times," he replied. "But not the horses of the bluecoats."

"Where did you get—"

"Ah, the blue coat. It is why your eyes gleam, Gallant. They gave me the blue coat too, a gift from the chief at Fort Laramie. No, Gallant. I did not take it from the body of a soldier in this treaty party that has come to steal land."

"A pity, a pity," moaned Gallant. "I thought I had an answer. Have you no news of them?"

"I have seen nothing. No man or woman of my village has seen them. I heard they had come to Fort Union, though. . . ."

Gallant wisely plucked an additional twist of tobacco from his kit. "Here, Coyote, is tobacco, as a gift. Take it as a gift from me personally."

Coyote grinned sardonically. "I am pleased with your gift," he mocked. "Come. I will show you a thing."

Gallant followed Coyote out of the lodge and into the warm bright day. They hiked along a flat on the southeast bank of the Missouri, past a forest of dun lodges, through rotting ivory snow, past squaws busily carting firewood and yapping gray curs and darting children playing with sticks and hoops. They trudged through charcoal cottonwood groves naked in the salmon sun, and at last out where the village horses nipped cottonwood stems and bark, carefully guarded by several Absaroka warriors, mounted and alert.

Coyote walked, slightly bandy-legged, deep into the herd scattering thick-haired dark ponies, until at last he paused before one, a bay whose winter hair grew almost black. "We found him across the river in the moon of the chokecherries, him and another with no master. He has no marks."

The pony was tame and the chief caught him easily with a bit of thong over the neck. "See, Gallant. No marks. He is mine."

Gallant ran his hands under the fur, finding nothing. An ear was notched. The soldiers had been mounted on American Fur Company ponies provided for them at Fort Union.

"Where?" asked Gallant.

"Near the Point of Rocks River, what whites call the Sun. Deep in the land of the Siksikas. Some of us had gone to steal horses from them."

"Nothing else?"

"Nothing. I will show you the other pony."

The other one, a spotted horse, seemed vaguely familiar to Gallant. The hair obscured its markings and it yielded no firm clue. But it reminded him a little of a pony he had seen at Fort Union.

"Ah! *Cher ami* Coyote! You have truly helped me. Here, *mon grand ami*. Take this!" He handed Coyote another twist of tobacco.

Coyote grinned. "Gallant, my dear friend, what would you say and do if I told you all of these horses here"—he waved expansively at a group of nine animals—"came from the same place, abandoned?"

"Coyote, *cher ami*. If you told me all these came from the same place, I'd call you a liar and give you no more twists."

Coyote smiled sardonically.

"You are a true friend of the Absaroka," he said. "and a true husband of our beautiful Owl Feather."

"That I am, my dear Coyote, that I am. By the way, where is she?

What lodge? I wish to renew my marriage with my dear wife, and get to know my dear children American Fur and No Father."

"I'm sure you do," said Coyote. "She is very poor and a burden on her brothers, who must hunt buffalo for her while you are on your travels. I trust you have brought her great gifts, heaps of powder and lead, blankets and pots, flint and steel, rifles and knives, yes?"

"Oh, I couldn't manage all that this winter, Coyote. But come spring, come spring, I will make it all up to my own dear Owl Feather. Truly, I will bring her even more happiness than I bring her now. But don't suppose I bring her nothing now. I bring her treasure and joy. I bring life and warmth to my own dear Owl Feather! She abides with her brothers, does she not? Where in the village is that, *mon ami?*"

He handed Coyote another twist of tobacco.

"And say, Coyote, may I borrow your lodge for the night? Would you and your good ladies permit me to enjoy a homecoming with my own dear Owl Feather? Have you not the lodges of your relatives and brothers and sisters for the night? Ah, *cher ami,* I have a little gift, *oui,* a little gift for the use of your warm and happy lodge for my homecoming. A pound of powder and a bar of galena."

"Gallant, my friend, you are a man," said Coyote.

Chapter Seven

It was an ungodly hour for the *El Paso* to depart, but Susannah didn't really mind. The sooner the better. The packet tugged at the hawsers pinning it to the levee at Leavenworth, its two chimneys churning out gray smoke that instantly lowered to earth and water in the icy night air of March. At the first streaks of dawn, its master, Ricardo Sandoval, intended to steer into the murky river, north, ever north, and west to the end of the world.

Few passengers loaded there. In fact, only Susannah and the inquiry party, Jay Constable in command of six men. But the riverboat teemed with people who'd boarded earlier at St. Louis or Westport and other points, many of them deck passengers only, who would travel up the great river camped on the planks of the main deck. None of them slept now, though night still lingered.

Susannah stood beside Nathan St. George on the levee, watching as the last of the military gear was hauled aboard by deckhands in the dim light of a single torch burning in a metal basket suspended from a spar. On board the dark boat a few lanterns glowed orange in their glass chimneys. Her father stood sternly beside her, disapproving, and she felt afraid and subdued, and yet yearning to be out upon the great black river, voyaging each day and hour toward the one she loved. His arm caught her shoulder and his hand found hers, buried in her shawl.

"I wish it could be someone other than Jay Constable," he muttered. "But I couldn't change that. Susannah . . . this is the worst mistake I've ever made."

"I will come home with Jed," she answered softly. A brave reply that concealed her doubts.

Colonel St. George grunted. "I have nightmares about this."

"I will be protected, Colonel."

"Will you?"

She clutched her reticule. Within it lay a cold derringer he'd given her. In a wicker basket on her arm lay pounds of hardtack; meals weren't always available on a crowded, filthy, teeming riverboat.

"I didn't grow up an army brat for nothing."

"It isn't just disease, cholera morbus and all the rest, that I'm worrying about, Susannah. What about other men, who will woo you, regardless of Jed? Or worse. What if Jed's . . . dead? What if Jed's wounded, or incompetent, or mad?"

"He told me wherever the river runs, there would he be," she whispered.

"Then go, and find your happiness." His voice broke, and she saw his tears, the seams of his weathered face wet in the flickering torchlight. "Godspeed, my girl, my last child."

She wept too. No trip up the great river was ever perfectly safe, and she might never see him again. Impulsively she hugged him and he flustered about uneasily. They had scarcely touched before. "Godspeed," he croaked again.

"Steam's up," cried a voice from above. White vapor pulsed and hissed from the escapement pipe.

"I'll put you on," the colonel muttered, escorting her up a narrow wobbling plank to the low deck.

"Off in five minutes, Colonel," said the purser. "I'll show you the way. Miss St. George is our only woman cabin passenger—some Indian wives of fur men, on the deck, of course. Women's cabins at the rear.

Six berths, but since she's the only one, we're putting your soldiers there. She and Lieutenant Constable will have staterooms on the texas deck, next to each other."

"Don't like that," muttered Colonel St. George as he followed along through shadowed crowds of rank-smelling ruffians in buckskins and up a companionway, past the boiler deck, until only the pilothouse perched above them, dark against the stars.

The staterooms, scarcely six feet wide each and with a narrow bunk occupying most of them, lay just back of the master's own quarters. Her trunk hulked inside, barely visible in the unlit, cold room. On the deck, leaning against the varnished rail, lounged Lieutenant Jay Constable.

"Lieutenant!" roared Nathan.

"Sir?" he replied, coming slowly to languorous attention.

"Keep her safe and comfortable, or I'll—I'll . . ."

Jay Constable smiled lazily, as if to say that an elderly quartermaster officer was not a line commander and almost powerless when it came to such things as discipline or promotion or military politics. "Miss St. George will enjoy her voyage of the heart," he responded in a soft Charleston drawl.

"See to it."

The whistle shrilled, steam bellowing into the night air.

"Susannah," Nathan said brokenly, and left, beet-faced, before she could embrace him again and before tender feelings could engulf them in the presence of others.

She watched him plunge smartly downstairs, plunge through shadows, never daring to look back. She watched the back of his graying head as he jerked stiffly down the gangplank, even as first light caught the water, turning it to iron, and caught the ivory mist of the river and the shore, making it as mysterious and obscure as her own strange journey.

She felt eyes upon her and turned. The lieutenant stood watching, with his usual amused and cynical and bright expression, missing nothing at all. She turned her back and pulled her heavy woolen shawl tighter. Men shouted below, and the gangplank rattled. Terrible coils of black smoke erupted from the chimneys above, and steam screeched into the night as the packet trembled and pulsed like a chained monster. Above in the wheelhouse she heard the master, Sandoval, shouting orders down the speaking tube. Deckhands loosened hawsers and tugged on their capstans, and the vibrating boat labored free. Her father had vanished, and suddenly she felt pierced with aloneness. A fragile woman, a lone woman surrounded by several hundred males who ran the gamut of humanity from savage barbarians without a thread of honor running through them to gentlemen. And a cynical, mocking, and no doubt unscrupulous young officer standing beside her, rejected suitor and chaperone.

She focused on Jed, remembered his rough face, coarse hair, inner strength, hard calloused hands, so much the opposite of the fragile and languorous and overly bright man assigned to protect her from—such as himself. She drew herself up, watching the riverbank slip away, and the silent comforting dark hulks of Fort Leavenworth up the slope slide behind the barren limbs of trees.

"Bon voyage," he said, smiling slightly.

"I hope so."

"Give or take high water, low water, sawyers, snags, bars, cholera, dysentery, pox, buffalo, Sioux, Arikara, Assiniboin, Blackfeet, exploding boilers, lack of wood, and passengers inclined to shoot deckhands, wild animals, or each other."

"You have it catalogued."

"I studied. I am to conduct an inquiry. They are very anxious in Washington City. Two high muckety-mucks vanished, probably dead, maybe a great outrage of the savages. Maybe ah, a problem of the command . . . ."

"I knew it wouldn't take you long."

He shrugged softly. "You suppose I'm envious of Jed; women think that way. I'm not. Neither do I give a lick about his command, his great chance at fame and fortune, captain of a treaty party—"

"But if you can find fault, you will, Jay. I know you will."

He leered gently, his face illumined by rising light. The hurrying river slid past them far below with small sighs and gurgles, and the hammering of the boat and its splashing side wheels seemed alive and fierce beneath her feet.

"I enjoy it," he said. "What could be more fun, finding fault? I'm without ambition, black sheep, actually. My life is a carnival, exotic and amusing."

"I've never believed that."

He smiled. "I am to protect you," he said. "How do you wish to be protected?"

"As little as possible."

He nodded slightly, his chocolate eyes mocking. "From what do you wish to be protected?"

She didn't reply, turning to lean on the varnished rail across from her stateroom. She tried to focus on Jed, her Jed, somewhere up this swirling river, Jed . . . The image wouldn't come.

A gust of air brought ash and smoke down on her, and she coughed.

"Are you hungry?" Constable asked civilly. "There must be a dining room somewhere. I see a small galley chimney aft."

She didn't want to eat with him. "You might attend to your enlisted men," she said.

"Why? They're lucky. Usually the army buys them deck space only. But we're important, and they got cabin space in the women's quarters. A long way from the paddlewheels, where they can enjoy the silence." He laughed softly. "The necessary conveniences hang off the side right in front of the wheels. Splash, splash."

She reddened. That was just like him, she thought. He always said something a bit off color if he could and watched the reaction.

He plainly anticipated her anger, and smiled lazily.

"I believe I will get settled," she said.

"I will guard your maiden's door," he replied. "Except for Jed Owen. Shall I guard it then? What are your maidenly wishes?"

She slammed her door shut and found herself in gloom relieved only by the illumination from a small skylight. No heat. Not a pipe or a vent. She sat down on a hard felt-stuffed mattress covered with a sheet and a gray wool blanket. No pillow. Travel up the Missouri into wilderness would be spartan, but she had been prepared for that. The throb and lurch of the packet hummed through her body, and she wondered if she'd sleep. Still, this would be a haven. She eyed the dead bolt that let her shut out the world. A thief could lift it in an instant, she knew. But it would be something anyway. She sat uneasily, absorbing the stark varnished pine quarters, feeling uneasy. Then she knew. She had no window. Jed might pass her on the river, going downstream on a mackinaw or a keelboat, and she'd miss him . . . .

Alarmed, she burst out of her tiny room and gazed up and down the glinting gray river, solemn beneath a cast iron sky. Nothing. The river rolled as empty and dark and swirling as ever, hiding its secrets from a loving and yearning heart.

Jed sensed a different mood when they led him to the council the next afternoon. When he entered the chief's lodge, he felt a wall before him, though each of the seven elders sat in his accustomed place, and all seemed familiar enough.

He did not feel well this day. He'd had a bad night, wondering about his future, if indeed he had a future. Wondering whether Kootenai tortured the way the Plains tribes did, slowly, to extract maximum pain before the mercy of death. He'd been haunted by images of his mother and father, Susannah, dying men, and lastly, the squash-nosed young woman who cared for him now. By dawn he felt drained and weak, his progress toward health disrupted by an anguished spirit.

"Read the rest," commanded Yew Wood Bow.

He did. There wasn't much, and it was more of the same. Elwood had artfully invented conversations with several soldiers, all of whom turned out to be bloodthirsty and eager to exterminate every last Indian man, woman, and child. Jed knew there were many in his command who felt that way: the attitude was not uncommon among the blue-clad troops of the frontier. No matter.

He read them the commission's official charge, to treat with the northwest Plains Indians and propose a reservation for them north of the Missouri. The papers made no mention of the mountain tribes, Kootenai and Salish, or the tribes of the Oregon country.

Dawn Killer of Piegans translated, and then silence descended. Jed waited for questions, but there were none. The elders sat quietly, passing a pipe among themselves, staring into the brisk flame that kept an unusually cold day at bay. He had decided to fight for his life, even if it meant talking himself hoarse. Even if he felt so sick he could barely sit up. He had read them the lies exactly as they'd been written, and now he'd explain them as lies and give reasons as best he could, and hope it was not beyond the skills of the translator.

"Tell the chiefs I have words to say about the writings of Elwood," he said. "They are lies. Clever lies. The sign marks can lie too, just as tongues can lie."

Dawn Killer translated.

"This man didn't like the army," he said, into a thickening silence.

"This man wanted to make the army look bad so that his own agency—ah, group . . . clan—could steal from Indians."

He knew that made no sense. Make the army look bad so they could steal? He tried to explain. Congress. Zachary Taylor's administration. Rivalry about Indian policy. Annuity goods, treaty goods for each tribe, given out by Indian agents, army or civilian. Cheating and corruption. . . .

Dawn Killer of Piegans wrestled with all this, not understanding, and finally said he didn't have words. Jed had run into a wall that could not be breached, a cultural wall. These Kootenai thought that killing every Blackfoot and Assiniboin and Crow and Gros Ventre might be a fine idea. Then they could hunt the buffalo unmolested. And stealing from others, especially horses, was a mark of honor, not shame.

Jed saw the blankness in their faces and understood it. His life lay at stake, but he'd be damned if he'd surrender it without a fight.

"What Elwood said of me, the thoughts he gave to me in his book— none of it is true," he said. "I have never desired to kill. I do not wish to wipe Indian people from the earth. I do not shoot women and children. I am a warrior and I protect my people in war, but the marks in the book about me, and about the other soldiers, are lies."

Chief Yew Wood Bow stirred and said something, which the translator passed to Jed.

"The chief says that the elders have no witnesses—it is what you say against what the book says about you. So the elders can never know."

"I read the words to them truthfully and didn't make them up. Doesn't that tell them something about me?"

They talked among themselves, and at last Dawn Killer of Piegans turned to him.

"They don't know that you read the words truly. One medicine man says you did, and he has vision into the spirit. Others ask why you would read words against yourself. It confuses them."

Jed wrangled with them a while more, getting nowhere. At last he said, "You now know that nothing in the blue bag is medicine of the white men. It does not say how to make guns and powder."

"They don't know that," the Dawn Killer of Piegans replied. "Some think that all you have read us of the little marks was a cloud to cover the true medicine in the blue bag."

"Let me read everything again. If it is not exactly the same as before, then you will know that I made great lies and did not read truly."

A barked command from Chief Yew Wood Bow halted the exchange; in a moment, Dawn Killer of Piegans translated softly.

"The elders have made up their minds. They did this one sun ago, not now. Some of them think you are an evil spirit sent from under the earth by the Dark People to confuse and kill us. Some say you are brave and honest, for you read the words in the book without fear, words that condemn you."

"I read truth!"

"Some say you have concealed the medicine. Some say you are brave and will not lie. Our medicine man thinks you are brave and true. Our war chiefs think you are from under the earth and lie. Some think you have hidden the medicine in the blue bag.

"We are divided. Some wish to kill you and cleanse our village of evil spirits that might destroy the Kootenai. Others say you are brave and a friend of the Kootenai, and want only to kill Blackfeet. They say if we kill you, then evil will fall upon us and destroy us. We are divided.

"But the chief has decided. Since we do not know whether you are friend or enemy, good or evil, spirit or man, we will do this: we will drive you from the village but let you live. We will not kill you because your spirit might make bad medicine on us. But we do not want you here. This very day you will leave us, and go far from the People. We will give you your things so you can make your way. We will give you carbine and ball and powder, your clothes, and a robe as well. And we will give you the blue bag with the papers. If you are a good spirit or good man, you will think kindly of us and bless the People. If you are an evil spirit, we will be glad you are not among us. That is the word of Chief Yew Wood Bow."

Death sentence. But it would take two or three wintry days before exposure and starvation and illness conquered him. "My horse?" he asked.

"No."

"I would like to have the herbs that your woman gave me that healed me. I will need more."

The chief nodded.

"She will give you some and show you where the plant grows along the streams."

"Where will I go?"

"Far away from the People."

"I cannot cross the mountains unless you know a pass."

"There might be a pass you can cross now. But you should wait until the sun is warm and the days are longer."

Jed knew little of this land, and that only through rumor. It had never been explored, though the fur trappers knew it well enough. To the south lay a long lake, and somewhere beyond it the Salish people, or Flatheads. Somewhere down that long wintry trail lay a mission called Saint Mary's which the Jesuits had established and abandoned, leaving the Flatheads semi-Christianized. There might be buildings, perhaps allies. A chance to live through a bitter season if he had a horse, shelter, and trail food enough to get there.

"You have spared my life," he said. "You will remember that I spoke truly and told you which of the black signs on the pages were lies. You have fed me and nursed me to health. I will see that you have your reward when I reach my people. You will be remembered kindly by the white men."

Yew Wood Bow nodded and motioned him out.

Later that afternoon he shouldered what they had given him: carbine and knife, clothing and robe, a packet of rose hips offered by the unsmiling woman, flint and striker, mess kit—and a blue haversack with its precious contents, some of them audacious lies. It occurred to him that he could burn Elwood's journal and the world would never learn of the lies on its pages. But some stubborn thing in him forbade it. He would take the last letters of his dying men to the east, take the wills and testaments east, take the love in them east, for he had pledged to talk to as many survivors, wives and children and parents, as he could. And he'd take the lies too and hope he had the ability to explain their purpose. If he failed, it'd mean the end of him, the end of his career, the end of his dream of Susannah.

They watched him leave, the whole village standing silently in their brown buckskins and black robes against gray snow and dark lodges. He turned to them and shouted against the biting wind.

"Thank you," he cried, and they stared back silently, and all he heard was the blistering wind in the naked branches. He had an hour or two of light and set his face south, tromping through cruel drifts of snow alongside the frozen and drifted gray lake, leaving a trail of footprints behind him that any Kootenai murderer might follow. He thought he might try the ice and leave no trail but soon gave it up. If they meant to kill him, they would find his white man's trail swiftly enough. A trapper might vanish into the wilds, but not a West Point officer without snowshoes.

The cold wrapped around him and he drew the curly dark buffalo robe over his shoulders. A sick man's death march. To the Salish if he could find them, and could feed himself in this gray waste, which held not even the hoofprint of a deer. To Saint Mary's, whatever was left of it, far, far away from the headwaters of the Missouri. He stared upward, into the forbidding white mountains that separated him from his own world and from Susannah, and wondered when he might cross them—if he lived long enough even to try. In this northern climate it would be June at the earliest, he knew. Unless he could find that lower pass Dawn Killer of Piegans had spoken of. He had months to wait, and a tiny amount of powder and lead with which to survive. Perhaps the Salish knew a winter pass. He felt weak and hungry, but grateful for the lengthening daylight that gave him time to find shelter. Still, he lived.

Chapter Eight

Jed managed to plow a mile before his weakened body rebelled, and he had to force himself to walk another few hundred yards on trembling legs to reach a spur of pine forest thrusting down to the lavender lake. He had come scarcely farther than the village ponies roamed, but he could manage no more. It had been less than a month since the moon-faced woman had started feeding him the potion and hot stews, less than a month since he had lain at the gates of death, and he remained frail beyond any weakness he'd known in his young life.

The buffalo robe lay heavy over his shoulders, but it kept the worst of the howling winds off him. He could roll up in it at night. The blue duck haversack bounced from his hip, an excruciating burden, as if filled with lead or cast iron instead of last wishes, love, and lies. He marveled at it, marveled that a small canvas bag with a few papers could weigh so much. But he would not ditch it. Not the bag, not the papers, not that clothbound journal with all the lies in Elwood's fine patrician copperplate.

No shelter. Nothing in sight but gray windswept ice, bleak drifts that sometimes reached four or five feet, and black forest thrusting down purple slopes. No rock, no caves, no cutbanks, no friendly warm lodges. The forest, then. Windbreak and firewood. Still a quarter mile off, and heavy drifts blocking it. He floundered through one, pushing waist-deep into crusted snow that collapsed with every step. He sweated in spite of the biting wind and fought the drifts one step at a time, plunging deep, extricating himself only to fall deeper the next step. His heart throbbed and his last reserves of energy vanished like the birds of autumn.

Still, that small arrow of forest meant life or death. And in the violet light of a late midwinter day—he had lost track of the days, and had no idea even what month it was—he knew he once again reached the lip of eternity. He could pace himself, he thought. Rest a minute and take a few steps, and rest again. This he did, making slow progress but avoiding the dizzy brink of collapse he had experienced when he struggled less patiently. He hit a windswept stretch and made a hundred yards easily but then confronted the largest drift, over his head. And beyond it, thick black forest.

He stood panting, feeling snow in his boots, chafing his calves. His military issue Hall-North breech-loading carbine weighed a ton and grew heavier by the minute. Sensation had ceased in his reddened hands; they'd outfitted for a summer expedition, not a winter one, and he possessed no gloves. He'd wrapped his hands in spare linen drawers and tucked them under his robe as much as possible, but it wasn't enough.

Might die, he thought. Given potion for the scurvy and meat for the body, only to die anyway. His stomach told him he wanted food too, yet he had none to eat. And not a sign of game, which had vanished, gone to warmer and more hospitable climes in the dead of winter. The forest. He tackled the last drift, floundering a few steps through crusted snow that scraped his shins and knees, even through his britches, and then his feet wobbled on solid rock. It wasn't a drift but a rocky spur, thinly covered with smooth granular snow. Even so, he could barely climb the ten feet to its crest, and on its far side he dropped into thick snow that had settled there out of the blast of the wind. Somehow, he wallowed out to stand among black pines.

Squaw wood. Dead branches, long dried, projected from every lower trunk, deprived of life and light by the flourishing limbs above. He pushed ahead into the forest, past an island of snow-capped red shrub, and found a barren place beyond, free of the bitter eddying wind, barricaded by brush and sheltered by forest. He sagged wearily to the cast iron earth and rested. His strength was slow to return, and cold ate at his last reserves. He sat numbly, stupidly, too tired to act in the waning light, until suddenly he realized he had to have fire, gather the squaw wood at once, before pitch blackness rolled in.

He staggered up and began breaking off wood, barkless sticks that cracked and snapped as he bent them. An armload now and more later. His hands felt nothing. Huddled under his robe he shaved tiny slivers with a knife he couldn't feel and struck futile sparks with a flint and steel that refused to stay in his frozen fingers. On one stick he found hairy threaded underbark, fine tinder, and he made a tiny pile of it and added a pinch of precious gunpowder, and struck the flint again. Soon he had sparks spitting in it. In ten minutes he had a small hot fire, and he lay beside it sucking air into weary lungs until he felt strong enough to prepare for the night. A trembling hour later, in the deepest of blackness, he had wood enough, and a cheerless blaze that failed to drive the numbness and pain from his hands. He huddled close to it, braving swirls of smoke to snatch its heat, the buffalo robe over his back.

He melted a bit of grainy snow in his mess cup, crushed some of the Kootenai woman's brown buds into it, and drank the medicine tea. The hot brew felt good in his belly. He found strength enough to break off more squaw wood in the flickering amber light which radiated orangely over forest snow and made black limbs dance. He started a second fire to warm his feet while he rested.

And yet it seemed all for naught. Just beyond the fire lay death, ready to claim him after all in spite of his luck. He was scarcely off his deathbed and his body would endure very little now. No food, no shelter, the Salish some vast winter distance away. Not so much as a rabbit to eat, his carbine and knife useless tools.

He'd been dumb about building the fire, he thought. Elwood's half empty journal had lots of blank paper for tinder. So precious had all those things in the haversack become to him that the thought of using the paper for tinder hadn't entered his mind. Paper. Death. Perhaps he ought to write his own final message. Some last word for Susannah. Not that the message would ever reach her. He'd die here in this vast place, a tiny speck of mankind in a sea of wilderness. He'd be eaten by wolves and coyotes, eagles and crows and magpies, until nothing but rags and bone remained. The bag would vanish, the papers fly away, and the vast empty wilderness would enfold him and leave not the slightest trace of his passage. Still, it was not in Jed Owen to give up so easily. Death, yes; he'd reconciled himself to that several times in the last few months. But he'd get his messages east, somehow, some way.

By the crackling pine-stick fires he contemplated it, turning ideas over in his weary mind. He could write his own message with a hammered out lead ball, the time-honored pencil of commanders. He'd noticed a natural trace along the lakeshore. He could hang the bag from a limb where the trail must be, where it would be seen, and hope for the best. He could draw pictographs instructing the tribesmen who found it to take it to a trading post. He could draw the sacred symbols on it, sun and moon, so they might respect it.

Writing with hammered lead would be hard, but he could convey two simple messages: he loved Susannah, and Elwood's journal lied. He could add the place and approximate time—he thought it must be February—of his death. The thought of messages comforted him more than food. But he would wait until morning.

Susannah. The thought of her filled him with a great tenderness. *Oh Susannah, don't you cry for me.* They were singing that, the ones rushing to California. Suddenly he had to live. He had to see her again, hold her, cherish again the sweet throaty voice that uttered bold, grave truths. He conjured her up in his mind, before his eyes, and caught her laughing, felt the gentle touch of her hand on his cheek, felt her honest direct gaze that said worlds to him. Susannah! I won't quit! I won't die! Not as long as you walk the earth in beauty and light, and your radiance touches me!

But just then he felt so tired he could barely will himself to fuel the fire and roll up in his curly dark buffalo robe. He felt a faint moisture rising from the forest floor, where the fire had melted the frost. He'd soon die, he thought; it didn't matter—or did it? Susannah! He pulled himself up and cut spruce bows with his knife, until he had a lumpy layer of them to lie on and perhaps keep his robe dry. He might die, but he wouldn't concede an inch while getting there. He'd seen too many soldiers quit and die when all they needed to live was some fight. Susannah! He whispered her name aloud, and it rang like bells. He heard her voice, silvery across the ether. "I'm coming home, Susannah! Wait for me where the river runs!" he cried into the blackness.

He scooped up some snow and set it to heating in his tin cup and drank the scalding water, enjoying the warmth. He did it again. He cut some of the branches from the shadowed thicket of shrubs and made a tea of the tender bark. Chokecherry, he thought, but he wasn't sure. He tasted the result cautiously, unsure about it. A bitterness bit his tongue, and he drank the rest slowly, waiting to see if his stomach would rebel. It didn't. In fact, the bark tea seemed to infuse life into his trembling frame.

Feeling somewhat better, he settled down for the night, listening for the sound of wild creatures. He heard nothing but the whip of air. Above he saw no stars, and the overcast worried him. Snow now would slaughter him in this nest. He made a pillow of the haversack, feeling the papers crush under his cheek, and stared into the wavering fires. He'd have to replenish them every hour or so, he knew. But they and the buffalo robe wrapped tightly around his weak body would get him through a night. One night.

"Owen," came a low voice out of blackness. "Owen." And Jed Owen sat bolt upright.

A delightful blizzard swept out of the north, burying the plains in two feet of snow on the level. Then the winds toyed with the green snow, whipping it into ten-foot drifts that ridged and eddied across the aching empty distances, halting all travel of man or wild creature.

Mon Dieu, a gift! Jean Gallant contemplated it joyously, studied the mounded snow that piled against the Absaroka lodges, studied the whitened prairie, humped endlessly like a shining sea, forbidding and endless. Ah, what joy! What paradise! Fort Union lay four hundred wintry miles east, and Fort Benton lay over a hundred northeast. Too much even for the American Fur Company's most intrepid and courageous and lion hearted engagé. Ah, the blessings that befell a virtuous man! Jean Gallant made the sign of the cross and clambered back through the door hole into the borrowed lodge, where Owl Feather sat quilling moccasins and No Father and American Fur fed the tiny fire and teased each other.

No, not even the company's hard masters would expect their own Gallant to travel across the snow-choked wastes in such weather. He had nothing to report anyway, save for two stray nondescript ponies found near the Sun River, and if the Sun River valley held any secrets, they'd be buried under ridged snow for many weeks more. He sighed. Food ran short. He'd traded his entire stock of geegaws and tobacco for food and the use of a lodge, but now he must go hunt and fill these bellies. It'd be an overnight trip, because all the game near the Crow village had long since been consigned to stewpots.

Like any proper woman of the plains, his own little Owl Feather had done all the work that mattered, butchering meat, cooking meals, making and mending his clothes with a fine steel awl she'd gotten at a trading post, gathering firewood from the endless cottonwood forests along the Big River, as these people called the Missouri, minding the children, softening hides, cutting thong, adjusting the wind flaps to the fickle winds, all the while laughing and chattering, pleased to have her own Gallant back. And the nights! *Mon Dieu!* Sometimes the afternoons, too! What else was there to do on a long winter's day? Did not every tribe of the northern plains repopulate itself during the winters?

He sighed, not wanting to hunt or face the cold or sit upon the protruding bones of his gaunt pony and steer it on down the river in search of a doe hovering in the cottonwood breaks. But it could not be put aside any longer: they were down to pemmican and jerky. So with many sighs, Gallant pulled on his new moccasins lined with rabbit fur, slid on his new red blanket capote which Owl Feather had fashioned for him of four-point wool, drew onto his hands the wolf-trimmed gloves of softest ivory doeskin she'd also made, and braved the elements, his venerable Hawken in hand.

Some instinct told him not to hunt the river bottoms but to steer his slat-ribbed pony out upon the snow-swept plains. A gunmetal blue overcast subdued the light and kept his eyes from watering with snow blindness. Out upon the empty rolling prairie, the great ditch of the Missouri vanished, and the village snugged into its bottoms made itself known only by a soft smoke haze hugging the land to the north. He rode quietly, feeling the resentment of the pony under him as it minced across snow-swept country never knowing what lay beneath the surface. Gallant sighed. Duty never appealed to him, especially the domestic variety. Let him be his manly self out alone, and he loved life. Coop him up in some squaw's lodge, and life palled.

He squinted at the surrounding hills, looking for the wily pronghorn. This time of year they ran in flocks, huddling together for mutual protection. And then, scarcely twenty minutes from the Crow village, he spotted them, forty or so, lounging on a south slope out of the wind, soaking up whatever heat they could. *Mon Dieu!* What blessings! He studied them, remembering to make a sweeping sign of the cross. They had seen him come but remained undisturbed by this wintry specter, their curiosity aroused. A poor meat, he thought, but a sight to see, with their white bottoms and rumps and tawny backs. He let the pony amble to a bare patch of ground scarcely two hundred yards off and easily dismounted, springing a bit on cold-stiffened legs. He pulled out his shooting sticks, tied together at their centers, and lowered himself to the hard olive clay, propping the Hawken's barrel in the vee of the spread sticks. Simple. Three booms of the Hawken, and three antelope lay sprawled leaking bright red blood into the snow. The band trotted off, barely alarmed. He loaded one flopping pronghorn over the rump of his nervous pony and skidded the other two along the snow at the end of a thong, and scarcely an hour after he'd braved the winter he clambered into his warm lodge.

"Ah!" cried Owl Feather, and set to work at once.

"A little gift from your very own Gallant," he said graciously, letting her catch up her knives and dress herself in her oldest skirts to begin the butchering.

"I'm glad you have come home to me, my very own Gallant," she whispered from beneath him in the dark of that night.

"My own little Owl Feather."

And thus the hardest months of winter passed, and Jean Gallant waxed fat and warm and fed them all. But the sun grew stronger daily and melted black circles in the white around the trees, stripped snow off the south side of slopes, and coaxed bits of green grass up in sheltered places. The yellow village curs turned playful and chased wolves. The warriors shot arrows and curried winter-starved ponies. And Jean Gallant grew restless. He could travel again.

"My very own Owl Feather," he announced solemnly one fine

March day. "I have my duties to the company. Now I must go and earn my little income from my masters."

"No, Gallant!"

"But I shall return!" he cried hastily. "Old trappers never die, Owl Feather. Here, my little wife, send the children outside and give me something for my memories."

She did, and afterward smiled stoically as she slid her softest doeskin ceremonial dress over her golden shoulders and pulled on her finest quilled moccasins.

"I will always remember, Owl Feather," he said hoarsely. "And you must remember what I have taught you of the arts of *amour,* and we shall enjoy them again!"

"You taught me much," she whispered. "I thought the Absaroka People knew everything, but I have learned."

He smiled beatifically and tied down the load on his packhorse. The geegaws were gone, but he had a load of prime furs to trade to the company in their stead. Some of them he'd won gambling, having become an expert at the bone game, which involved sleight of hand. He'd cleaned his brother-in-law Makes Arrows out of two richly dressed robes.

He hugged his own Owl Feather good-bye, while the village watched contemplatively, and then he rode off into the winds of March, trotting his tough ponies across mud-slick hills under a coy sun and blustery heaven, leaving tears and entreaties behind him. *Mon Dieu!* It was always hard to leave them!

Fort Benton didn't interest him, so he rode straight toward Fort Union, where the Missouri and the Yellowstone met, across wind-lashed prairies, braving late storms, fighting a pack of wolves that followed him, avoiding a village of Assiniboin he didn't want to deal with because he had no white man's gifts and they would have no news, straight east until the mountains behind him shrank into the horizon and his only world was cottonwood-lined creeks and snow-patched rough prairie. Then, over a month later, he rode toward the stockade of Fort Union, crown jewel of the American Fur Company, where Kenneth McKenzie had invested years and a small fortune bringing civilized amenities upriver and shipping beaver pelts and then buffalo robes down to distant St. Louis.

McKenzie was long gone, along with the beaver trade, but his son

Owen still lingered here. Pierre Chouteau rather than John Jacob Astor owned it now, and Alec Culbertson ran it, or James Kipp, or Malcolm Clarke. Jean Gallant would report to one of these, though he never knew which because one or another was always running down to St. Louis, escaping the wilderness that Gallant loved even more than he loved women.

He thought of riding first to his own little nest, a log cabin outside of the fort where his own Assiniboin lady, Owl Song Woman—he must remember not to call her Owl Feather—awaited him eagerly. But duty before pleasure, and in any case she had grown old and lacked the nubile attractions of his younger wives. So then, always duty. He rode into the great yard within and drew his pony to a halt before the comfortable house where his *bourgeois* lived and ruled, remembering to compose his dark features into a somber and dignified expression.

"Monsieur Kipp!" he exclaimed, "Your very own Gallant has returned safely, through the hells of winter."

Kipp waited patiently, as he always did for Gallant.

"*Oui*, I have visited every village, and I have suffered—ah, monsieur, how I suffered from the winds and cold. My thermometer read minus forty-nine once. *Oui*, try being out in that, eh?"

Kipp sighed patiently.

"But I made my way, suffering frostbite and cold and starvation, from village to village, chief to chief, making wise use of small gifts, always asking, eh? Asking. Asking . . ."

"Asking about your wives, Gallant?"

"Ah, no Monsieur Kipp. My mission was ever before me, and duty came before pleasure. Asking about the lost soldiers. No word, Monsieur Kipp. No one had seen them. Poor creatures, they vanished from the face of the earth. *Mort.* Dead, I am sure."

He thought to tell Kipp of two nondescript ponies found by Coyote's band on the Sun River, and decided not to.

"I am so sorry," he sighed. "It came to nothing. Except for a few pelts I won—ah, bargained for. Which of course I will trade to the company."

"Very well, then, Gallant."

"Is that all you have to say? After so much suffering?"

Kipp eyed him quietly. "You look fat, Gallant. You wear fine new moccasins, splendid wolf-trimmed gloves, a beautiful blanket capote, an elkskin shirt of Crow design, and you bring robes you say are your own. Your suffering was—formidable, Gallant. Yes, you are our best man."

"I knew you'd see it that way," said Gallant. "And now my own dear Owl Feather—ah, Owl Song Woman—awaits me, Monsieur Kipp!"

Chapter Nine

Jed clutched his carbine and swung it up, unsure whether it was loaded and capped. In his haste and weariness he had neglected to check.

"Jed Owen. We are coming. Do not shoot."

The voice pierced through the blackness beyond the wavering amber of the fires.

"All right then," he replied. He lacked the strength to fight anyway, and whatever fate brought would be his lot.

He heard horses first, the gentle snuffle and the unique crunch of hoofs on snow and frozen ground. Two horses, one heavily laden with his own and Charbonneau's army gear. Then three people, led by Dawn Killer of Piegans. In the corduroy light he recognized them all. One was the moon-faced squashed-nosed woman who had cared for him. The other was the youngest and quietest of those in Yew Wood Bow's daily council, so junior that he had said little and done nothing but gaze contemplatively at Owen through those long readings.

They wore capotes made of bright striped Hudson's Bay blankets and somehow managed to look cheerful even in the somber winter night. Jed sat up and drew his buffalo robe tight, even as they settled themselves close to his fire.

"This is Diving Hawk, a war leader of our people. He sat among us."

"I remember."

"And the woman, Medicine Sagebrush, you know. She is the woman of Diving Hawk."

Jed smiled at the one who had nursed him back from death's door.

"Diving Hawk was with me when we captured you and the one who is dead—we must not speak his name—and won your horses and things."

Faint memory stirred in Jed. Diving Hawk had risen out of nowhere, along with Dawn Killer of Piegans, counted coup on Jed and Gabriel, and took them across the great mountains, far, far away from the drainage of the Missouri.

"Diving Hawk had had a vision. The Beyond People came to him and told him that the Old Things are passing away and the New Things are coming, and the white men hold the secrets of the New Things. He saw you teaching him the things of your people, the meanings of the signs on paper. He has come with gifts, the things that belonged to you and the one who is dead. And also pemmican and jerky, because there's no game in cold times.

"He has a request: he wishes that you would stay with him in his lodge until the warm times come and the sun stays long, and he wishes you will teach him all that you know, so that he may lead the People wisely when the time comes of the vision he saw. But if not, these things are yours."

"But I've been banished from your village by Chief Yew Wood Bow. They fear I'd bring evil upon them. They would oppose this."

"Diving Hawk has moved his lodge to a place outside the village. He has told the elders of his vision. No one goes against a vision, not even the elders and medicine men. You will not enter the village, for that has been said, but you will stay in the warm lodge of Diving Hawk and Medicine Sagebrush, and you will teach. And I too will come and learn of your ways."

Jed eyed the packhorse contemplatively, seeing his army tent halves and bedrolls, and even his own privately purchased Colt's

Dragoon hanging from the saddle. Safety and comfort; a tent and better weapons.

"If I should choose to go, I am free?"

"Diving Hawk has given you freedom and all that you and the one who died possessed. But it is a long time until the passes through the mountains open up."

"What about the Salish, to the south? That's where I—"

"Many days along this lake. Then a river that cuts through mountains but turns west, away from the Salish. You would have to find the right way, along another river, to the valley of the Salish. And you will be far away from the Big River you call the Missouri."

"Tell Diving Hawk I'll come and teach him. I'll need you to translate. And tell him I wish to learn the ways of the Kootenai people."

The Kootenai talked excitedly among themselves, and then they helped Jed into the familiar saddle of his horse and led him through the stygian darkness, their journey made possible only by the dim starlit snow. They hewed to the frozen shoreline, passing the darkened village set back beside a bare-limbed forest, and on toward the northwest, Jed gathered from an occasional glance at Polaris. There, perhaps a mile from the village, rose a solitary lodge with smoke drifting from its wind flaps. Curved around it rested a windbreak of brush, gathered from the dense aspen grove nearby. A mound of firewood rested blackly near the east-facing door flap. A large frozen carcass, he didn't know of what animal, hung from a tripod, well above the snapping teeth of wolves.

Jed dismounted and fell in a heap, his legs too wobbly to carry him. The woman helped him up and supported him. They crawled into a warm, snug, comfortable place lit by a bed of red embers. She smiled and helped him to the place of honor, where he sank into a mound of soft warm robes. Diving Hawk and Dawn Killer of Piegans carried Jed's possessions in and placed them carefully around the periphery of the lodge. An infant coughed and wailed, and it surprised Jed. They had left it sleeping in its cradleboard to come fetch him. The woman, Medicine Sagebrush, hastened to the child and bared her umber breast to it.

At last, with Jed's possessions stored and his horses set out among aspen and cottonwood to gnaw a winter's living from bark and twigs, the two young Kootenai settled themselves in the lodge, and the master of this home withdrew a pipe and tamped tobacco into its red pipestone bowl.

Ceremony, then, Jed thought, so sleepy he could barely keep his head up.

"We will smoke and then I will leave and you will sleep," said Dawn Killer of Piegans. "This must be."

The next morning, a blinding, sunny one, Jed remembered puffing once on the pipe, but that was the only thing he remembered. Beyond that, only the soft warmth of a buffalo robe, the comfortable marvel of a lined tepee set inside a windbreak, and floating images of Susannah, smiling.

He knew from the way the light lay in the smoke hole, that it must be midday. Lazily he watched Medicine Sagebrush sew moccasins with an awl and thong. The child, a chunky boy named Soldier, crawled nakedly about on the warm skins, intuitively staying away from the fire pit in the center. Jed marveled at the child's nakedness in bitter winter, but the lodge encased warmth, and its inner lining acted as a flue guiding outside air upward to draw smoke out through the smoke hole into the azure-black sky. The woman noticed him staring and smiled.

Perhaps an hour later his host and Dawn Killer of Piegans seated themselves cross-legged before him, and the great enterprise began.

Words first, Jed thought. Teach them to speak English first, and then tackle spelling and writing. The task seemed formidable. But Diving Hawk had other plans.

"He says he will adopt you and give you a Kootenai name."

That surprised Jed.

"He says that from this moment on you are his adopted son and a member of the People. He gives you the name Tobacco Runner."

"Tobacco Runner?"

"It is what you call 'messenger.' We send runners with a gift of tobacco to other villages with news. Now you are Tobacco Runner, one of the People. And now no one of those in the village will touch you, for they will never harm another Kootenai."

"I am honored to have Diving Hawk as my father and Medicine Sagebrush as my mother, and this one here"—he gestured at the child—"as my brother."

That done, they smoked again.

"Now when the blue-coated soldiers came to kill all the People, as you told the council, kill the Piegans, kill the Assiniboin, kill the Kainah, kill the Absaroka, even as you told us, you will not kill your father and mother and brother, and our people."

Jed felt saddened. They had believed Elwood's lies about himself and the army. Well, he'd try to explain.

"Some in my army think that way," he told Dawn Killer of Piegans. "But many do not. The government, the great chiefs, do not. Some of the white people do, those that want your lands, but most do not. The religion—the medicine beliefs of the whites—forbids it, says no to killing. You have been misled by the words I read, the words of the headman called Elwood. Tell my father I will explain. Tell him it will take many days, and he will need to learn new words and make new pictures in his head. But even if it takes until the snow melts, I will give him understanding. I will tell him why the man Elwood lied—so that he might become rich."

The pair of them talked at length in the tongue of the Kootenai and at last turned to Jed.

"You read things that were not true? You gave us lies?"

"I read truly. I read what the words said."

"We do not understand," said Dawn Killer of Piegans. "All of us in council believed you spoke only truth."

Across from Jed, his new father glared darkly, and Jed did not know how to explain.

Each day Jed stared at the white crowns of the mountains, but nothing changed. Sun warmed the air, stripped snow away from the long valley, melted the green ice cap on the lake, nurtured tender verdant grasses and coaxed out lime green leaves on the aspen and cottonwoods.

He grew mad with impatience. He had to return! They would think him dead! Susannah would surrender at last and find someone else! That thought was more than he could bear: Susannah losing hope, mourning, and finally discovering some other man, while he remained trapped here on the wrong side of the mountains, far from the great Missouri and all its headwaters, where he had promised her he would be. He thought only of the wide river and its crystal waters fed by these Rocky Mountains, the river that would take him to Fort Leavenworth.

But each time he asked, Diving Hawk said no, not yet. In the passes would be snow, three times, five times the height of a man, and cold streams cascading meltwater out of the mountains, streams that would rip a horse's feet from under him, hurl a man down a mountain in moments. No, not yet, white man. Do not be impatient to leave us.

But he was. He paced the greening fields, stared bitterly at the purple barrier to the east, forbidding and sawtoothed, watched vicious gray clouds boil up each day and dump their blizzards, feet deep, on the distant ridges.

"I'll go south then, to the Salish. Surely they have passes to the Big River that are easier."

Diving Hawk nodded. "You could do that. The way to the Salish is open now, and they could take you from the country of the Bitterroots to the country of the Three Forks, where the three rivers come together to make the Missouri. Yes, you could do that now but you would not save time, for you would go far out of your way. In one more moon you can cross here, if you are strong and brave."

"I will wait."

Diving Hawk smiled. They had long since learned of Jed's love.

A prisoner in paradise. In truth this land of the Kootenai with its azure mountains and white peaks, its glowing long lake and verdant slopes, its spring zephyrs and dancing game, caught his soul at every glance. Except for buffalo, these Kootenai people had everything mortals might want, and a fresh sweet world scented with sage for a nest.

For seventy-five days by his count he had taught and learned in the lodge of Diving Hawk, word by word, Kootenai and English. The alphabet and numbers, the combinations of letters that made words. Bit by bit the magic signs, the medicine signs in the blue haversack made some sense to Diving Hawk, Medicine Sagebrush, and Dawn Killer of Piegans. Even then, Jed found himself unable to explain that writing could lie. Neither could he describe the cities and nations of the whites. When he told them that a hundred thousand lived in a single city, they laughed. Could white men be so numberless? And how would such a mob be fed? He did little better describing the government in Washington City, its branches and departments. In the end, he knew that these Kootenai only half understood Elwood and his purposes. And they still believed that Jed Owen and his soldiers would some day kill all the Indian people save for themselves, who had adopted him.

Jed gave that up as a lost cause. At least he could teach them enough so that when it came to treaties, they could deal intelligently with any commissioner Washington might send to them.

"Tell me the earliest day."

"Your horses are not yet strong. The mountains will test them and maybe kill them—and you," replied his host. "But I will invite Dog here."

Dog. Ancient shaman of the Kootenai village, respected among them all for visions, for seeing the unseen, for telling of what would come. Dog, Jed's sole ally in the councils of Yew Wood Bow, who told them Jed read truly. Dog would come here because Jed could not enter the village. During all these days and weeks, the Kootenai had carefully not noticed him, stared the other way, passed silently, no matter that he had been adopted into the tribe. Dog would tell him the time when he could head for unseen passes.

That soft evening Dog came, and Jed gave the ancient one a small brass telescoping spy glass that had been Charbonneau's, and the shaman's old face broke into a wrinkled smile.

The old man was given the place of honor, to the left of Diving Hawk, who waited quietly with Dawn Killer of Piegans. The old medicine man seemed to know why he'd been summoned. He closed his eyes, rubbed fresh new sagebrush leaves over his cheeks and lips, and dropped the leaves on the coals, perfuming the air.

"When the sun rises tomorrow you will leave, Tobacco Runner. You will go slowly for five suns to the pass that Diving Hawk will show you. This is the Kootenai warrior pass. To the south there is a low one that is easily traveled; Two Medicine Pass, the Piegans call it. But they lurk at its mouth to kill you and take your things. You must take the high pass Diving Hawk shows you. There at the foot of it he will leave you, and you will go to your people of the east. And your heart will quake in you at the sight of the snow and ice rivers above, and the black clouds that await you. And your horses will be afraid. You will cross on slanting ice long before it is safe, and on top you'll find chasms to snare you and poor footing and death at every hand. I do not see all the things that will be."

The man's quavering voice fell silent.

They waited, but he was done.

"I honor you, Father Dog." The Kootenai had no exact synonym for the gratitude he wished to express. "But the Piegans won't kill a white soldier who has come to make treaties. And the lower pass, Two Medicine Pass, is easy, you say."

"You are alone. Have you a translator? Can you make your fingers talk? Do you have tobacco and medals and gifts? Will the fierce Piegans believe a lone man has come to make a treaty with them? No. They will kill at once. And if they find you alone on the prairies, they will kill without mercy to take your horses and guns."

"I'll take your secret high pass."

"You are true, Tobacco Runner. Take good word of the Kootenai to the fathers of your people."

The old man left the lodge like a wraith, leaving a ghostly presence behind him in the quiet.

"Tomorrow we shall see you no more," said Diving Hawk. "You will risk the wet mountains for your woman Susannah."

"A part of me will stay here, and my heart will be on the ground because I leave you, father and mother," he replied. "I mean to come again to see my parents."

He found gifts among his things and Charbonneau's, a knife, a tin cup, some gunpowder, coins, sugar, tobacco, salt. All these he laid before them and watched their eyes flash joy. From his field desk he took paper and a pencil stub and wrote out the alphabet and numbers, a few hundred English words.

"Mother Medicine Sagebrush, you gave me life with your herbs. We call that disease scurvy and know only that it comes when something lacks in our food. I will remember you and your medicine."

She smiled, her eyes dancing.

They left when the sun was well up and searing the last of the frost off the bright grasses. Diving Hawk circled widely around the village, where people watched their progress solemnly, somehow knowing of the white man's departure. Yew Wood Bow had donned his ceremonial buckskins, bonnet and his finely wrought high moccasins, and he held his staff of office. He watched the two horsemen and the packhorse amble leisurely to the northeast. No one moved. Jed watched them standing like statues in the golden sun until he could see them no more.

Each day, as they probed toward the shoulders of the mountains, the climate changed. They had started in late May or early June, Jed thought, but as they steered their animals along a slick wet trail patched with decaying green snow, they receded into April and then March. Not an inch of dry land existed anywhere. Creeks thundered, driftwood and logs rocketing down them. Each fording wrought terror, as the smashing wall of ice water slammed horses broadside, upsetting them, drenching packs. The worst, a thirty-yard-wide deluge of water and ice floes, tumbling rock and slippery logs, they negotiated only when Diving Hawk stripped naked and lashed his terrified pony into the vicious water, clinging to its mane while it fought its way across to pull itself out exhausted, far downstream. Then, with a rawhide line, he helped Jed and his animals through the torrent.

On the fifth day, even as Dog had said, they reached a small plateau at the head of a cirque. Vaulting upward, a snow-covered grade lifted into fog and dense dark clouds. From every pore of the mountains water dripped and green ice hung.

"Here is where I leave you, Tobacco Runner," Diving Hawk said. "You will need a strong heart for what comes. On the far side of Lone Walker Mountain you will come to the Two Medicine Lakes and then the River, and that will take you to Marias River, as your people call it. No game up above, not yet. You will have only the pemmican. Keep some with you, not all of it on the packhorse. I leave you now. Be close to One Above, whom you call God. We will await word of your safety."

He turned swiftly back, wanting nothing of the emotion flooding them both. Jed watched his father vanish in the foggy gloom. He turned in the dripping silence to the path ahead and felt stricken with dread. It vanished white and dripping and murderous into a bank of iron-dark cloud. But beyond, beyond the unknown January above, lay the plains, the great Missouri, and the chance of delivering his messages.

Chapter Ten

Sometime after they'd churned past Council Bluffs, the solid phalanx of trees that had hemmed the murky river since Leavenworth surrendered to grassy banks and longer vistas. The budding trees had been a faint green haze, but the windswept prairies lay brown under an April sun that had not yet coaxed the grasses to life. Rotting snow lay upon blue northern slopes, soaking up sudden showers from the restless sky.

Susannah swiftly mastered the daily ritual of the packet and ceased to notice the throb of the twin steam pistons propelling its splashing wheels. They stopped frequently for wood, wherever the woodhawks on the shores had stacked it in long lengths. When the woodhawk was on hand, the master, Sandoval, paid him cash; when the woodcutter was off somewhere, the roustabouts loaded the crooked hardwood aboard anyway, and Sandoval left a letter of credit and made a special notation in his log.

She lost no time making the master's acquaintance; his quarters lay just forward of her own. She sensed in the wiry dark Spaniard with the patrician nose a security and power that comforted her far more than Jay Constable's languorous mockery.

"The farther we go up the river, the worse the wood," he told her one day while she idled in the wheelhouse. "Below, there were good hardwoods, but ahead, soft cottonwood for the most part. It takes more cottonwood to make steam."

On occasion they snared floating debris, trunks and roots, pulling it aboard with pikes and setting it to dry. Anything to keep the hungry firebox burning.

They had little trouble with sandbars, with the spring runoff so high. The river flooded twice, Sandoval explained; first from the prairie runoff, if there had been snows in the northwest, and then again in May and June, when the mountain runoff peaked. This year they churned through opaque gray water that ran high and washed giant roots and logs which Sandoval called "sawyers," down the endless river. He feared them, and when the pilot sighted one, Susannah heard a clamor of bells and felt a sudden veering and the shudder of reversing paddles.

"They'll punch a hole through the hull in an instant," he said.

"Will that sink us?"

"Usually not. But we have to lay to for repairs, patch the hole." He eyed her. "Your safety is my first concern."

"I think the safety of the boat and all its people and cargo are your first concern."

He smiled blandly and bowed slightly.

She saw her first buffalo that day, a solitary bull on a distant knoll. A few greenhorns tried to shoot it while Sandoval eyed them watchfully from above.

"They always try," he muttered. "Later we'll have good haunch of buffalo. We depend on them, and shore hunters, for our larder."

"You don't take food enough for the journey?"

"Staples. Not meat. We can always get fresh meat. Unless there's Indian danger and our hunters can't work along the shores. From now on, though, we'll be picking up carcasses they'll leave in sight on the banks for us."

Two days later she asked him a question that had been simmering in her. "Can you marry people? I mean, as a ship's master, can you—do it legally?"

His brown eyes danced. "I can, but I never have. I lack even a ritual."

"Would it be legal and proper?"

"Legal, I imagine; proper, more or less. Depending on your religious convictions." He cocked an eye toward her. "Have you someone in mind? That slouching lieutenant?"

He said it frivolously, she knew. Word of her purposes had somehow spread everywhere aboard the *El Paso*; as the lone white woman aboard, she was the cynosure of endless gossip and observation.

"No, not him," she said, staring out upon the endless, empty plains. "I don't much care if it's proper, just so that I keep the gossips at bay."

He laughed suddenly. "You are a bold woman, and I admire that. He must be a splendid man, this Jed Owen you come up the river to marry. I hope he's worthy, and as bold as yourself."

She saw the faintest flicker in his eyes and knew he had stopped himself from saying the rest: if your Jed Owen is still alive.

"There's the mountain marriage. The French call it the country marriage, *mariage du pays*," he said. "Down below on those decks those engagés and their squaws, the fur company ones, are bound by such wedlock. Unless some priest has wandered along."

"Maybe that's what I'll do," she announced, watching Ricardo Sandoval's face twitch with unspoken words. "A mountain marriage. I rather like the taste of it."

She laughed boldly, but he averted his gaze. Well, she thought, when was an army brat ever respectable?

She spent her days everywhere except her blind dark stateroom, where she couldn't see the river. The wheelhouse felt best, and she found herself welcome there, whether or not the master was present. From its high perspective atop the texas she could watch the great river from bank to bank, sheltered from rain and sun. One day they did spot a mackinaw, one of the long low rough-cut boats built upriver to drift down with cargo. Six black-bearded men in greasy buckskins manned it, skirting the bales of black buffalo robes in its belly, and her heart lurched at the sight of two who might be Jed. But they were French, engagés of the Opposition, Harvey, Primeau, and Company.

Sandoval came to her aid. "We are seeking news of the army party led by Captain Owen," he roared at them through his speaking horn.

Gallic shrugs. *"Non, non,"* one of them yelled back. They vanished around a broad bend, and Susannah slipped into a melancholy and scarcely noticed Lieutenant Constable grinning up at her from the deck below.

"You live here in our pilothouse so that you can watch the river," Sandoval said gently. "Ah, how you watch every bend for Captain Owen. There's no need, Miss St. George. I've long since asked my mate and steersman to hail every mackinaw or keelboat or canoe, and every horseman on the riverbanks besides."

"I—I didn't know."

"But if you enjoy our company here, stay on, my lady. We are honored by yours. And it's a haven from Lieutenant Constable, yes?"

She grinned ruefully. "I am more obvious than I supposed."

"I see only true love," he replied gallantly. "And what delights the soul of a man more than that? I confess I keep my eye on your escort and protector."

"He was a suitor."

"So I gather."

"Jay Constable's brave and bright," she said tentatively.

He stared out upon the misted horizon. "Perhaps," he said slowly. "Perhaps we will see. The river brings out the essence of men. Did you know that? Bring a man up this endless river, into the unknown wilds, and the truth of him will show sooner or later. Before we dock at Fort Union, we'll know."

"He's left me alone, mostly. Except for his eyes. His gaze follows me. They notice, of course—the passengers. Let one talk with me at table or say a word on deck, and there he is, gazing. I suppose that's what he was told to do by my father."

"You've met our passengers?"

"They delight me. Wild as these prairies. They have no manners but something better, I think: a natural honesty."

Ricardo Sandoval laughed heartily. "You're a romantic," he said. "I suppose you're right. They're honest wild men, honest murderers, honest rascals, madmen of the mountains, without deceit."

They swept a curve, the tumbling current driving them against the outside bank so that the wheelsman had to point the stem inward as the boat quartered. Beyond, across silvery water, lay a wooded flat, dense with cottonwoods not yet budded. At its upper end was a rude mud levee with cords of long-cut wood stacked on it, dark in the low afternoon light.

"*Bueno,*" said Sandoval. "They have a little. The *Mary Blane*'s ahead of us, getting wood first. It burns twelve cords a day. We burn eleven. If we don't buy it, we stop and cut it ourselves, crew and all the passengers—except ladies, of course. You cook."

He barked swift commands, and the packet slipped sideways somehow as his steersman wheeled and the engineers down below slowed the engine. Racing current tugged the boat, threatening to spin it clear around, and for the time being the master and pilot Sandoval was too preoccupied to explain things to Susannah. Then it hit calm water, save for the sucking eddies of the muscular river, and the boat chuffed easily toward the bank, where rough men waited and watched.

"A lot of men and not much cordage," Sandoval muttered.

His deckhands threw out lines, and in moments the packet was made fast to stumps. A great quiet settled over them while deckhands and woodhawks stared at each other.

"Got some cordage," yelled one red-bearded giant in filthy buckskin britches and red calico shirt.

Sandoval nodded, and the crew lowered the wobbly gangplank.

"Three cords, and some looks green," Sandoval muttered. "We may be cutting our own tomorrow."

A dozen burly woodhawks. It surprised Susannah; usually they encountered one or two at each stop. These rough men boiled aboard, each with a three-foot chunk of cottonwood, while the deckhands stacked the cordage and the teeming passengers watched. One of the woodhawks, a slat-thin one with a full blue beard and bright eyes, spotted her as she stood at her railing above and stared much too long.

She lacked beauty, she knew. Too long of face. But she might be the first white woman to venture into this wilderness; she'd heard of no other. She must be an apparition to him.

Uneasily she turned her gaze elsewhere and spotted Constable grinning again, missing nothing. As much as she disliked him, she felt momentarily protected. He said something to his six soldiers below, and they spread out to station themselves at the companionways. But they weren't armed, she noticed.

It took only a few minutes for the rough men to heft the huge logs aboard, and then they gathered around the mate, sweating and rank even in the cold air.

"Hyar now, we'll be takin' our wage in spirits. Ye'll be settlin' for a keg or two," said the slat-thin one who'd stared at Susannah. "Plumb dry up hyar, and we'll be havin' a fandango. I think we'll churn up the river with ye and have us a dance and all. It gits tiresome cuttin' trees out in some patch days on end."

"Three cords we make it, and here's gold," replied the mate, Walleye Ralph, amiably.

"Naw, we'll have us some spirits."

From above, Ricardo Sandoval addressed them quietly. "We can't bring spirits into Indian country. You know that. This packet was searched at Leavenworth."

The blue-bearded woodhawk grinned. "They allus miss a little, and they allow some for ship's use. I think maybe we'll have us a little search."

"You'll stay right there," replied the master. "You have your pay, and there'll be no fandangos while we're under steam."

"Haw!" exclaimed the woodcutter, his sharp eyes on Susannah above. She felt chilled. "This child's going to have spirits and a fandango."

Walleye Ralph grinned and nodded to his deckhands. His massive fists closed and unclosed. Joy lit his face. He hawked and spat. The crew edged toward the woodhawks, who leered happily, ready for the fun to begin.

But for a moment only torsioned silence prevailed as men eased themselves into various positions, selecting opponents to maul, and passengers either slid away or stood their ground, ready for the brawl.

"Stop," barked Sandoval from the texas deck. He clutched a baby dragoon revolver.

"Off the boat. Once you're on the bank, I'll toss you a gallon jug from my ship's stores. But if you think we're carrying illegal kegs, you're mistaken."

"Haw!"

"The one that starts a brawl gets shot," Sandoval snapped. "Let that be a warning."

Susannah watched unhappily. The woodhawks, men rougher than she'd ever seen on the river, all had knives. Some had revolvers at their hips. The burly deckhands had nothing but their fists. She glanced at Constable, imploring him. His enlisted men weren't armed either.

"Gentlemen, gentlemen," said Constable, unwinding himself from his usual slouch. "I don't think you'll wish to tackle the army, sirs. The army might just tackle you."

The lieutenant walked forcefully up to the woodhawks' leader, who stared up and down at the slender, delicate-looking officer and bellowed. The man's ham fist cocked and exploded, knocking Constable backward, and instantly the brawl was on, a seething howling mob.

A shot. Sandoval had fired over their heads hoping to stop them. Too late.

"Ralph!" he bellowed to the besieged mate. "Cast off." The mate glanced upward, and then he snaked through the brawl toward the fore hawser. Sandoval ducked into the pilothouse and shouted down the speaking tube. Susannah felt the vessel shudder under her feet. "Miss St. George, into your stateroom at once, and lock the door," he snapped. She backed from her railing reluctantly.

But the woodhawks weren't on board for the joy of a brawl. They pulled knives and heavy revolvers out, and backed the deckhands and passengers off almost before the fistfights began in earnest. Shots now, puffs of powder smoke. A bullet spanged the pilothouse a foot from Sandoval.

As if prearranged, groups of woodhawks sprang to action, several into the hold to hunt for kegs, one party toward the galley and ship's stores. A group of three, led by their blue-bearded chief, pounded up the stairs, silvery knives and black revolvers in hand.

Frightened, Susannah backed toward her door, reluctant to shut it and miss anything. Below, Jay Constable, nose bloodied, clambered up and began snapping orders to his six enlisted men: two clerks, an interpreter, a cook, and two roustabout privates. Not much help there, she thought bitterly. But the blue-shirted men ducked out of the brawl and trotted aft toward their cabin.

"Hooraw!" bawled a buckskin-clad passenger, a graybeard out of the mountains and grizzly wild, smashing hard fists into a woodhawk and gouging eyes and ears with all the practice of a dozen rendezvous behind him. He laughed maniacally.

Walleye Ralph freed the boat and it slid away from the bank, spinning cockeyed. A shudder, and the great paddles at the sides cranked into water and steam belched from the escapement.

"Mate," yelled Sandoval, pointing at the firebox. "Wood. We lack steam."

Susannah wondered why he'd pulled clear. The blue-bearded one had gained the boiler deck and sprang upward toward hers. Sandoval shot, his dragoon snapping lethally at them, then clicking empty. They shot back as they roared up the companionways, grinning. Fear laced through her. She backed into her doorway. She could shut it in an instant, she thought. The shore spun dizzily. The *El Paso* corkscrewed in the current, lacking steam.

Below, a woodhawk stabbed, the Green River knife a silvered streak that vanished into the belly of the old mountain man. He coughed, clutched at gouting blood, and sank to the main deck. His squaw shrieked.

From the aft cabin the soldiers boiled out, rifles in hand.

"Steam," snapped Sandoval above. He yelled something at his steersman and the packet slowly turned, still sliding downstream with the current, and headed toward the near bank. Susannah watched horrified.

"Brace," he said softly above her.

The woodhawks gained her deck, and she ducked inside her stateroom, slamming the door and bolting it. Howling laughter outside, and heavy feet on the narrow planks. A pause, and then a wild crack, and her door collapsed inward, shattering as it ripped from its frame.

"Haw!" roared the blue-beard. "We'll have us a fandango, lady. First time I set my eyes on white lady-flesh like yourn since I be a tad."

She thought of her derringer too late. He plunged forward, grabbed her, and yanked her out of her narrow cabin as if she weighed less than a feather. She felt the seams of her bodice part and air eddy in.

The two other woodhawks with him plunged into the master's cabin and raked its mess shelves of his private stocks of spirits, whooping with joy.

"Hyar's the stuff!" one bellowed. "Hyar's happy times!"

For the moment, they ignored Sandoval and his steersman up in the pilothouse.

From the main deck more whoops ripped the air. They'd found the remaining whiskey, a keg in the mess, kept under lock for sale to passengers. Woodhawks frolicked and pranced, bandying the keg out onto the deck. The mate saw the rising shore and slipped forward, lying flat on the deck.

Deckhands crowded forward, out of the brawl. Most of them spotted the shoreline and the vector of the ship, and flattened themselves. Passengers saw and braced. The woodhawks scarcely knew the ship was under steam, and began tapping their keg, using a few cups from the galley.

Blue Beard lifted Susannah over his shoulders and tromped down the stairs, laughing. She pummeled his back with her fists, and bit him savagely, sinking her teeth into his earlobe. He bellowed. She kicked and squirmed, heart in her throat.

"You sonofabitch," she hissed, and tried out the rest of her Regular Army tongue. He howled. She felt massive hands pawing her legs and rear.

Around her she heard the boom of army rifles. A scream. Cursing. Her captor made the boiler deck, laughing. Before them, Lieutenant Jay Constable loomed, nose still gouting, revolver in hand.

"Put the lady down," he said in a voice deceptively soft.

For an answer, the howling woodhawk bulled straight toward Constable, and Susannah felt his lumbering gait jolt her. Constable stood his ground, lowering the barrel of his revolver slightly. At the last instant, it bucked in his hand. She felt a shudder spasm through the woodhawk, felt him fold toward the deck, grunting, felt herself careening onto the planks.

At that moment the *El Paso* skidded up a sandy bank of the Missouri, and everything loose on board, including the mortals riding it, catapulted forward.

Chapter Eleven

Jed watched Diving Hawk vanish around a bend in the trail and felt his solitariness in the unknown, desolate mountains. Above him loomed the most forbidding landscape he'd ever seen, slick with gray ice and wetness, all of it overlaid with mist. Mysterious booms echoed down the canyon, and he couldn't fathom the source of them. Wind pummeling the peaks, he thought, or avalanches of rain-soaked granular snow greasing its way down. The upland was a writhing thing, a cold snake pouring vicious gusts of bitter air and mist down upon him.

A decision that struck him as biblical faced him: he could ignore Diving Hawk's counsel and find that lower pass to the south, to face whatever Blackfeet lurked wherever it debauched upon the plains, or he could struggle upward into the forbidding peaks, risking his life with every step.

He hated to make a decision like that. There might be no Blackfeet at all along the lower trail. Or they might prove to be perfectly friendly, and eager to share a smoke and a gift. But his instincts told him otherwise. He'd be alone, without a translator, unfamiliar even with the hand language of the plains, with booty any Piegan warrior would prize and a scalp there for the taking. The danger wouldn't stop at the end of the low pass, either: he'd have to travel alone clear to Fort Benton, hoping no hunting or war parties picked up his trail in the soft spring-wet clay.

Temptation tugged at him. Ahead lay cold and misery and heart-stopping terror. Yet he chose it, because it seemed best. He'd never chosen the easy way through life, and he wouldn't start now. He eyed his drooping ponies and came to a quick decision: he'd walk, leading his horses. And he'd divide his gear and provisions equally between them, in case one lost its footing and slid to its death. He examined their unshod feet, knowing how easily those slick hoofs could slip on wet ice. He wondered if he could cut notches in the hoofs themselves, cleats for traction. With his knife he tried it on his own pony's off forehoof, but the effort exhausted him. He settled for cleaning out the frogs.

Carefully he distributed the loads on his pony and Charbonneau's and tied them down tightly over the riding saddles. He took time to achieve balance, and to make sure that food and gear were divided between the animals. One thing more baffled him. He saw not the slightest forage above, and wondered how his horses would survive several days—more, if a blizzard struck—in a land of naked rock and small pines.

Nearby some stunted cottonwoods grew, and he decided to carry a bundle of twigs, heavy with buds. He cut an armload of them, pitiful fare but better than nothing, and then a second armload, and lashed them down atop the packs.

"Well, my friends, let's be off," he said, taking the first reluctant step up the muddy trail. Some residual weakness from his brush with death remained with him, and he had to pause every hundred yards or so to catch his breath in the thin air. The breathers seemed to do him good, enabling him to plot his next steps and prepare himself. Thus he climbed for a mile, through soggy snow, past dense pine forests, until a dun cliff wall hemmed him closer and closer to the tumultuous creek tumbling down the bottom of the gulch. The trail forded the creek at the bottom of a narrow gorge, now choked with boiling gray water. He saw no way across. A sheet of ice as slick as glass covered the trail. He picked up a small rock and set it on the ice and watched it zip into the tumult below. A similar sheet of glassy ice rose on the far side, and the water in the gorge looked to be ten feet deep or more, and boiling so fast

94

it'd rip him and his animals down the mountain no matter what he did. He squatted there and studied it, seeing no way around the barrier. He walked back, looking for a game trail up the cliff wall that hemmed him on the right. He found one, also ice-laden, and beyond the possibilities of packhorses. He backtracked further, looking for a way to the ridges, finding none. He led his horses down the trail, hearing them mince over ice behind him, until he came to the lodgepole-clad slopes that might permit a detour. He plunged into the forest, heading relentlessly upslope until he encountered vaulting walls of snow that had been trapped there by the trees and hadn't yet begun to decay. The rest of that afternoon he probed for an opening, finding the way locked and the mountains impregnable along this warrior trail of the Kootenai.

The other pass, then, and the fate that awaited him at its end. The gray light had dimmed, and lavender mist filtered over him. Sunset, somewhere. He retreated downslope, finding no level spot to camp, not even a place large enough for a small tent. The hard going wearied him. If anything, the downhill hike on ice and greasy mud drained more energy from him than the uphill trip. But at last, when the dimming light had begun to alarm him, he found himself in the bottom of the cirque where he'd said good-bye to Diving Hawk. Cottonwoods and aspens flourished there, and old dun grass poked through patched snow.

Finding dry wood proved to be a problem, but at last he'd broken off enough dead lower branches, as gloom settled in. With a bright fire going he tackled the next problem, sleeping dry on the sopping wet ground. He did not even want to lower his packs into the muck and finally hung them both from limbs and picketed the hungry horses. The ground oozed under his cold, soaked boots, turning his feet to ice. He yearned for dry land, a place to hunker before his cheerful blaze and dry himself and his boots. His best bet for a dry bed would be pine boughs, he thought. Small-needled firs and spruce, laid thick. But the nearest pines rose a quarter mile away, and darkness had descended.

At last he struck upon an idea. He lashed the grommeted corners of the narrow half tent to four aspen, using what little line he had at hand, including the braided horsehair reins from his bridles. He sat gingerly in the hammock; it held, although it sagged more than he wished. That night he slept awkwardly but stayed dry, his blue haversack there inside his bedroll. By morning his makeshift hammock had stretched a foot lower, but it remained a few inches off the mucky ground.

He scarcely knew how to find the lower pass, and the constant gloom of banked clouds upon this west slope kept him from getting bearings. So he followed the rushing creek back down to the larger river in the wide valley below, which he followed south. It was a fork of the formidable river that led back to the long lake of the Kootenai. Here he made good time. He thought perhaps this river itself would lead into the pass he wanted, and that proved to be the case. He took his time, letting his winter-gaunt ponies feast on the emerald shoots of grass that had progressed an inch or two toward the sun. His heart hurried him along, but as he rode one horse and then the other along the easy trail, he devoted himself to watchfulness, and planning. If he could manage it at the far side of the long pass, he would leave his horses and walk ahead to reconnoitre. Diving Hawk's warnings loomed large in his thoughts.

The wide valley scarcely seemed like a pass at all, and if he'd remembered it, he'd have attempted to reach the plains a month or two earlier. At Fort Benton he'd heard talk of a low pass called Marias, but he'd paid no attention. He hadn't been bound for the mountains. Now, as he walked his ponies along level river bottoms, he felt sure he traversed Marias Pass. He didn't know he'd crossed a divide until he found a creek near him racing east. He reined his pony, feeling joy radiate through him. This was drainage of the Missouri! This rushing creek tumbled toward his own nation, and its water would flow into the Mississippi, and ultimately pass by New Orleans and into the Gulf of Mexico! The image of Susannah filled his mind at once. Now at last he had returned to the river.

The pass took him generally in a northeast direction, and he realized as the mountains dwindled and the country turned dryer that no clear line demarked the end of the pass and the beginning of the plains. And that hostiles could lurk anywhere. He'd already ridden too far into the jaws of death. Chilled, he steered his ponies toward a copse of new-leaved cottonwoods, leaving prints in the soft earth. In the blue shadows of the trees he dug into his field kit for his spyglass and scanned the country anxiously, seeing nothing but antelope and a few mule deer. Time now to think and plan. Time to study the earth for fresh trails, to travel at night, to reconnoitre from nearby hills and hope the Blackfeet weren't doing exactly the same thing.

He picketed his ponies in the deepest shade he could find and hiked cautiously up a long shallow coulee, heading for a ridge on the right, wishing all the while that he'd become cautious a lot sooner. Still, he saw nothing, but that didn't mean they hadn't seen him, with those Indian eyes that could pick out movement and identify it so much better than white men's could. He approached the ridge cautiously, badly winded, and eased his head over the rounded shoulder to peer into the country beyond. Puffball clouds against an azure sky cast moving shadows upon the broken country ahead, making the world seem alive with energy and direction, ever changing. He saw nothing. He opened his telescoping spyglass and slowly scanned the country, starting at the extreme north, and covering each ridge and valley, especially stream courses where cottonwoods massed in long lines. Then he focused on the river he thought must be a branch of the Two Medicine, which he had followed easterly to this edge of the pass. The glass slid by something, and he drew it back and stared. There, perhaps two miles off, lay a large village, brown lodges nestled along the river. Anguish ran through him. He searched closer then, finding the country alive with horsemen, hunters, horse herders, squaw parties digging roots, children racing ponies, and warriors afoot, arrows nocked in their bows. Piegans, Bloods; he didn't know. He only knew that he confronted a wall of death.

A giant hand clawed Susannah forward, lifting her bodily from the weakening grasp of the woodhawk and tumbling her along the deck until she skidded into Jay Constable, who'd slammed into the curved railing next to the companionway. The woodhawk's body crashed into her, flopping boot clipping her chin. The other two woodhawks had been on the stairs, and the jolt had flipped them down to the main deck, where they sprawled and twisted, groaning.

She heard a thundering of cargo in the hold, smacking forward. Aft, pots and crockery clattered and clanged. Screams. Passengers tumbling, people skidding along decks. She gazed at the carnage, and then at Constable, who squirmed under her, laughing wildly. She felt his arms and hands, his legs wrestling the weight of the woodhawk as well as her own, and she primly pulled free, gaping at the chaos below.

Even while the woodhawks tumbled and skidded, the deck crew had leapt up and disarmed them. The mate, Walleye Ralph, pounced on a knife-wielding woodhawk and flattened him with a single smash of his massive fist. Above, Sandoval watched calmly, revolver in hand. In moments the ship's crew had disarmed the floundering woodhawks, stripped them of knives and clubs and revolvers, and began manhandling them into a heap on the foredeck even before the woodcutters had recovered their wits.

Only then did she understand it had been no accident, that the ship's crew had known exactly what to expect, had prepared by lying down and hanging on, to leap upon the staggering, careening woodhawks, who were so busy brawling and carousing they hadn't known the packet was about to plow up the sandy bank and scythe them all down.

Soldiers and passengers picked themselves up slowly, examined bruises, stared bewildered at the items torn loose by the collision. Constable pulled himself up, wincing, and shouted at a private, who picked up a rifle that had slid into stacked wood and then joined the crewmen holding the woodhawks at gunpoint.

Susannah stared in horror at the body of the old buckskin-clad mountain man, which had slid grotesquely into the cordwood, leaving a wide streak of blood along the deck. She found blood all over her skirts, where the blue-bearded leader had gouted upon her. He lay on his back now, eyes admiring the sun and lips expressing awe. In death he looked smaller and less menacing. Wild men, she thought. These men simply turned into wild creatures out here, far beyond law and civilization.

"You are all right, Miss St. George?" asked the master from above.

"I think so."

"It was the only way," he said. "They sometimes get a little frisky out here."

Below, passengers were bandaging scrapes and cuts, and some of them growled at the mate. Walleye Ralph ignored them and set most of his deckhands to cleaning up. Several plunged into the hold to begin shifting cargo aft. He detailed others to the galley.

"Very good, Mr. Ralph. When you're able, report to me with damage, injuries, losses, and so on. And we'll need a burial detail. How many dead?"

"Three, sir. That passenger there, the woodhawk shot by Lieutenant Constable, and one of those that fell from the texas deck. The other's got a broken shoulder, I think."

"Any other injuries?"

"Scrapes, sir. None of the crew. We were braced."

"I'll have you in court when I get back to St. Louis, Sandoval," yelled a young man with a gashed elbow.

Sandoval nodded. "Mr. Ralph, when a man's free, send him to my cabin to clean up, my mess, the charts, and all. But not now. And set a man to straightening up the luggage of any passengers who request it. Miss St. George?"

"I can do it," she replied wearily.

"Lieutenant, one more thing, if I may. We're beached, and it'll take a few hours to free up. That means we're vulnerable to any sort of Indian trouble."

"My clerks and translators will protect you," Constable retorted, the amusement back in his face. "I've already rescued Miss St. George from a fate worse than death."

That startled her. Was that the woodhawk's intent? Wasn't he just forcibly hauling her to a wild fandango, mountain-man style? And did the man have to die? Uneasiness filled her. Perhaps Jay Constable had saved her honor. Perhaps she'd have been thrown down the companionway with the others if—if that bullet—

She turned to see Constable mocking her again. He barked orders, and his soldiers deployed themselves, one up at the pilothouse, two others on land, hiking toward the bluffs. One private had lost his rifle; another had sprained a wrist and was clutching it.

"There, Mr. Sandoval. The army's at your service."

The master stared blankly at the amused lieutenant.

It galled Susannah that she probably owed her life to Jay Constable. And her honor. He'd had no compunction about that during his brief courting. He peered at her now, reading her thoughts with eyes that missed nothing.

"I suppose I should thank you," she said reluctantly.

"Your sentiments are most generous and clearly wholehearted," he replied, his mouth twitching with amusement. "Perhaps Mr. Sandoval's measures were a bit drastic. Wouldn't you say so, Mr. Sandoval? Endangering life and property, a costly packet? Risking lawsuit?"

"Did it once before. It works."

On the foredeck the ten living woodhawks sat sullenly, guarded by two revolver-wielding crewmen.

"I think your guests are contemplating ways to escape your hospitality, Mr. Sandoval," said Constable, delight in his voice.

He was right. Jay Constable enjoyed being right.

The master glanced down and then addressed the mate. "Mr. Ralph, see to the prisoners. And set a man on shore to see about more cordage. We'll take it for damages."

Through the next hour Susannah watched sweating crewmen and volunteering passengers restore order. Down in the hold she heard the scrape and thunder of crates and cartons being dragged aft. Passengers with shovels began gouging shallow trenches in the grassy riverbank. "Ought to just shove 'em in the river," one muttered.

Susannah wondered how the crew would free the packet, whose stem had slid fifteen or twenty feet up the soft slope of the bank. She had an inkling when she felt the hull shift under her as cargo piled up at the rear. Several hundred yards upshore, passengers were dragging cordage they'd discovered in the woods out upon the crude levee, while the woodcutters watched bitterly. The bodies of Blue Beard and the other woodhawk were dumped unceremoniously in the trench and covered with mud.

The engine idled, and steam belched lazily from the escapement, with little more than embers in the firebox heating the boiler.

They came for the body of the wiry old mountain man, but his squaw sprawled over it, jabbering in Cheyenne, and wouldn't let them touch it. She wept brokenly, smoothing the seamed old face and sobbing. They pulled her up gently, but she broke into a torrent of words, crying against it.

A burly French engagé of the fur company hollered up at the master. "She's saying not here, not here with these woodcutters. Let her off upstream a way, the woman and her man. Let her off later with him, and she'll make a scaffold for him in the way of her people."

Sandoval nodded, and they left the old squaw to her grief.

Crewmen herded the prisoners down a makeshift gangplank to the shore and guarded them there. Then Sandoval began snapping instructions. Firemen chunked the huge logs into the firebox. Crewmen swiveled the two forward booms outward and dropped spars from them, planting each spar upon the riverbank to either side of the prow. Then the boatmen began turning the capstans with long poles, slowly winding in cable that pulled the booms downward and piled weight on the spars. Susannah watched, fascinated, seeing the answer to her questions.

"It's how we pull ourselves off sandbars in water," said Sandoval amiably. "Only now there's much more strain on the spars, because we're on land. Something could snap, so stand back."

The vessel creaked under her and swayed as the river current toyed with the floating aft portion of the hull.

Slowly the prow rose until it rested clear—or nearly clear—of the bank.

Sandoval snapped a command down his speaking tube, and the great paddlewheel thrashed in reverse, while the boat shuddered. The boat backed a foot, then another, and finally five or six feet before the tilted spars dropped the prow back into the mud again. The crew unwound the cables, reset the spars closer to the water's edge, and repeated the process, and this time the shuddering packet floated free, bobbing in the river even as Constable's riflemen raced wildly down from their bluffs, their hoarse voices carrying over the throb of engines and the tumult of cheering passengers.

"Injuns!" one howled.

Chapter Twelve

The sun was his enemy. In darkness he might slip around the village, assuming he could elude its night herders and its ever vigilant roaming warrior police. His ponies were not shod, their tracks could not be distinguished from those of the Blackfoot ponies. But he wore his army boots, and a single heelprint in the soft earth of spring would give him away. He suddenly realized he had left just such prints climbing the coulee to this ridge. He glanced behind him and saw nothing, not even his horses hidden in the lime copse of cottonwoods below.

Jed trained his glass on the orange country he had just traversed, fearing hunters had seen him. He peered back, clear to the mouth of Marias Pass, studying the slopes and the bottoms methodically. He took his time. Careful observation could save his life. Nothing. Still, he could expect trouble any instant. On a fine spring day like this the Blackfoot village would be half deserted, and the country around it would be alive with hunters, warriors, firewood gatherers, root diggers, bow-and-arrow makers, vision questers, eagle trappers, and all the rest.

His best bet would be to wait in that copse of trees with his ponies until dusk and then make a wide loop southward. He eased off the ridge and slid down the lavender coulee a few yards, his gaze sharp upon the hills behind him. When at last he peered into the sunny bottoms he arrested his progress at once. A horseman rode a spotted brown pony easily, and beside him walked a woman. Villagers. They followed the trail into the throat of the mountains.

Jed eased his telescoping glass around and steadied it on the couple. The young man wore only a red breechclout and leggings and dark moccasins. Two glossy braids fell over his coppery back. A boy, without a coup feather in his hair. The slender young woman beside him wore a doeskin dress without ornament, and beneath it those high black moccasins that gave the tribe its name. Lovers. They saw none of the surrounding world, but only each other. Jed sighed with relief. A young courting couple would wander by and miss him entirely. He lay immobilized above them, in plain sight if they cared to look, but they didn't. They followed the river.

Then from the cottonwoods one of his horses whinnied greetings. Jed watched in frozen horror. The youth drew up at once; the girl whirled and ran toward the distant village. The unarmed boy located Jed's horses and urged his pony toward them cautiously, ready to wheel and run. Jed thought to shoot, but he lay far beyond revolver range, and killing the youth would be a fool thing to do. The youth reined his pony a rifle shot from the cottonwoods and waited. Making medicine, Jed thought. Trying to discover who and what hid in the cottonwoods. The boy lifted his arms to the sun in some gesture of supplication, arching his young lean body. Jed's pony whickered. The sound of it galvanized the Blackfoot youth, and he heeled his pony into a fine lope and raced straight toward Jed's horses. Scarcely pausing, the boy leapt down, freed the reins and halter rope, and raced off with his booty, howling triumph at the sunny universe. Jed's ponies dragged behind the boy, their drab packs bouncing. He watched his carbine vanish as they rounded a shoulder of land. Worse, he saw his blue haversack, tied to the cantle of his military saddle, vanish too.

The world turned silent. Jed heard not a bird, and the wind ceased, as if God had held his breath. The racing puffball clouds stopped midstride, the shadows arrested on the slopes. In minutes a warrior or hunting party would boil through, looking for the owner of those horses. Caught by lovers! Chagrinned, Jed tried to face the decisions he had to make. Run? No, not on foot, with heavy boots dimpling the ground under him; not with scores of mounted Piegans or Bloods after him. Hide? Nowhere to hide. A naked slope. His bootprints leading clearly to himself. Fight? He had a loaded Dragoon revolver, and a Barlow knife in his pocket. Good for ten seconds of resistance.

Fear swept him, a leaden force that weighted his limbs and crushed his heart. He'd weathered cholera and scurvy, starvation and cold, hostile Kootenai and winter, only to come to this. He would never deliver his letters. Sighing, he stood up and dusted off his frayed army uniform. He had dignity left, and it might purchase him enough time to bargain a little. The blue haversack—if he could somehow get them to take it to Fort Benton . . .

He walked slowly on buckling legs down the slope without seeing a soul and continued on toward the village on the distinct trail that emerged from the pass. He forced each leg forward, feeling it tremble under him. He wished he had courage, but it had deserted him utterly, and he walked as a lamb to the slaughter. Ahead, pinpoints of distant movement materialized as racing warriors. Trembling, he unfastened his belt and set his holstered Dragoon on the gray earth before him and stood at attention, erect, terrified but not wanting to reveal it.

Five of them. Powerful, large warriors in their prime, nearly naked in spite of the chill spring air. They raced up to him on frenzied ponies that threw their heads about. Each carried a bow with a nocked arrow. Their opaque agate eyes peered sharply at him, at the revolver on the ground, at his blue tunic with its brass buttons and worsted epaulettes displaying the gilded thread of his rank, and at the yellow trim on his britches that said *dragoons* to those who knew. He wore no hat. Like most frontier soldiers he'd abandoned the visored pom-pom that the War Department decreed and adopted a felt slouch hat instead. But even that had vanished at the time of his capture.

He waited, fainthearted, for the arrow that would pierce him. He saw the marks of their manhood upon them, the breast scars that told him they'd paid homage to Sun and Courage, the coup feathers jabbed at careful angles into their bound hair, and the scars of war hideously deforming the flesh of arms and legs and shoulders. A warrior society, the village's current police.

Some instinct beyond his own imaginings lifted his arm, palm forward, in a gesture that suggested peaceful intent. Those glittering agates of eyes saw.

"Do any of you speak English?"

Silence.

"*Parlez-vous français?*" he asked, suddenly grateful for a tongue West Point had given him.

Something changed in the eyes of two or three of them. French. The engagés of the fur company were mostly French. One of the warriors slid off his pony and cat-walked forward. Jed braced himself, but the warrior only wished to finger the fine brass buttons on his navy blue tunic, and then the gilded thread of his epaulettes, his captain's insignia. But they wouldn't know that. They'd never seen an American soldier. The warrior muttered something, gestured, tugged. He wanted the tunic.

"No," Jed replied intuitively. Then, switching to French, he told them the tunic was his; he was a runner, an *ambassadeur*, from the government of *les États-Unis*. He wished to be taken to the village headman.

The warrior settled for the holstered revolver on the clay, and the band prodded Jed forward, nocked arrows never wavering from his torso. Some surge of energy gave him strength, and he walked ahead, dreading his fate. Torture. If they tortured him, as well they might, he would wish a thousand times over he had kept his revolver and put a bullet through his brain.

Fine ambassador he would make, he thought bitterly. He hadn't a single gift, not one twist of tobacco left. And not an interpreter in sight. None of the accoutrements of an official party—guides, translators, the brass medallions to be given to chiefs—none of it. He spotted the youth who'd caught his horses, and as his entourage walked by, the youth joined it, with Jed's ponies—and the blue haversack. A desperate thought came to Jed as he stared at that small bag of blue duck: *grab it.*

The boy headed the parade proudly, leading the trophies of war, two fine ponies piled high with white man's things. The villagers gathered as news of this fine thing flashed ahead. Dogs sniffed and howled and snapped at Jed's boots, and naked brown children chattered like jays, but the adults seemed lost in deep silence, eyeing Jed and his strange uniform with visible curiosity but saying nothing. One old squaw lifted a knife and grinned hideously, obviously awaiting her turn at the torture. The women did that, Jed knew. Expertly. Inflicting all the pain they could manage without killing the victim. Knife slices, burning brands, eye gouging, tongue severing, severing digits one by one, toes and fingers. Then the things more terrible, too terrible to think of. *Oh, Susannah, don't you cry for me* . . .

The quiet procession entered the village proper, and Jed stared at somber cowhide lodges, smoke-blackened at the top and golden below, many decorated with medicine symbols in bright colors. He'd expected cacophony, but now even the yellow dogs slinked along and the tongues of children stuck to their throats. The rank odor of human waste caught him, and decaying offal, and smoke and leather. From tripods before many lodges hung medicine things, and scalps, a few brown and one yellow, and the befeathered skulls and claws of small animals.

Silently the party proceeded through the great village, past twenty, fifty, eighty lodges, until at last it drew up before a larger one where two eagle-feathered coup sticks reared up from moist earth, insignia of great rank. Before that lodge stood a massive, virile, cruel-eyed man wearing only a blue breechclout and high black moccasins. Jed's escort stepped away, leaving him to stand alone, staring back at the chief who would decide whether he would live or die, be tortured or not, be set free or not. Jed said nothing. The chief said nothing. From all over the village, people thronged to see and hear, amidst an amazing silence.

They took the measure of each other.

"I am Captain Jedediah Owen, United States Army."

Nothing.

"*Je suis Capitaine* Jed Owen . . ."

Nothing. It struck him that they knew the sound of French but not the substance of it. Just as well. He scarcely remembered a word of it.

"Take me to Fort Lewis—ah, Fort Benton," he said. "Take me to Alec Culbertson there."

Some subtle thing changed in the chief's eyes. Perhaps he understood English well enough.

"I am honored to be your guest," Jed said quietly. "I am in need of help. My government sent me out to your people to begin talks about treaties. We would like to invite you to a treaty council, you and the Crows and Assiniboin and others, to a council at the trading post. I came with gifts of tobacco and presents from my government in the east. But we suffered disease, death, and finally . . ." He decided not to tell them of his captivity. "I've lost my translators and guides, and would like an escort to—to Culbertson."

They listened intently but he couldn't tell whether they understood.

"If I'm not welcome here, I'll take my ponies and leave."

Still no response. He thought of another tack.

"I am a messenger, come in peace. If harm comes to me, you will anger the trader Culbertson, and he will close his window to you. Then you will not have powder and lead, or hoop iron for arrowheads, or blankets, or kettles."

They stood quiet as statues, and it exasperated him. Beside the chief stood an old man with a seamed brown face, crowned with a special horned buffalo head with feathers and red trade cloth dangling from it. Medicine, probably. Jed turned toward the others, war chiefs, subchiefs, heads of warrior societies and clans. And beyond, a mass of silent villagers, hard-eyed youths, grinning old crones, stoic, dour women.

They focused now on the youth who'd captured his ponies. The boy undid the olive canvas pack of the rear horse, letting things spill to earth, including the pemmican.

Kootenai!" someone hissed, spotting moccasins.

"I wintered with them."

The youth turned to Jed's saddled pony and pulled the haversack off of it.

"Don't!" snapped Jed.

They turned toward him, faintly surprised.

One giant warrior slid the Hall-North breech-loading carbine from its saddle sheath and hefted it happily.

"It's loaded," Jed barked.

For an answer, the warrior, apparently a subchief, swung it toward him and drew back the hammer. Jed refused to flinch, though the bore pointed at his chest.

The youth unbuckled the haversack and peered into it.

"Young man," Jed said sternly, "put that back on my saddle. Those messages are no concern of yours."

The youth continued to rummage, while Jed felt something inside of himself tense like a wagonspring. The young man clutched something and pulled it out, a string of enameled black beads . . . Private Coppola's rosary. Its silver crucifix, tarnished now, snared the sun. The youth handed it to a woman Jed took to be one of the chief's wives, who held it high, exclaiming.

"I am delivering that to his people. That was his dying wish," Jed snapped into uncomprehending faces.

The youth pulled out a letter, examined the black marks upon it, and tossed it to the earth. It seesawed down and caught in trampled grass.

"Don't!" cried Jed.

The young man ignored him, pulled out Elwood's blue buckram journal, and riffled the pages, curious. They meant nothing to him. He tossed it on the ground, where it cornered into mud.

"Put it all back!" roared Jed with such force that people stared, amazed. He didn't see them.

The lad found another letter, the one Jed had drafted for Private Harrison, and tossed it to the wind.

Something snapped in Jed.

With a feral roar he sprang at the youth and knocked him to the earth with one massive thrust of his fist. As the boy fell, Jed snatched the haversack from him, ripping its shoulder strap where it had been riveted to the bag. With three catlike plunges Jed plucked the letters and journal up and thrust them in. He caught the wrist of the woman holding Coppola's rosary, twisted it until she wailed, and grabbed the rosary from her, jamming it back into the bag.

They jumped on him then, finally galvanized by the wail of the chief's wife. The chief himself, a giant with bulging chest and arm muscles, landed on him first, smashing him backward. Jed, berserk, butted the chief with his head, heard a grunt, and then flailed him with his own massive fists. Arms gripped him, snatched at the haversack. Jed ignored them all, his mind only on the haversack. He shrugged off smashing blows and grabbed the bag, clutching it to him. They tripped him, toppled him, landed on him then, and his sole thought was still the bag, which he clutched to his belly with all the power his arms possessed.

From above somewhere he heard a sharp command. Reluctantly seven murderous Blackfoot warriors clambered off of Jed, each with a parting shot of some kind, a fist to the head or a moccasined foot to his ribs, that jolted him, turned him nauseous, sent wild red pain flaming through him. But he held on to the bag.

He hugged the haversack, too battered to move. Above him they snarled and snapped in a tongue he didn't know. Not the chief; it was someone else's voice. He turned, foggily staring up to see the old one with the buffalo horns barking something at them all with a strange authority and dignity that brooked no resistance. Shaman. Having his say. No doubt they'd torture Jed now. He hated the bag in his grasp. It hadn't been worth it. Killing himself for a bunch of messages he could just as well deliver orally. Stupid.

The old shaman harangued them while Jed slowly caught his breath and the searing pain in his lungs subsided. The mud under him greased his britches and smeared his tunic and pressed coldly on his flesh. The blind red rage that had impelled him faded, leaving him weary. As his own body sagged into calm, he grew aware that the shaman had finished and the whole village stood around him quietly. The chief caught his eye and bid him stand up. Jed did, glaring severely at the chief and headmen.

The chief raised an arm and pointed. "Go," he said in English.

"I want my horses and things," Jed retorted.

"No. Go." The chief pulled a long, wicked knife from a beaded antelope-skin sheath one of his squaws handed him and thrust it directly toward Jed, halting the blade just before it pricked Jed's belly.

Stay and die, the chief's eyes told him.

Jed nodded. He addressed the shaman. "Whatever you told them, thank you. I came in peace."

No comprehension illumined the shaman's brown face or glittering eyes. The old man's gaze dropped to the bag.

Jed limped—something had knotted up in his left thigh—southward, clutching the blue haversack with its broken strap. The villagers let him through, but just barely, reluctant to see someone they would love to torture to death leave them. But the shaman's iron command held them like a hoop held barrel staves. They padded silently behind, a mass of tall, powerful people in brown buckskins and bright trade cloth and the ever present black moccasins, driving him from their village.

Why he lived he didn't know and didn't even want to guess. What had the old shaman said? What had he believed? If Jed lived, perhaps some day Culbertson or another fur trader might find out. Courage? He wasn't aware of any in himself. Magic? Something to do with the haversack? Maybe. But no matter. He limped along, never looking back. Everything ached. His head rang. His filthy tunic and shirt and britches scratched. His ribs, probably broken, hurt so much each breath tortured him.

He passed beyond the outermost lodge while the village guards watched, swinging eastward along the Two Medicine River—at least he thought that would be the stream—and plodded onward. They rode behind him on their ponies. He thought they might drive an arrow into him, here away from the village and its taboos, but they didn't. After a few minutes of shadowing him they turned back, and he stood alone, alive, with the haversack clutched to him and all its contents intact. Something in him gladdened, and he recovered hope. He'd deliver his letters.

He paused to take stock. Somewhere far ahead lay Fort Benton and the Missouri River. He lacked food and shelter. Nights still felt cold, close to freezing. He had no flint and steel, no firearms, no robes or blankets or canvas. It was early for berries and fruits and nuts.

Well, yes, he thought, he did have something: the folded Barlow knife in his britches pocket. He could whittle a lance . . . and yet, what could he catch with a lance? He wished he'd learned woodsmanship, traps and snares, but he knew nothing of those things. He catalogued the whole of nature and found his prospects dismal. Birds, fowl, large game, rodents, beaver, muskrats, buds, roots . . . Roots. From the ridge he'd watched squaws dig roots, employing only a sharp stick. But what root? He paid attention now to the ground and eventually found what he'd been looking for, sharp gouges in the soft earth near the swift river, and a few torn floppy leaves. He found a plant they'd missed and eased it out, using his knife. Ugly black root, twisted and carrot-shaped. He snapped it, and found the inside white. He bit into it cautiously, swallowed a little, and waited.

Chapter Thirteen

The report seemed greatly exaggerated. Susannah watched the racing privates scramble down the tan eastern bluffs, shouting unfathomable words. But nothing rose up along the horizon behind them.

Galvanized into action by the shouting, Sandoval barked commands from high up on the texas deck. Below, passengers scurried to the portside rail or ran for rifles stowed in cabins or in the heaps of dun cargo on the deck. Lieutenant Constable languorously clambered up to the texas, squatted beside his sentry there, and studied the eastern shore, laughing amiably.

Upstream a couple hundred yards the several passengers who were dragging black cordage out upon the crude levee, paused, wondering what the commotion was about.

"Get aboard," Sandoval roared to his crewmen guarding the sullen woodcutters.

"Give us our weapons," yelled one of the prisoners.

Hoots greeted his plea, but a nod from Sandoval changed that. Wall-eye Ralph pitched their knives to them, but held the revolvers. The woodcutters scrambled for the glinting knives.

Now every eye on board scanned the eastern bluffs. Passengers barricaded themselves behind piles of cargo on the deck and pointed the large bores of percussion lock rifles toward the slopes, where Constable's two soldiers scrambled breathlessly toward the boat.

"Firemen, give me fire," Sandoval snapped from above. No one was minding the firebox, but at last one crewman pulled himself loose and began pitching the rough logs into the glowing furnace.

Susannah watched the crewmen who had guarded the woodcutters scramble aboard and yank the plank up.

"Put it back," commanded Sandoval calmly. "We'll wait for those soldiers."

Upstream, the passengers on the mud levee fathomed danger at last and peered anxiously at the bluffs behind them, catching glimpses of the racing bluecoats through the cottonwoods.

Still nothing. The shouts of the panting sentries vanished in the shriek of building steam and the scrambling of passengers.

"Let us on!" bawled a woodhawk.

Sandoval ignored him. "Mr. Ralph, when we board those soldiers, cast loose at once. We'll proceed to the others up there."

The mate sent men fore and aft to free the lines when the moment came.

Susannah, standing on the white boiler deck where it curved around the fore cabins, watched with mounting puzzlement and dread. Nothing. And yet the two privates gesticulated wildly, their shouts lost in the chuff of the engines and the uproar.

From above, Sandoval addressed her quietly. "Miss St. George," he said. "You are not watching a carnival."

"I'm an army brat."

The arrow caught him square in the chest, piercing up to its fletching. He staggered backward.

She screamed. He toppled slowly to the boiler deck, rolled, and plunged past her to the main deck. Another arrow skewered the steersman in the pilothouse, piercing his neck. He tumbled out of sight behind its half walls.

The arrows hadn't come from the east; a black-wooded spit of land to the west teemed with warriors. Not a soul on board had fathomed it, not from that quarter. Susannah stared horrified. Up on the west bluff, beyond rifle range, stood a whole migrating village, a vast tawny line of people, brown ponies, travois, dogs, silent golden children.

Up above she heard Constable laughing again.

An arrow slashed through her hair and buried itself in the wood behind her. Again she screamed.

On deck, arrows buried themselves in passengers whose backs were exposed. A brown-feathered arrow sizzled into Susannah's skirts with a faint ripping sound. She stood there on that high deck, more exposed than anyone on board, and the marksmen on the west shore made sport of her.

"Turn your butt around, soldier," she heard the lieutenant say above her.

At last a few passengers, the fur company men mostly, understood. "West bank," they bawled, "Take cover," "git around."

A few of their pieces boomed, this time at the howling, tree-hidden mass of shadowy warriors across the silver channel.

"Yanktonai," bellowed a riverman below her. "Or Santee Dakotas."

"Miss St. George."

She peered upward, startled, to see Constable's head poke over the texas deck, where he was lying.

"I'm sure you enjoy showing your maidenly form to the savages, but they have other things in mind than admiring your attractions." An arrow punctuated his words, clattering off a brass fitting and ricochetting into the smashed door of her stateroom.

He laughed.

Frightened, she sprawled to the deck. An arrow smacked through the space where her body had been.

She lay on the deck, completely exposed, too frightened to move. A shot from the west shore buried itself just above her. She saw its smoke drifting up from the brush there. Around her now she heard return fire. Crawl! Crawl to safety, but she couldn't. She sprawled there paralyzed, inviting vicious fire from the far shore. It didn't seem to matter at all to them that she was a woman. Grinning, the lieutenant scrambled along the roof above and then dropped over its lip, landing lightly beside her.

Something stung her *derrière*.

Jay Constable laughed, sprang for her, lifted her easily with those delicate hands, and carried her around to portside. Across the water, fusils banged and indigo arrows followed them. She felt wood splinters lash her face. But a moment later Constable let her down slowly.

"Why, you have a Yanktonai arrow dangling from your maidenly rear."

She slapped him. His head flew back.

"They have the right idea," he said, mocking.

She sank, trembling, to the shadowed deck, too weak to think, weeping. Oh, Jed . . .

Dimly through her tears she heard the battle snarl around her. Walleye Ralph roared commands now. Ropes sailed free, the packet slid backward, tugged downstream by the harsh green current. Firemen braved arrows and shots to build steam. The mate scrambled past her up to the pilothouse, pulled the body of the steersman out of it, and grabbed the helm.

"Forward slow," he barked into the speaking tube. From the sides a splash of water and the shudder of the great wheels as they bit into the river.

On the shore the woodsmen scattered, whooping at their luck. Ahead, the passengers still on shore hunkered behind the cordage they'd piled on the mud levee. Except for a revolver or two, they had no arms. A party of Yanktonai warriors had swung north and peppered them now from across the water.

She heard Jay Constable slurring soft orders to his men. The two winded sentinels climbed past her in a whirl of blue, the others following. Constable deployed all his men on the texas, where they lay prone. Only four had rifles, but these began methodical and effective sharpshooting at the howling Dakotas across the channel.

The bastard had saved her life.

Her terror turned to rage. She slid a hand around her jade skirts and found the arrow buried in them. The instant she touched it vicious pain radiated out from that part of her she could barely name.

The packet slid close to the woodhawks' mud levee, guided by the mate, who yelled commands down the speaking tube even while he tugged at the varnished wheel.

In the safe lee of the still-moving boat, the remaining six passengers, all of them fur company employees, scrambled out from the cordage and splashed into the river. They had no plank, but with a good leap they were able to swing themselves up.

Across the water the silent Yanktonai sent death raining down. Those with fusils or flintlocks banged at Walleye Ralph, who stood exposed in the pilothouse. Arrows sailed at him too, clattering onto the texas. But Constable and his soldiers drummed back, protecting the mate.

"Forward, fast," bawled the mate into the speaking tube, and the packet shuddered out into the main channel, angling closer to the dangerous west shore. Deckhands scurried for cover, letting ropes trail in the water.

"Pull in the lines," Ralph demanded quietly. "Keep them out of the wheels."

No one obeyed at first, but finally a deckhand dashed to the starboard side. An arrow caught him flat in the back and he collapsed, groaning.

On the main deck, a pool of red carmined the planks around Sandoval's body. Susannah stared, a sob caught in her throat.

The Yanktonai fire focused on Walleye Ralph now as he steered the boat through the choked channel. She glimpsed his face above her, and then it vanished.

"Oh, no," she groaned.

Two deckhands raced up the companionways toward the pilothouse, but arrows and fusil balls caught them both, and they tumbled down the steps onto the boiler deck near Susannah, groaning.

Behind the boat, the woodcutters scrambled into the cover of cottonwoods, while Yanktonai whooped down to the water's edge and peppered them.

Along the bank Yanktonai horsemen easily kept up with the packet, loosing arrows at the pilothouse. They struck its half wall, and death-rattled down onto the texas deck. Walleye Ralph's head bobbed up and vanished again, but the spokes of the helm turned slightly, centering the boat in the channel.

"Mate!" cried a deckhand from behind some cordwood. "Keep yer haid down. I'll tell ye whether t'right or t'left. A tad right, now."

She saw the helm turn mysteriously. Thank God, she thought.

The Yanktonai saw it too, and watched in silent frustration, ignoring the occasional shots from Constable's soldiers.

The packet rounded a bight and slid past a towhead that masked the boat from the shore. On the distant bluffs, the villagers watched.

"Hit the village," Constable drawled to his men above.

They popped shots into the distant forms, some three hundred yards off, doing no hurt but sending them scurrying out of sight behind a ridge. The warriors below noticed and gave up the fight. A silence settled over the river, save for the occasional shouts of the deckhands up to the crouching mate, and the groaning of the wounded.

"It's over," muttered Constable. "They thought they had a prize."

Susannah scarcely listened. Fiery pain radiated out from her rump, blotting out the rest of the world.

"You've an arrow dangling from you," mocked Jay Constable.

She refused to reply.

"It seems to have entered a little north and west of Jed Owen country."

"I'll kill you."

"That's what I admire about you northern women. In Carolina, they'd coo."

She rolled the rest of the way onto her stomach, feeling the dangling arrow sear her.

"You'll need some minor surgery. I'm sure you'd prefer to have Captain Sandoval do it, but—"

"Not you. Anyone but you," she snapped. "The mate."

"'Fraid he's a little busy. Fear not. I'll need to slice a bit of your skirts, but I'll expose only a few pink inches of you. Why, even Jed couldn't rightly complain."

"Stop that!"

He laughed amiably. "Here I've saved your life, and my reward is snarls, not kisses."

She buried her head in her arms, filled with despair. The image of the dead master, Sandoval, sent a shudder through her. She felt a gentle hand on her skirts, a hand taking no liberties, and then a sawing, the sound of fabric parting. Then a last cool air—there.

"Metal arrowhead, hoop iron, about an inch in, is all. Not past the barbs on the end. Not much blood. Rather narrow. Reminds me of Jed."

Susannah clenched her fists. She meant to smack him when this was over.

"Shall I pull fast or slow?"

She kept her silence.

"Women prefer slow," he said. He wiggled the arrow slightly, triggering a groan from her in spite of her clenched teeth. He didn't pull slow. He yanked. Fire, and then a dulling ache.

"I'll need to wash and bandage."

"I'll do that in my cabin," she snapped. She sprang up and raced for her stateroom, scarcely noticing the carnage below her, where people on the main deck wrestled the dead aside and bound up the wounded.

She slammed the shattered stateroom door behind her, a door newly perforated with two holes where balls had pierced the thin wood. She undid the long line of buttons down the front of her gown, tugged the grimy dress off, wincing at every move, and stood in her grubby petticoats, considering what she should do.

A knock. "I brought water and soap," he said.

Furiously she opened the door a crack and took the pitcher and the ball of yellow soap and slammed the door again, angry that he'd anticipated her needs. She scrubbed viciously, except in the tender area, where she laved herself gently, feeling it ache with every move of her body. She wondered how she'd bandage such a place. The bleeding had stopped. It had not amounted to much.

Exhausted, she lay on her side, unable to do anything, feeling the comforting rhythm of the engine and the churn of the paddlewheel aft, and hearing the occasional shouts of men restoring order. She would be in the hands of Walleye Ralph now. Could he pilot? Did he know the river? Who owned this packet now that its master lay dead? She wept, while refusing to weep. Her eyes leaked wetness into the small hard pillow, even while she hated the weakness of tears.

Susannah on the forecastle, her legs pressed against its coaming, watching the desiccated, lonely land parade by in the late sun. Two hours to Fort Union, they'd told her. For weeks they'd churned up the emerald river, through a strange, desolate, amber land that grew more and more mysterious and lonely with each passing day. Never had she imagined plains so vast and silent, hiding their secrets in emptiness. Hiding Jed somewhere in their endless reaches. She'd pierced into a new world so far removed from the outposts of civilization that it changed something inside of her. She felt less secure, less certain of her station in life, more inclined to depend on the hard men around for her safety.

What news would Fort Union hold? News of Jed's death? No news at all? She felt the folly of her long trip and didn't know why she'd come. The romantic vision—finding him here, being folded into his arms—had died in the daily passage through endless grassy steppes, vast bronze ridges, and more recently, sharp red bluffs. On rare days they'd spotted solitary Indians sitting their ponies and watching the strange fireboat laboring up the turquoise river, whose water ran clearer here, fed by mountain snows. Jed seemed a mirage, a dream, unreal in this harsh place where only tribesmen roamed. She knew he'd died. When Jay completed his official inquiries—a matter of a few weeks, she imagined, she'd go down the endless river empty-handed and empty-hearted.

For several days after the fight with the Yanktonai, she hadn't spoken a word, or even acknowledged Jay's presence in passing. But he'd smiled amiably, the mockery never far from his eyes. That first day they'd steamed as far as they could before the wood ran out, and then they'd anchored beside a desolate and silent cottonwood flat. The mate sent crewmen and passengers alike ashore to cut wood, while he detailed several others to dig a common grave on the riverbank, at a point of land just ahead. There they buried Ricardo Sandoval at sunset, together with three crewmen and two French engagés of the fur company, lowering their long forms, sewn into unbleached ship's canvas, into the cold earth.

Walleye Ralph couldn't read, so Lieutenant Constable did the honors, reciting passages from King James with a quiet dignity that surprised Susannah. Some who stood there wore bloodstained bandages, and back on the packet lay one crewman in a coma. It surprised her that mocking Jay Constable could become humble in the presence of death, and at that moment she found it hard to loathe him.

There'd been no further trouble, but each day brought new challenges. A massive flowing herd of swimming buffalo halted them once. Another time they struck a sandbar, and she watched with fascination as they sparred the ship—"grasshoppered," they called it—over the hidden shallows. They feasted on choice hump and tongue of buffalo now. The world she'd known slipped behind her, and along with it her vision of Jed. The endless land had swallowed him.

One day, at sunset, Jay had stood beside her, saying nothing.

"I'm sorry," she said impulsively. "I've never thanked you. You looked after me and protected me."

He grinned, and for a moment she thought he'd mock her. But he didn't, and he remained polite through the following weeks.

The ship felt different under Walleye Ralph's command. Ricardo Sandoval had been a New Orleans patrician who'd conversed with gracious ease; the mate had risen from lowly estate, and while he seemed strong and able, he treated Susannah deferentially, as if a colonel's daughter lay beyond his competence.

They passed the yawning mouth of the Yellowstone in a wide, empty land and churned steadily up the diminished Missouri, past the Opposition's adobe Fort William, where rough men boiled out to watch them, firing their pieces and whooping their delight.

Word seemed to fly ahead somehow, and gawking tribesmen lined the banks here and there the last four miles.

"Assiniboin," said Jay softly. She'd scarcely been aware of his presence.

Then they cleared the last bight, and the stockaded tan rectangle of Fort Union glowed before them in the low gold sun. A cannon boomed, and again. Over the top of the palisaded walls she glimpsed a long peak-roofed house and a variety of buildings, all golden in the afternoon light. Purple shadows lanced up each nearby coulee, and the prairie skies ran from sea green at their zenith to indigo on the eastern horizons.

Fort Union shimmered with power. Here lay the heart of John Jacob Astor's western empire, now owned by Pierre Chouteau of St. Louis, built by the formidable Kenneth McKenzie, who imported the luxuries of the civilized world and exported beaver plews, and then finely tanned buffalo robes.

Susannah searched anxiously for Jed Owen among the throbbing crowds and didn't see him. She wept, somehow sensing she would not find him here. Above, she heard Ralph barking commands down the speaking tube, and she felt the pulse of the paddles slacken and a hush fall over the packet.

She stared at the great post and saw no love there, and she tried to fight back her tears.

Chapter Fourteen

The Two Medicine nurtured Jed, gave him water and occasional shelter under a cutbank. He whittled a digging stick and dug up the black roots with the tasteless white meat in them. He found wild roses and added to his diet the hips that had healed him of scurvy. He sampled the slimy umber roots of cattails and found them edible and starchy. The summer was too young to supply much else.

The roots and bulbs never filled him, never stopped the gnawing in his belly. He knew he was losing weight again, but still the food sustained life somehow, and enabled him to trudge eastward day by day through the bottoms. On sunny days the dark blue tunic caught the sun's heat and warmed him, but nights sucked the heat from him. He lacked fire, and tried to nestle somewhere out of the endless, restless prairie wind that whipped unhindered across the vast, empty land.

Some days he shivered under a herringbone heaven while powerful arctic winds whistled. If he couldn't hole up, he walked briskly to stir his blood. Once it poured all day, a polar deluge that drove him to claw a slim hollow out of a coral clay cutbank with his Barlow knife and sticks, and even then he half froze, lying cold and wet and trembling for hours.

He worried about animals, the wolves that trailed him, bears, coyotes, the painter tracks he'd seen once. He found an arrowhead one day and pocketed it, wondering what sort of weapon he might make with it. He had no way to anchor it to a shaft. But with his knife he fashioned the end of a good green willow lance into a sharp point, hoping he could keep a wolf at bay with it. He doubted wolves would attack him, but he wanted to be ready.

His boots disintegrated, the uppers pulling away from the soles, and he knew he had come upon grave trouble. He flapped along, feeling the air pulse in and out of his boots, wondering what to do. With an awl and rawhide thong he might repair them, but he lacked the tools. The wide blade of his Barlow knife wouldn't help. He kept a sharp eye for dead buffalo, the hide of which he might use, but he found nothing. He studied the cottonwoods that occasionally massed along the river bottom, hunting for burial scaffolds, and once he did find one, but it was so ancient that everything on it had turned to dust and fiber and bone.

He couldn't help but leave a trail behind him in the soft spring turf, but he did his best to conceal his passage, sticking to rock and harder ground or grassy areas. He slid down the river like a wraith, ever alert for hostile tribesmen. Often he climbed the russet ridges and slowly studied the endless land, whose horizons seemed to recede beyond the lip of the universe. The emptiness of it awed him. He saw nothing, though one day far to the north he thought he discerned smoke.

The Two Medicine joined another river and swung north, and he feared it drained into British possessions, but he pursued it doggedly. Eventually it emptied into a larger river that ran southeast again. The Marias perhaps, though he couldn't know. That day he stumbled on a root, the sole of his right boot ripped off. It lay on the grass, a useless thing, his bare foot encased ridiculously by the worn upper. He picked up the sole, wondering what to do, thinking he might manage a sandal. He spent that day under a marbled gray sky cutting straps from the leather of the upper and threading them into slits he had painfully cut in the sole. It took an entire day, but by sundown he had a serviceable sandal. That night he felt desperately hungry. The roots and bulbs failed him, and he sensed his deepening weakness.

The marbled sky proved to be the prelude to one of those northern storms that lower out of the west, dropping the temperature to somewhere close to freezing and pouring needles of sleet down upon young leaves and tender grass. He found a sandstone hollow full of gray animal offal and sticks and ancient dun leaves. Sleet turned to wet snow that clung heavily to cottonwoods and chokecherry bushes and box elder. It numbed him until he knew he couldn't last much longer without warmth. If only he had flint and steel . . .

Maybe he did have flint and steel. He dug in his tunic pocket for the arrowhead, wondering what it was made of. It had been chipped from a fine-grained glossy tan stone that looked like flint. And the steel blade of his Barlow knife. He pulled it open, dreading that he might dash the flint too hard against it and break his knife, his one lifesaving tool, which could whittle sticks and cut leather strips for sandals. He dashed the arrowhead across the steel, as close to the haft as he could. A single orange spark arced outward. Joyously, he yanked a blank page from Elwood's journal and dashed orange sparks into it. They burned tiny black holes in the paper but failed to ignite it. He tried fiber, dry inner bark from one of the sticks under the cutbank, and the sparks lodged there, smoldering. He nursed an ember and cooed over it, and in a while he had a small hot fire and felt comfortable for the first time in days. He let his mind turn to the letters, and the possession of them gave him courage. This river would take him to Leavenworth, carry him to those widows and kin . . . .

This stream meandered north and south and even west on occasion, but its true course ran southeast, toward the great Missouri. Jed weakened swiftly and could no longer hike a whole day. By noon he felt done in, but he struggled on for another hour. His vision had grown bad, and the horizons seemed a blur. His tunic had frayed at the elbows and his britches were rent in places, and he feared he'd soon be naked. While he rested he spent his hours cutting the remains of his boot into useful thong, which he wrapped about his left boot where it threatened to fall apart.

He discovered fresh prints of unshod ponies one day, and ahead in the bottoms a large herd—a village herd. He settled quietly into the red river brush, and soon saw herders, coppery bare warriors in breechclouts, well armed with bows, arrows, and trade fusils decorated with brass tacks hammered into the stocks. Almost without thinking, he made a fateful decision. He stood, walked out of the brush and shouted at the herders. They stared a moment, and then they trotted their ponies to him, hard-eyed men with heavy cheekbones and gleaming oiled jet hair that either fell loose or was bound in two braids. Their gaze swept from his sandal and patched boot to his frayed clothes, settling long on the blue haversack Jed clutched fiercely to him and the whittled lance that doubled as a staff and walking stick.

"I wish to see your headman," he said. His voice cracked; he hadn't used it for weeks. They escorted him silently into the village. At its edge the town crier found him and whirled among the tawny dark lodges to sing the news. Tall, handsome, proud people swarmed about him, staring curiously at his gaunt figure and loose-hanging tattered clothes. He felt vaguely ashamed. Any of these people could have survived easily the journey that had drained him almost to the point of death. Still, he hobbled among them, past gawking bright-eyed children who peered solemnly, past whispering, giggling young women, past serene old grandmothers with ochre skin like the neck creases of buffalo, past muscled young warriors whose gaze dismissed him as no threat at all, and maybe future sport.

Still, Jed sensed a courtesy here, the hospitality of the village, a politeness mixed with rampant curiosity. They guided him past circles of east-facing lodges until at last the headman greeted him in an open area, almost a village plaza. He stood tall and lean, with intelligent gray eyes studying him from either side of a flattened wide nose. He wore only a breechclout, and yet radiated a gravity and power Jed had never seen upon a mortal man.

"Captain Owen," he said.

"Sir? You know me?"

"You are the long-lost Jed Owen. Do the others live?"

"I—no. They died of cholera. Most of them. Gabriel Charbonneau died of something else. And one was killed by the Kootenai," Jed stammered.

"I am Pi-inakoyim, of the Kainah. I am the brother of Natuyi-tsixina, the wife of Alec Culbertson. The white men call me Seen From Afar, and call her Natawista. We have looked for you for many months."

"Seen From Afar? Culbertson's in-law?" Jed stared bewildered at the great Blood chief, one of the greatest of all the Blackfoot chiefs. "We had hoped—we had hoped to invite you . . ." He faltered.

"You are weary from long travel," the chief said. "Come and smoke."

Still dazed, he followed the Blood chief to an imposing lodge, larger than Jed had imagined a lodge could be. Within the great dark cone an amazing bevy of beautiful women sat quietly, watching Jed.

"We will smoke the pipe that bonds friends, and then you will tell me your story, Captain Owen."

While the chief serenely tamped tobacco into a long calumet with a gray pipestone bowl, Jed gaped at his surroundings. Thirty lodgepoles, he counted. Perhaps forty cowhide skins for a cover. And everywhere within, luxurious dark robes, brilliantly painted parfleches, blankets and capotes trimmed in snowy ermine and wolf, a bow and arrows in a fine beaded quiver, gleaming rifles—and squaws, some young and slim and exquisite, some older and possessed of serene authority.

Seen From Afar lifted his pipe, invoking the blessings of the cardinal directions and of Sun and Earth, and then he smoked calmly, passing the pipe to Jed as he exhaled. Jed did the same, until the charge of tobacco had burned.

"We have learned that treaty makers from the whites always come to take something from us," said the chief blandly. "But if I am wary about all that, I am not wary about you, a brave soldier and chieftain of your people. Let us talk in perfect friendship, Captain Owen. Begin at the beginning."

Susannah wondered why she'd come. She walked hopelessly through the musty wooden corners of Fort Union, through the warehouse and trading store, past the quarters of the engagés, and out upon the sun drenched high plains that stretched beyond the rising and setting sun. Empty. Impulsiveness and a forlorn love had driven her here, and now amidst the reality of the empty plains she faced Jed's death and quietly grieved.

She'd instantly been welcomed in the amazing palatial home of the chief trader, James Kipp, and his quiet Mandan wife Ipasha, or Good Eagle Tail, daughter of a great chief. She could scarcely believe such a peak-roofed mansion could rise so far from civilization, or that the

Kipps' table could yield endless amber and cerise wines and delicacies hauled clear from Missouri.

The *El Paso*, under its mate Walleye Ralph, departed for points unknown upstream. It held cargo for Fort Benton and would steam as far as it could up the unexplored river and unload on a riverbank. From there, Fort Benton rivermen would haul the goods west. She watched the packet chuff into the unknown, cautiously sounding its way along the cerulean oxbows of the great river, and wished she might be aboard. But it could not be. She was beholden to her father and her chaperone to stay in the safety of the fortress.

"I'm sorry he's not here," said Jay Constable, sounding almost civilized. He'd slipped up beside her on the riverbank as they watched the steamer disappear into the great unknown.

"How long will you be? When do we return?" she asked.

"We're here for show. It's the army's way of telling Washington City that it's doing something. We could probably take all the testimony in an afternoon—what's there to say, after all? Get Kipp's story. Find out what the fur company's done. Record the dates that Jed's party stayed here, and at Benton. You know; make a record and go."

"Back on the *El Paso*."

"Maybe. We'll stay long enough to look industrious and thorough." The mockery had returned to his face as she studied it. "Then we'll depart on another packet if one comes, or a keelboat. Oh, you'd enjoy a keelboat."

The lieutenant conducted his inquiry in the dining hall of the engagés, and it went even as he said: within an hour or two, he and his clerks had extracted every bit of information that existed at Fort Union. The only shred of news came from the fur company's voluble bald man, Jean Gallant.

"It is on the Sun River they found *les chevaux*, the horses. Two horses. Maybe fur company. Nothing else," he said grandly. "I could perhaps go back, now that the snow is gone. Go back and hunt for graves, *oui*?"

Susannah winced.

She listened disconsolately to the rest—the tale of this Frenchman's hard winter trip to the Blackfoot and Crow villages, his battle with winter and cold and starvation. His opinion: dead, all dead, sirs.

She caught the thin bald trader outside in the plaza.

"Ah, mademoiselle I have my eye on you there. Such *beauté, oui*. Such sweetness of the eye. Such a handsome fine figure—ah, form, so womanly, yes. Ah, how I suffered for you, coming so far for your gallant *capitaine*. Ah, never have I set eyes on one so sweet and loyal, so beautiful, so wise, so virtuous and innocent. Ah . . ."

His gaze roamed boldly over her lips and breasts and thighs, and at last she colored. "Mr. Gallant," she rebuked him, "I am promised to the man I love."

"Ah, *mon Dieu*, how fortunate is he—if he lives. Ah, he has won the prize, the glory, the honor of the most beautiful *femme, fille*, woman in all creation, the perfection of the entire female race—"

"Mr. Gallant—"

He patted her arm grandly. "Whatever you wish—whatever. Even the smallest thing, mademoiselle. Gallant is at your service. But nod your head and I will travel to the ends of the earth to serve you. A wild rose I would bring from the Pacific Ocean, if you ask it of Gallant, mademoiselle."

"Take me to the Sun River. I would like to see Jed's grave," she said.

"Oh, *Mon Dieu!* My employers would—resist. Your lieutenant who guards your virtue, your honor, your sweet chastity—ah, he'd be mad as a grizzly and have me shot! Ask Gallant anything, but not that!"

She scarcely knew what possessed her, and yet she continued. "Take me. I will pay well. But you must promise to—to be a gentleman. I am betrothed. Will you promise?"

"For you I promise anything. The stars, the sun, the moon. All this I promise, mademoiselle. For pay? How much, eh?"

She didn't reply. "Promise me as a man of honor that you will protect my—virtue. Always."

"*Mon Dieu!* Such a hard thing! You are a magnet and I am iron. How can a poor mortal man make such a promise?"

"Gallant!" She laughed in spite of herself.

He laughed with her. "I make no promises," he said. "Never do I promise a lady so beautiful anything like that. You make a man of Gallant. *Oui*, a man!"

"What would happen? If I employ you and we leave, would the fur company send men after us?"

"Ha! They never catch Jean Gallant. I make to disappear with you— vanished. The soldiers, maybe. They come after, led by the young lieutenant who mocks you. Ah, *oui,* I observe everything, yes? But they are innocents. The blue soldiers. Ha! They come from the cities, from the civilization of *les américains.* Poof! We vanish, we go to the Sun River. And I make love, I woo you, beautiful mademoiselle, all the way!"

"You must stay on the river if we go."

"The river? *Non,* it is no good."

"He told me that where the river runs, there would he be."

He stared, bright and curious. "The river," he said.

"Have you considered everything? Will you be fired if you guide me?"

"Ah, mademoiselle, what is employment? Nothing. What is a wage compared to guiding a beautiful virtuous maiden to her *capitaine*? Nothing! And besides, I go to work for the Opposition, *oui*?"

She couldn't resist a brief smile.

"Tonight we leave! Ah, mademoiselle, how beautiful you will look in the pale light of the moon. I shall gather all things, *les chevaux,* the food. You bring a little clothing. Just a little, not much. The less you wear, the more *magnifique* you are, *oui*? Trust Gallant to keep you warm."

Gallant beamed at her, finally melting the severity of her glare. "I will choose my clothing carefully, and for all weather," she said. She planned to take a lot of it, and especially her Derringer.

They agreed on a fee of a hundred dollars in gold and set the time of departure for midnight, because the June sun lingered to eleven. The great front gate would be shut, but he'd handle all that. She should wait on the Kipps' veranda until he beckoned.

Filled with misgiving, she gathered her things together in the bedroom the Kipps had given her and bundled them into a canvas bag supplied by Gallant. She could not explain her own conduct. She scolded herself—she would bring grief to the Kipps, to the American Fur Company, to Jay Constable, to everyone else; she'd betray her father and mortify and worry him half to death. And yet . . . and yet . . . The thing that tugged at her heart could not be denied.

Jed, oh, Jed, if you live, I must find you. If you are ill or captive, I must help you. If you lie dead, and my heart dies too, then I must know, I must stand beside your grave wherever it is on these endless plains . . . .

Still, she could leave a message behind. She could exonerate Jay and her hosts, the Kipps. She could take all the responsibility and blame. She could write her father that the decision was her own, that whatever the price, it would be hers to pay as well.

She found a nib pen, ink, foolscap, and an envelope, too, in Kipp's office in a wing of the great house. There she penned her note to Colonel Nathan St. George, concluding with that sentiment she had read somewhere and enjoyed: The heart has reasons that reason knows not of. She addressed the envelope to her father but left it unsealed so that it might be read. She carefully didn't say where Gallant would take her, but they'd know: the Sun River.

She and Lieutenant Jay Constable were the dinner guests of the head trader and his wife that evening, but she toyed with her buffalo tongue, said little, and finally pleaded a headache and fled to her room. Four hours later she sat astride a wiry Indian pony, her skirts hiked up, trotting behind a shadowy fur company engagé under a clear warm sky, riding down the Milky Way toward the edge of the universe.

Chapter Fifteen

No one followed. Gallant took her down a beaten path that swung north of the river and then west, the trail to Fort Benton. She sat her fat pony sleepily, feeling its rhythm under her. Behind, two packhorses burdened with canvas-wrapped loads followed reluctantly.

She saw a shooting star, and then three more. The bowl of heaven seemed alive, a living ceiling stretched over an infinity of black treeless land. *Jed is dead,* the streaking stars told her. The idea simply lodged in her head, and she believed it. Ahead a few paces the bald guide rode alertly, and she felt safe in his presence, safer than with a platoon of dragoons. He'd never stop romancing her, of course. Conquest was a male game an army brat knew all about. Gallant might woo, but Gallant would never win, and the wooing promised to be amusing during a time when she had nothing else to brighten her life.

She didn't particularly worry about what she'd done—this scandalous trip, accompanied only by a fur company engagé. Her father had always known he'd reared a headstrong daughter, and her letter would exonerate the Kipps and Jay. Still, when she checked off in her mind all the things that might happen—capture by hostile Indians, disease, death, losing Gallant somehow in this vast emptiness, maltreatment, by any male—she wondered how she'd dared to venture out upon a trackless land in search of a man she loved, no doubt dead.

She grieved quietly, hearing the soft clop of hooves as the ponies carried her and her goods over the breast of the plains. A certain desolation settled upon her, and anger too. If Gallant forced his attentions on her, she'd bite his head off. She glared suspiciously at the thin hulk riding ahead, but then she settled down. The one thought that kept returning to her was the sheer foolishness of all this. Unless she found a grave and put her gnawing doubts to rest, she'd accomplish exactly nothing. She sighed. Love impelled her, that aching need, that dear close joy that Jed meant to her, that simple admiration she felt for him, had catapulted her out upon this waste. She wouldn't even try to explain it. She just had to do it, and that was all.

She trotted her pony forward. "I asked you to stick to the river."

"*Mon Dieu!* That would take forever, riding along each bend and out each headland. If we miss your *capitaine,* he will get news of you soon enough at Fort Union. Follow the river! You don't know what it is you ask. Not this river."

She had no answer.

"*Le bateau, El Paso,* it is up there a way, yes? If your *capitaine* is on the river, they will find him."

"Will we come to the boat?"

He shrugged. "Who knows? The mate, Ralph, takes it to new waters—for *an bateau grand.* Maybe it strikes a rock and sinks. Mostly we are many miles away from the river."

Dawn pried open the black east like a silver knife blade piercing an airtight, but still they rode onward. A numb weariness settled over Susannah, and she dozed in the saddle, feeling it chafe her thighs. She desperately wanted rest but she refused to complain. Army, that's what she was, and she'd show the Frenchman how she'd been bred. She hunched low, one hand on the pommel to steady herself, and ignored the howling of her body. She pushed pain away and fiercely concentrated on Jed, the big rough warmth of the man she loved.

The umber plains stretched grayly away, rolling to russet rocky ridges and dry coulees and bunchgrass flats. Thirst caught at her, but still Gallant didn't stop. The rising sun faintly warmed her back, and that felt good. She felt her pony weary under her and knew they could not keep up this relentless march much longer. But still Gallant hurried on, into midmorning. Then at a high place he paused. Two or three miles off—she never was much good at distances—a thin jade band of trees lined a watercourse.

"Maybe we rest the ponies, *oui*?"

She nodded, and they covered the last distance in an endless half hour. She dreamed only of getting out of the saddle and curling up somewhere, and of water. She'd never wanted water so much.

"The Big Muddy," he said, leading her off the trail and south a quarter of a mile or so, his sharp brown eyes studying the distant amber slopes.

He helped her down, his strong hands a shade too familiar, and she headed for the river. She splashed the icy gray water over her face and drank some hesitantly from cupped hands. She found Gallant sitting in a sun-dappled glade, surrounded by young cottonwoods and brush. The picketed ponies grazed.

"No one is following?" she asked.

He shrugged. "Kipp, he tells the lieutenant that to follow Jean Gallant is to chase wind. No one follows Gallant. We let the ponies graze an hour and maybe we go again."

"I need sleep."

"We go," he said. She sank into the tender grass and he handed her a strange sausagelike thing.

"Pemmican. A strong food for the trail."

It tasted a little rancid. She detected ground meat, fat, and berries of some sort marbled through it.

"Why are you in such a hurry?"

"Gallant is always in a hurry. To see the new land and meet the new ladies, and make love to beautiful women, as many as there are."

She smiled and curled into a ball on the warming earth, trying to ease the ache of travel-torn flesh.

Too soon, he was shaking her. "Beautiful mademoiselle, we go now to find your *capitaine*. Ah, what a sad and beautiful journey, yes? A journey of the heart, a journey of love, a journey of hope. We'll go now, and find your *capitaine*."

She stared up at him. He hunkered over her, his soft brown eyes shining warmth and joy. Behind him, the drooping ponies stood on cocked legs, packed and ready.

"Never have I been so honored, to take a beautiful young highbred lady to her true love. Ah! It floods the heart, yes?"

She laughed, fighting back the weariness that weighted her like bullet lead.

He helped her into her saddle, and she adjusted her skirts, full ones of teal blue, which she had chosen because she needed to hike them up to ride astride.

"Ah! What calves, mademoiselle! What petite feet and lovely rounded legs!"

She reddened. Nothing in her life had prepared her for compliments of her legs, so carefully hidden from men back at Leavenworth. Ankles perhaps. She enjoyed the faint indecency of it, and laughed again.

He led her across a benign day, while sun and wind chapped her flesh and pinked her nose and neck. Little of it stayed in her mind, which bogged with weariness. Jed could ride right up to her and she'd scarcely notice, she thought, fighting to keep her wits. But Gallant remained alert, his liquid umber eyes reading the land with some knowledge beyond hers, studying the flight of hawks and crows, the movement of antelope, the faint gold of rising dust, as if to discern what lay over the bronze ridges and down in the lavender draws. Even in her weariness, she sensed that a master plainsman was protecting her.

By late afternoon great towers of white cloud had built in the southwest, turning the sky into a city of gray caverns and ivory ramparts.

"That one over there, she will descend. But I know a place," he said, "a few hours. Maybe it makes rain first and we get wet, and the clothing, it sticks to your beautiful form."

"Stop that, Gallant. I'll not have you thinking or saying things like that."

"*Mon Dieu!* How can a poor *homme*, a poor man like me, help it, eh? I take a vision of beauty to her *capitaine*, and I tell myself, Gallant, she is a pearl beyond price! I take a mademoiselle of perfect form, sad, sad eyes, long shiny hair, petite ankles, happy laugh, and a heart filled with love—I take all this along the trail, just this most beautiful mademoiselle and myself, alone together, and I go half made with desire, ah . . ."

"Gallant. Take me back."

"*Mon Dieu!* I will control myself. I will hide the longing in my eyes, yes? I will say nothing! I will turn my gaze elsewhere so you will never see the *tristesse*, the yearning, the sighs of hunger, the dreaming of one small kiss—on the cheek, on the beard of my cheek—one petite kiss, *oui.* I will hide all this from you, *chère* Susannah, and we will go on to your *capitaine.*"

She refused to smile. Gallant had begun to alarm her, and she feared for her safety.

They hurried silently westward under an indigo sky, trotting weary ponies into a freshet of wind that had knives of ice in it. Above, the boiling clouds vaulted to the gates of heaven, higher than mountains pile on top of each other, ever changing, sometimes pierced by bold bolts of rose sun. Susannah peered at the empty land around her, spotting nothing but swelling dun prairie and rocky ridges, cactus and amythest sagebrush. Occasionally, off to the south, she glimpsed oxbows of the great river, silver now in the chalky light.

Rain came, in cold gusts at first, and in moments drenched her cotton dress and shawl and soaked icily through the linens of her underthings, cold and cruel on her flesh. The lashing water sculpted her soaked clothing to her, matted her hair, dripped icily off her nose. Chilled, she trembled violently in the sudden blackness of the raging storm. Lightning cracked, startling her witless, blue bolts searing down just ahead.

Gallant trotted the soaked ponies down a sudden grade and into a bottom while the storm shrieked overhead and the icy rain sucked the last heat from Susannah's body. She closed her eyes and hung on to the pommel now, quaking with cold. Rain turned to hail, pea-size stones and then lead bullets that smacked and stung and raked her iced flesh. The hail clattered off her saddle and every branch and piled in blue heaps in the battered grass. She lost her sense of which direction they were moving in but saw dense stands of water-blackened cottonwoods, a rising river, and beyond it amber rock cutbanks. One had a hollow, protected by an overhang of stratified stone. Someone had laboriously walled off its north side, making a sheltered dry ell.

"Mademoiselle, we are arrived, the river called Wolf," Gallant yelled over the roar.

She dismounted stiffly and fell in a heap in the mud, her numb limbs refusing to work.

"*Ici!* Inside where it is dry, mademoiselle. I'll bring the packs. Take off your clothes, mademoiselle, before you die of the ague! Do as I say, yes? I will find you a blanket and we will make warm."

She stared helplessly at him, her body convulsing violently.

"No," she shouted.

"Do as Gallant says," he barked, "or the fevers will take you away from your *capitaine* forever!"

Reluctantly she turned her back and with trembling fingers began to unfasten the hooks of her blue bodice.

The scarecrow of a man slumped in a chair before Chief Trader Culbertson scarcely resembled the one who had passed through Fort Benton the previous summer.

"You could use a month of fattening on buffalo hump," Culbertson said.

Jed nodded. "Your brother-in-law fed me well."

A small party of Bloods dispatched by Seen From Afar and led by his friend Small Weasel had brought Jed here and returned at once to the Marias, explaining that the chief would wait there for the trading to begin because he feared white men's diseases.

"All dead," Alec Culbertson said.

"Cholera. Gabriel Charbonneau died of some other fever. A private was killed by a Kootenai arrow. I almost died of scurvy, but they decided to let me live."

Culbertson surveyed the man's ragged britches, shredded tunic, and makeshift footwear. "I'd give you clothing off our shelves, but I have none. Trade goods aren't in yet; any day now. We've traded everything in the place, right down to bedsheets. But in a few days . . ."

Jed smiled wanly. "I can wait."

Outside the adobe fort, four hundred lodges of Blackfeet and Cree forested the flat, and perhaps three thousand Indians awaited the new trading season.

"I can have some of the squaws make up some buckskins and moccasins for you. Even trade off your worn duds for something. I can fetch you something for that blue bag." The man seemed weary and possibly still very ill, Culbertson thought. Not ready for any strenuous travel; not for a week or two yet.

"Not the bag. No, I'm keeping that."

Some harsh thing in Captain Owen's voice puzzled the trader. "What's so special about the bag, Captain?"

The gaunt man sighed, ran a rough hand through unkempt shoulder-lengthy black hair. "I'm bound to take it back down the river." He fixed the trader with a wild, almost mad stare. "It's got a few messages in it. That's all."

"I've heard things," prompted Culbertson. "Some of the Piegans camped out there told me about a white man who went crazy when they took that bag from him."

"Some of them are here?"

"My people. My Blackfeet. My wife, Natawista is a—"

"I know," muttered Jed. "Met her last year. A lovely woman. No, Mr. Culbertson, I'm not crazy. I'm just keeping my promise. These are letters I wrote for most of my men when they lay dying of the cholera. A few wrote their own, such as the two treaty commissioners, and there's a journal that was kept by one of them. And some small things: rosaries, a ring or two, tintypes, locks of hair. That's all. But I made a promise to deliver them if I had breath in me. I promised them. I watched them die. I saw peace come over them when I promised. Saw it . . . had to keep it. Had to do for them what I'd want done . . . message to Susannah if I'd had to write one."

"Susannah?"

"My fiancée, at Fort Leavenworth."

"You fought them for that?"

"Yes."

Culbertson sighed. "Should be news any day now. I have goods coming here on the *Mary Blane* and the *El Paso*. Army inquiry party's coming, I understand, to look into your disappearance. No doubt they'll have news of your people at Leavenworth. My keelboats are down the river picking up the trade goods, but I haven't heard anything. The packets are pushing farther upstream these days, above Fort Union, shortening the distance we have to keelboat or wagon the goods. Anyway, we're all waiting here, Captain. Waiting for goods, waiting for news, waiting to open the trading window."

"An inquiry party? Do you know who?"

"No. The army contacted us in the fall, and I sent out my best man, Jean Gallant. He got to most of the villages in the middle of one of the coldest winters, but he came up with nothing. I guess the army wants to make a record of some sort to satisfy all the politicians in Washington City. That new Indian Bureau's set up a howl. All the army's fault. Of course, they don't want the army to take over Indian affairs again. Myself, I'd prefer the army. For obvious reasons."

"I have Commissioner Elwood's journal," Jed said. "He attempts to discredit me in it—discredit the army. Make us look so bloodthirsty that . . ." Owen's voice faded away.

Alec Culbertson gaped. "You brought back a journal intended to discredit you?"

The hollow-eyed man across from him nodded.

"Why, man?"

"Way I am."

"May I read it?"

Jed stared, reluctantly. "I suppose," he said. "In my presence. I won't let those papers out of my sight."

Culbertson lifted the haversack from the reluctant captain, who glared, fire-eyed. "Eat. You can eat while I read. Then I'll take you over to Natawista and you can have our spare room."

Jed Owen shook his head and stared.

"Suit yourself," the chief trader said. He peered out the small glass window, brought almost two thousand miles from St. Louis, into the silent sunlit yard surrounded by gray adobe walls. Quiet now. When the trade goods arrived, bedlam.

The good-byes, the letters from the dead, some of them water-stained now, touched him. One by one he parsed them, sensing something of Captain Jed Owen's mission and strange passion. He peered up from the plank desktop and saw that the man had dozed off, weariness overwhelming him. Culbertson read them all, pausing to absorb the letters of the two commissioners, one an honorable man, the other a cauldron of greed and machination.

Damn them! The trader saw the future, saw the fate of his Blackfeet, who'd be hounded into smaller and smaller reservations, their buffalo commissary slaughtered, forced into dependence on government annuities and then cheated out of the annuities by crass opportunists like Elwood. He pulled the commissioner's blue buckram journal out last and began skimming its pages, ignoring the routine entries, looking for the things Captain Owen said would be there. Well into the middle he began finding them, aspersions on Owen's character, insinuations, lies.

He read through the quiet afternoon hour, granite-faced.

Owen sprawled across from him. Comotose. Exhausted. Burn Elwood's damn journal. Easy enough. But Culbertson couldn't. He felt as honor-bound to deliver the thing as Owen had. The trader stared at the man, seeing exhaustion that sleep didn't erase. Long coarse hair over his shoulders, scraggly black beard. Hollow cheeks. Long grim creases at the edges of his stubborn mouth. A man. More than a man. A rock, like Saint Peter.

He arose softly, stuffed the papers back into the blue bag and set it gently beside the captain. Then he slipped out, going past the warehouse, redolent with baled buffalo robes and packs of beaver pelts, past the engagés' barracks, toward the silent sunny place he and beautiful, quiet Natawista called home. He found her there in her favorite red taffeta, slim and jet-haired, darning stockings.

"Natty," he said softly. "Captain Owen's done in. I'll have him carried over and put to bed. Probably won't wake up for a day. I'll have Malcolm Clarke pull those rags off him. We haven't a stitch for him, not until the keelboats come. I'd like you to go out and find some women in the lodges who'd like a pair of four-point blankets in trade for some good moccasins, some buckskin britches—not a breechclout—and a shirt and the rest. They can have his rags, too. Get his size from those, and from what's left of his boots."

She smiled. She understood him in English but usually spoke her Blackfeet.

"I know just the ones," she said. "I'll bring them."

"Natty, one thing more. This man, Captain Owen; I've never met his like. He's a man, given a trust, who keeps it unto death. He's a—a man, Natty," he said hoarsely. "Tell the women that. I want those buckskins decorated to match the man. This Napikwan, white man, carries Sun and the power of Sun. He's chief above chiefs. He's medicine above medicine. Tell the women, Natty. Tell them that their dyes and quills and beads and cloth trim—tell them to make it all sing of Jed Owen."

"Has he a woman?" she asked, smiling shyly.

"He's engaged to a Susannah."

"We will make this clothing his wedding suit," she said softly. "He will shine like Sun in her eyes."

"Do that, Natty," he said, fighting back an unfamiliar emotion that blurred his vision.

Chapter Sixteen

Gallant handed her a thick brown blanket. Susannah opened it gratefully and wrapped it over her shoulders, sliding her sopping teal dress down underneath until it lay in a heap at her feet. That was as far as she'd go: she'd live with her icy chemise and petticoat.

"Ah, beautiful lady, the blanket, she keeps your lovely form from my yearning eyes," the Frenchman said woefully.

It angered her. Would this never cease?

She settled down against the rear of the hollow, feeling harsh rock jab her back. In spite of her wet underthings she felt a thin warmth enfold her from the tightly wrapped blanket. Susannah let Gallant do the work while she squeezed water from her thick hair.

He unloaded the packs and hauled them in and then vanished into the drizzle and returned with semidry sticks he'd snapped from trees. Miraculously he had a fire crackling in a few minutes, encouraged with a pinch of gunpowder. He hobbled the four horses and turned them loose in the grassy bottoms to feast on young grass. And all the while he glanced boldly at her, dining on her with his eyes, thinking noisy thoughts that she heard unspoken.

He vanished again into the twilight with a hatchet, and when he returned he carried a load of wood, slick with water, and set it near the fire to dry. She waited until he was gone and then wrung her blue dress and stretched it over the packs to dry. Icy air eddied around her, sometimes sucking away the radiant heat of the small fire. Awkwardly, clutching the blanket tight, she dug into her own pack for a dry petticoat and chemise, found them, and began to change, huddled under the blanket. He returned with more wood just then—naturally he would, she thought—eyed her dolefully, sighed languorously, and departed again.

But she couldn't pull her soaked chemise off without dropping the blanket. He seemed to be out of sight. She made her bitter choice, hating to be put in such a position, and stripped off her soaked underthings and pulled on the dry ones, resuming her seat with the blanket about her, warm at last.

He returned with more wood and a beatific joy upon his face but said nothing. Settling under the ledge, he began camp chores in the cold, sighing gently. Just beyond, water sheeted off the lip of rock that sheltered them, and the storm growled like an old man in nightmare.

He boiled a gruel of heaven knew what, and it filled and warmed her. He finished his kitchen chores and unrolled his robes while she waited coldly.

"A cozy night, yes?" he said softly. "Ah, the joy of sharing a small haven in a storm with a woman so beautiful . . . ah, mademoiselle, why don't you—"

"Gallant," she said wearily. "In one way, your attentions are flattering and amusing. What woman doesn't like being wooed and complimented?"

He smiled and peered at her with heavy-lidded eyes.

"But you only make me angry," she snapped. "Lust is no compliment. You flatter me with the hope of spending your lust on me. You seduce me for conquest. Your thoughts are not of me, but of your pleasure."

"Ah, mademoiselle! It is not so! I'm hopelessly in love! Never have I been so lovesick!"

She might have laughed some other time, but now she contemplated him with rage. "My love belongs to Captain Owen. His arms are the only arms that will ever hold me. I pray to God that he lives, but if he's . . . gone . . . I need to sit at his grave and know and understand my loss. What I have with Jed is sacred and holy and honorable. I am—a virgin. And if he lives, and if we marry, our union will be more than—than lust."

"Ah, Mademoiselle St. George, how I envy you. I am only a poor fur trader finding *petit* pleasures where I can. I should be honored if you would but comfort me with a *petit* kiss, a hug for a lonely man of the wilderness, a—"

"Stop!" she yelled, and kept on yelling, some feral rage exploding in her lungs.

"Mon Dieu!" He looked startled, and then impressed.

"You will stop this—this verbal assault—this rape with your eyes and voice," she snapped. "You will not touch me. You will respect my privacy. You will stop your—talk, this lustful talk, this seduction. You will not compliment me again. Not my form, not my mind, not my eyes, not my words. Not anything. You are escorting a woman who loves another, and if you ever forget it again, I'll—I'll make your life miserable in ways you can scarcely imagine."

"Mademoiselle, I am honored," said Gallant. "I am only a lonely engagé, far beneath a colonel's daughter."

"Stop that!"

"I hope your *capitaine* lives and you have your happiness. But mademoiselle, if you have happiness, pause some day to remember poor old Gallant, the humble engagé who led you to him. And if he doesn't live"—he sighed sadly—"I'd be honored if you would think of me kindly in your generous heart, and say a small prayer for a man who worships at your feet."

She giggled. She stared at the incorrigible Frenchman and howled. He looked hurt at first, but then he guffawed and chortled, and they bayed at the cold night.

They continued west the next day under blue enamel sky, through air so clear it made ridges fifty miles away seem close and huge. They traversed long treeless slopes, and the only foliage she saw lay in coulees. These sere Indian lands seemed vaster than ever, and Jed smaller than ever. The trickery of transparent air gave rise to mirages and visions. Once she saw Jed in the sky, black-bearded and dressed differently, in strange golden skins, looking like an Indian. They passed outcrops the color of apricot, bluffs of burgundy sandstone striped with chalk. They startled caramel antelope sunning in a silvery green sea of sagebrush. By midday the sun glared so white it turned the heavens white. And still they walked their shaggy little ponies westward, knowing no sound but the zephyrs in their ears.

"Ah, mademoiselle, do you know that your very own Gallant will be famous one day? Yes! History will know me!" he said, walking his pony beside hers into the distant afternoon.

"I'm sure you are a great man of the wilderness, Gallant," she said.

"*Oui*, yes. Yes, I am that. But this fame, she comes from another thing. I am making absolute zero."

"You are making what?"

"Zero. Absolute. No heat. Not a particle of heat, yes?"

She stared, puzzled.

"That stupid Swiss, Fahrenheit. He crawls up into the Alps across the sea, yes, and he hangs up his mercury thermometer and waits, and when the mercury goes no lower he calls this reading zero, yes? Nothing. No heat. Zero absolute. But he's an idiot. He's nowhere near zero, yes? Here we see the mercury go much lower. It goes down, down, twenty, thirty, forty degrees below what he says is absolute zero. How can anything be less than zero, eh? It makes no sense, less than zero heat. But your friend Gallant know true zero. Absolute zero. It is fifty below. Already I have seen it go to forty-nine below, yes? In my packs I always carry a thermometer that goes to sixty below. But fifty below, she is the bottom. Someday soon I prove it. Maybe I go up into the British lands to prove it. I wait until it goes to fifty below, and then I tell the world, see? True zero. We make new thermometers with true zero at fifty below, and water, she freezes at eight-two warm. And we call the new system Gallant. Zero Gallant, not zero Fahrenheit—we discredit that imbecile and throw him away, yes? We have the Gallant system, yes?"

"I hope you're right, Jean."

"Jean! You call me at last by my given name. Jean! See what fame does! I am on the brink of fame, and already people call me Jean and make smiles! I will not let fame turn my head. I will remember you, Susannah, long after I am rich and famous, yes?"

"I hope you do. And I'll always remember you."

"Ah, what joy! To be remembered by a beautiful lady," he said, trotting his pony ahead.

They topped a long soft ridge and discovered beyond it a flat valley with a large river oxbowing its way south and into the distant blue Missouri. Susannah sat her pony, feeling the brisk June breeze toying with her rain-softened hair, dismayed by the giant land and her own smallness.

"Ah! See there, Madam Owen. It is the *El Paso*, yes?"

It took her time to see what he saw so far off, or to make sense of the tiny dot on the Missouri, which could at first to her eyes have been anything. But in time she made out the packet anchored at the north bank, and beside it the forms of two smaller dark boats.

"Keelboats," he said. *Le bateau* comes this far to the Milk River, but now she goes back. They unload the trade goods for Fort Benton, yes? Soon a bunch of engagés, all muscle and no brain, they pole the keelboats up the river, fighting the current. Or sometimes they take out ropes and cordelle—they pull the boat up the river by walking along the bank. Hard work. Only the dumb French will do it, yes?"

"I think they must be very strong."

"You want to go down there? Find out about your *capitaine* from the ones who have the keelboats? They come from Fort Benton."

It tempted her. Above all she wanted news.

"If I go they might force me back on the *El Paso*," she said. "And cause trouble for you, because you are with me. But I do want news. Could you go yourself? I'll wait here. I'll find cover where no one will see me or the ponies. You can go ask. Two hours each way, I think. And if you're alone, seeking news, no one will say or think anything."

"At your service," he replied. "That crease in the land there. You wait in it, yes? I will be back before dark, with news. Yes or no, the *capitaine* has been found or he has not."

She settled into the young bluestem and watched him disappear down the long slopes to the river. She had never imagined the world was so large, or that she could be so alone.

She kept her vigil uneasily through the long afternoon, feeling the eddying breezes, the chapping sun, the rough texture of gravel and bunchgrass on her buttocks and back. She peered warily from the lip of the coulee, seeking signs of life and danger, tribesmen who could easily carry off a lone woman and use her or sell her or trade her. Once black and white magpies exploded from a clump of sagebrush, chattering alarm. She studied the area, not knowing what had disturbed them, discovering nothing.

She watched the horses crop. When they lifted their heads and pricked their ears forward, she peered uneasily about. In the dense solitude she wondered again why she'd come all this way. She didn't know Jed anymore. They'd been separated longer than they'd been together. He'd transferred to Fort Leavenworth, courted and won her in seven months; they'd been separated over a year. He must be dead by now; was there any other possibility? Could the treaty commission simply be taking its time among these far tribes in this vast land? No.

She knew so little about him. All the time of discovery, of learning the intimate details of another mortal, had been cut off by this separation. What did she love, really? A pasteboard image of a rough, commanding, competent man with some sterling quality that shone in him. But what else? How did he feel about her? Did he simply lust, like Gallant? Would he be harsh and oppressive as a husband? Did he anger swiftly? Would he be tender after years had passed? Kind and wise with their children? Would she love him ten years from now?

She had no answers. The future lay as empty as these endless prairies, as hollow as the azure bowl over her. Surely Jed lay dead somewhere. If she could find a grave, what more could she ask? The not knowing, that would be more than any woman could bear. Maybe this wild trip would be worth something after all, if it could just end the uncertainty . . . Oh, Jed.

She spotted Gallant far off, an expanding black dot making his way up the long gradient from the Missouri bottoms. Beyond, on the river, the *El Paso* belched black smoke from its chimneys and swung east, apparently heading downstream. Gallant must have caught the keelboat crew just as they finished loading. The packet slid swiftly out of sight, a tiny dot of civilization, and the terrible sense of being a small speck of humanity engulfed her.

"Nothing. They have no news. All friends of mine, so I know. In fact, they say the *bourgeois*, Culbertson, tells them to watch the riverbanks sharp when they come, yes?"

She had expected that and felt nothing. A certain numbness that comes from surrendering hope had settled on her over the afternoon. "I would like to find Jed's grave," she said softly. "Or at least some graves, if the others are buried somewhere."

"The Sun River. I know to look there, but nowhere else."

"This land is larger than I had ever imagined. We'll never find—"

"Ah, Mademoiselle Owen, we might. Men travel this land by the waters, by the rivers where they water their horses and themselves. So that makes it small, you see? *Petite?*"

She nodded, not really believing him.

"We'll go to the Sun River now. Far to the west, beyond Fort Benton. But now we follow the Milk River instead of the Missouri. Soon the country around the big river gets rough—mountains, canyons, great difficulties. We go the easy way around the mountains, yes?"

"I want to follow the Missouri. Jed said—"

"The rivermen, they'll see Jed on the banks. I have told them Captain Owen's beautiful fiancée has come up the river."

"Very well."

"You are a different woman than when I ride down to *bateau.*"

"Perhaps that is so."

He peered at her closely, and then he unhobbled and loaded the packhorses and saddled her pony. They camped on the shallow wooded bottoms of the Milk that night and the next day followed a clear wagon trail that Gallant said led to Fort Benton. It took them farther and farther from her river, but it no longer mattered. She looked only for a marked or unmarked grave.

For days on end they followed the Milk River, always finding easy passage over gentle ground. They passed north of a small blue range of mountains Gallant called the Little Rockies and then swung around a much larger and closer range, full of chalk and coral and lemon colors under its green cover. The Bear Paws.

"We've seen no Indians," she said to Gallant one day.

"They're here. Many of them have gone to the forts—this is the trading season, when *les bateaux* bring the goods up the river. But maybe a few are out, *non?* The Cree. They mostly stay in the Queen's land, but sometimes they come. The Blackfeet name for the Cree is Lying People."

"This is Assiniboin country too."

"Yes, but now they are at Fort Union, trading with James Kipp."

"Still, I see you looking, watching the trail we make."

"I don't like surprises."

One day he shot a buffalo cow and they enjoyed tender hump meat and tongue, leaving the rest to the gray wolves. North of the Bear Paws they rode through dazzling fields of wildflowers, lemony daisies, bold blue lupine, and carpets of purple blooms Susannah couldn't identify. They startled a band of mustangs and watched them race southward into rough olive-hued country. The bay lead mare raced up a sentry knoll and stared imperiously, then vanished. One moonlit night they heard the roaring of an enraged bear, and another night the bellow of buffalo bulls continually rattled the peace. The vast high plains no longer seemed empty to her, but teeming with life.

Where was Gallant taking her? Day after day they rode along the meandering river. Beside the campfire one night she asked him some pointed questions, observing his surprise.

"The Milk? She runs to the British land and then curves south again into this country. She curves like the teton of a woman on her back, *oui?* But we don't go that far. Soon we come to Big Sandy River, and that take us almost to Fort Benton. The Milk, she's a good river to travel. Buffalo and grass and water. The Blackfeet call it Little River, *Kinuk Sisakta,* but she is not so little, no?"

Gallant no longer plagued her, but she knew his thoughts were never far from his lust. She no longer cared. She had slipped into a deep quiet, preparing herself for the worst. The intimacies of camp life no longer troubled her, and she washed and dressed herself almost unaware of her guide and turned into her buffalo robe at night without any thought of where to place it. He sensed her distance and at least feigned indifference, though his gaze often slid over her like a caressing hand. It didn't matter. Her body remained her own.

They turned down the Big Sandy along a well-defined trace lying west of the Bear Paws and across an endless rough land of chalk and lemony grasses.

"We'll go to Fort Benton, yes? We are maybe ahead of the keelboats. We'll talk with the *bourgeois,* Alec Culbertson, and you will stay with his family, his Blood wife Natawista. She is a woman to make a man sigh and groan . . . . They'll make you stay, and I'll go up to the Sun River and look."

"If they make me stay I don't want to stop there, Gallant. How can they make me stay? Will they treat me—"

"No, no. They'll say it's very dangerous for a woman, and Gallant is just the one to look at the Sun River, yes?"

"Then let's go around Benton. I've hired you to take me to the Sun River."

He shrugged. The next day they left the Big Sandy behind them and traversed dry prairie in a hot chafing wind, sliding down cedar-choked coulees as they approached the Missouri again.

"Tomorrow at sunset, we are at Fort Benton," he announced that night. They had made camp within sight of the glinting river.

"But I'd rather—"

"Fort Benton," he said.

"I'll find a way to leave," she retorted. "If there are graves somewhere on the Sun River, I must see them."

He shrugged. "I hear from the Crow about two stray ponies there, and you turn it into graves."

Chapter Seventeen

The murmur of voices penetrated through Jed's sleep, and he rolled over, drifting back into the fog. A gentle hand shook him, a hand upon his bare shoulder. The voices would not be denied. He rolled again, yawned, and opened his eyes upon a shadowed unfamiliar room. The call of nature came strong upon him. Voices. A woman's voice.

"Jed. Oh, God, Jed."

He turned, finding a woman sitting on his bed and seeing blurred faces beyond, all peering. Susannah, with tears rolling down her face. A mirage.

He sighed, closed his eyes, and drifted away from cruel mirages into his sleep world. But the hand caressed his shoulder and ran over his full black beard. A woman's hand. He grew aware of his nakedness underneath the tan blankets. He opened his eyes again and met Susannah's intense gaze. Leavenworth? How did he get to Leavenworth?

"Jed! Jed! Oh, Jed! You're alive. I didn't have enough faith. Hold me, Jed, hold me tight."

"Susannah?" She peered at him from a face sheeted with wetness. It could not be.

He focused at last on those around him. Culbertson, bulbous-nosed and grinning; Natawista, watching quietly with some unfathomable joy in her dark face; a bald man in buckskins, lean and hawklike, with heavy lips. Fort Benton, not Leavenworth.

Susannah threw herself against his chest, hugging him, pressing her wet cheeks into his rough beard. Susannah. Susannah! He folded his bare arms about her, fathoming at last the solidness and softness of her body, the thin blue fabric of her dress, the fierce clutch of her hands and arms. She trembled in his arms, and he felt her sobbing convulse her.

"Oh, my darling Jed. I gave up hope. I thought you were dead," she cried. "I didn't have faith. I didn't have faith . . . . Is it really you? Are you well? Are you hurt? Are you wounded? I want to heal you with my love. Oh, Jed, let me heal you!"

He didn't have an answer to that. He hugged her, feeling her love, feeling her yearning, feeling the sheer reality of her, feeling her lustrous hair against his face. He enfolded her in brawny bare arms, feeling the crush of her soft breasts, the thin fabric, the shape of her back under his palms, the utter reality of her. He peered up at these strangers, watching so intently, aware of his nakedness under the sliding blanket. But he couldn't let her go. He couldn't fathom this wondrous thing, nor was he sure it existed. The trembling woman clutched at him, her hands discovering him, sliding over his shoulders, touching his bearded cheeks, burying themselves in his hair. She pulled back and gazed through wet eyes, reading him anew, learning him, memorizing him, loving him.

"I came to find your grave," she said, her voice muffled in his ear. "You're the only one alive. The only one. What a terrible ordeal you've had. Oh, Jed, I cry inside."

Culbertson must have told her. Jed needed suddenly to dress and answer nature's call.

"Susannah. Give me a minute."

"You look so strange," she whispered. "So gaunt. The beard. So different. Hair to your shoulders. But it's you!"

"I'll get my things, and—" He peered around wildly. "Where are my things?" He saw no tunic and britches.

"*Mon Dieu*, the man wants to put on clothing!" exclaimed the lean bald man. "*Idiote!* Mad as a loon."

"My things!" cried Jed. He saw the blue haversack on a chair, but not his tunic and britches.

"Forgive us—they were used up," said Natawista Culbertson in slow English. "The women have made this." She pointed at a folded pile of buckskin clothing, topped by handsome black moccasins.

He peered up at her, at the clothing, and at the woman sobbing softly in his arms, and smiled.

Culbertson cleared his throat. "We can leave you two alone for a reunion if you—"

Susannah's convulsing body stilled in Jed's arms. She pulled free, a haunted look upon her glistening wet face.

"Hurry!" she said softly. "I can't bear even a minute."

They filed out, the bald man last. Dizzily Jed sprang from his covers and found a chamber pot under the rough-hewn bedstead. Then he pulled the buckskin clothing on, scarcely noticing the fine trim, dyed quills, trade beads, the bold images of Sun on the breast of the buckskin shirt and the other rich designs. He felt the rankness of stale sweat on him and wished he might bathe, wished he might present himself clean and fresh and outfitted in a fine blue tunic with gold epaulets and polished black boots.

Everything fit perfectly. He peered down at himself, at the soft high black moccasins, the buckskin britches and thigh-length shirt. At the dyed belt he had cinched at his waist.

I'm a stranger to myself, he thought. I'm a dragoon captain, not . . . this. And yet, these things had been sewn and beaded with loving hands. Susannah flooded through him. The mystery of it! How could she be here? Where was Colonel St. George?

They awaited him in a small parlor. Susannah stood swiftly as he entered, her eyes searching his, her face dry now, and radiant with softness and vulnerability and beauty.

"You eat," said Mrs. Culbertson softly, steering him to a table with coffee and a steaming gruel of some sort.

He sipped the coffee, savoring its aroma, wondering how long it'd been since he'd tasted any.

"Tell me," he said hoarsely. "Tell me everything."

* * *

They walked hand in hand along the riverbank, past the great village of Blackfeet waiting to trade. He scarcely noticed the bright lodges, the scampering naked boys and yapping dogs, the smouldering cookfires, the squaws who peered sharply at the fine designs on his buckskin shirt, done in lemon and black and apricot tones, and covered their mouths with their hands in wonder.

His thoughts were solely on the woman beside him, whose warm hand he held; the softness of her brown hair and the tall, clean-limbed figure within her blue dress. They hadn't talked much, discovering they were really strangers. He scarcely knew her and couldn't think of much to say. She'd turned shy and reserved, stealing glances at him as if at a stranger, afraid to look boldly. It troubled him. Had he changed? Had she? Did they love each other?

She hadn't said so; neither had he.

Strangers. Different. He knew the long journey and the ordeals had changed him, but he didn't know how. She seemed different too. It shocked him that she had come here, insisted on it, badgered her father, fled from the safety of Constable and his troopers, hired that obvious voluptuary of a man to guide her. She'd said little about that, she and that fur company man traveling alone, unchaperoned, across hundreds of miles of prairie. She'd said too little.

The ribbed white sky lay low, keeping the day cool and anonymous. He'd get used to her, he thought. Even if she'd been reckless and head-strong, coming up the long river, fleeing the safety of her chaperones. Susannah would be . . . difficult. Flattering in a way, this daring trip of hers.

She walked beside him, her glances upon the silvery river and black cottonwoods and the endless parade of tall people hurrying on their errands in festival finery that glowed brightly even under the white heavens. An ancient woman paused, squinting, and then muttered something Jed couldn't understand, her old claw of a hand tracing and patting the sun symbol on his chest, exclaiming sharply.

"I don't know what that's all about," he said. "Maybe we shouldn't get too far from the fort."

Susannah didn't reply, but her hand tugged him onward, away from the village, past the last of the squaws digging roots, past brown boys in loincloths herding shaggy ponies, past dark islands flocking with magpies, until at last they'd escaped the villagers. She said nothing, but her eager hand had pulled him there beyond the safety of the fort, pulled and tugged.

Then at last, when cool privacy enveloped them, she relaxed. "Tell me about the letters, Jed. And the journal."

"It's nothing," he replied. He didn't want to tell her; she wouldn't understand. There were things that bonded men together; hardship and death. Honor. How could he ever explain his need to deliver Elwood's journal to his superiors?

"Is it a secret?"

"No, a bond."

"What's in Elwood's journal? You said it contained things against you. You said it lightly, wanting it to slide by me."

He felt annoyed by her probing and couldn't answer.

They stood silently in the still afternoon, aliens.

"I'd like to know," she said firmly. "I'd like to understand. I'd like to read the letters you wrote for those dying men. Please share this with me, Jed. Please. We've a life to share. And—I'd like to know what happened between you and Mr. Elwood. Did he hate you? That journal—why are you . . ." Her voice faded into nothing as she sensed his anger.

"I do what I have to," he replied sharply. "If you can't understand that, then you don't understand me."

Susannah didn't reply. She pulled apart, putting distance between them. "Are we still engaged?"

"Of course," he said shortly. He couldn't imagine why things were going sour. Had he changed? Had she? Had they each been living on illusions and fantasies, blind to each other's nature?

"Do you love me?"

It angered him for some reason. "Why ask? Do I act like I do not?" he parried.

"I'm a—maiden, still," she said softly.

He spun her around and stared into her eyes. "Why did you say that?"

"So you'd know," she retorted coldly. "Because you doubt."

"I haven't doubted!"

She smiled wanly. "Jay Constable. Jean Gallant."

He let her go and went to stand on the riverbank, peering into the murky water, feeling the grayness of the afternoon. She didn't belong here. A lady, an officer's daughter. Here.

"Jed," she whispered softly. She tugged him around and opened his arms and slipped between them, hugging him, pressing herself against the length of him until he felt her melting against him, felt her hands tugging at his shoulders, sliding to his waist, drawing his buttocks hard against her loins. Desire flared in him. She kissed his lips, not liking his beard but finding his lips and pressing hers to them.

He hugged her tentatively, his big rough hands feeling the linen fabric, the contours of her back, the bumps of her spine, the smallness of her waist . . . Was this Susannah? Here? Two thousand miles from Fort Leavenworth?

She lifted her lips to his ear. "I love you, Jed."

He hugged the stranger harder.

"We're alone," she whispered.

"Yes," he said hoarsely. She was giving herself to him.

His own desires raced through him, and he kissed her hungrily, caressing and demanding.

Until she wept. She pulled free, sobbing, her hair disheveled, sinking at last to her knees in the soft grasses, tears welling steadily from despairing eyes.

At last she calmed herself and looked up at him. "Let's go back," she said. "You've shut me out. It's over."

Jean Gallant didn't fear Alec Culbertson, even if the man headed the Upper Missouri Outfit and was a partner of old Chouteau himself. The *bourgeois* frowned up at him from behind his cluttered plank desk in the shadowed, redolent office.

"Did Kipp send you?" Culbertson asked.

"*Non,* the beautiful lady, she ask me to take her. I look at her, I see a beautiful woman in distress, a young woman eager to find her *capitaine,* a young woman needing Gallant's help and understanding, and love, and a good strong man to—"

Culbertson grinned. "How much?"

"Hundred. She offer me a hundred to take her to the Sun River."

"I'm docking you twenty, as long as you were on her business and not ours."

"I'm still ahead, *oui*? I thought maybe I would join the Opposition."

Culbertson laughed. "The keelboats will be here tomorrow. Gallois says they're ten miles down. Tomorrow, the bedlam starts, and I won't have time to look after our guests. I'm turning the keelboats around immediately, as soon as the trade goods are shelved, and I'm sending Miss St. George and Captain Owen down on them. Separate keelboats. You too. Kipp needs you at Union. We still have five hundred bales to go down, and trade goods to bring up."

"Ah, a pity. Angry lovers make a bad journey. You put Owen on one boat and the beautiful woman on the other. I will chaperone the beautiful woman, yes? I am very good at consoling the broken heart of a woman."

"I'm sure you are, Gallant. Are you perhaps the reason for their quarrel?"

"*Moi? Non, non,* she wouldn't let Gallant touch her. Not even pat her arm. Not a pinch. Not a hand on her saucy *derriere.* Not even kiss her good night. Not even help her out of her wet dress when it makes rain."

"That's what I thought, Gallant. Thanks to you, we've got a pair of bitter lovers and a broken engagement."

"Hah! It's nothing. Lock them in a room and it will all come out fine in a day or two."

Culbertson glared. "You're going down on Owen's boat, not hers, Gallant."

Dismissed, Jean Gallant wandered into the quiet yard of the somnolent trading post and watched a youth unload cordwood from a cart. Tomorrow, the madness. Today, the waiting. He glanced at Culbertson's house, where Susannah St. George, her face pinched and drawn, cloistered herself with Natawista. The captain had removed himself and stayed in the engagé barracks, wandering out in the Blackfeet village with thunder in his face.

Mon Dieu. There were wives to visit out among the Piegans and Bloods, but the *bourgeois* was sending him straight down the river! Ah, well, he would console the widow St. George—almost a widow. Let her weep in his arms. That seemed compensation enough. That and making eighty dollars in gold, even after losing his pay.

He found the captain brooding on the riverbank up near the Opposition's Fort Campbell, the blue haversack clutched in his hands as always.

"Ah, Capitaine, it is a hard thing losing a woman, yes?"

Owen didn't answer, staring at the sliding waters with a face of granite.

"What you need is a sweat. It makes all the poisons of the body go away. It makes the mind new and the soul new, yes? Maybe I talk with the medicine men, yes?"

"I prefer my own company, Gallant."

"The steam, it make your rivers run. You rub the sweet grass and sagebrush too, makes you clean and smell good. The medicine men sing the songs and pretty soon the bad goes away, all the woman thoughts, and you are new."

"Leave her out of it."

"I'll go find the medicine men. You do it now. Tomorrow the keelboats arrive and then they take you back down to Fort Union. Right away they go back for more trade goods. You and—You each go on a different boat, yes?"

"I don't want to sit naked in a sweat lodge and—"

"Ah, it makes you new. They will be pleased. They know you are a brave man, carrying the letters from the dead. They will be pleased to sweat with you."

Captain Owen stared into the blinding river, not resisting.

"Trust Gallant," the Frenchman said, rising.

Gallant bestowed a small gift upon Hatchet, a young medicine man of the Small Robes Piegans. He watched the limping youth summon squaws and elders to begin preparations and then walk down to the riverbank and settle silently beside the somber captain, beckoning. Slowly Owen stood and followed.

A sweat for the *capitaine!* Gallant himself preferred a woman, but these English-speakers, for them a sweat could be better. *Oui*, a sweat and a medicine chant could drive a woman out of the soul. Or permit her to enter it. One way or the other. It drove his Gallic mind wild to see them separated by hurt and pride, or whatever it was. Gallant would cure. He, Gallant, was wise in all matters of love. Let it begin, let it end; one way or another. Now who among all the Yankees would have thought of the true cure, a sweat? In the sweat lodge of Hatchet's people? Ah, it took the Gallic soul to see the truth of the Blackfeet way. Ah! Was ever a man so experienced at love as Gallant? Was ever a man so generous, sacrificing his own desires so the *capitaine* and his lady might find love? Cupid!

That Culbertson, dour Scot, putting lovers in separate *bateaux*. Ah! Puritan! Fou! As soon as Fort Benton disappeared behind them, Gallant would make a switch. The *capitaine* and his lady in one keelboat, with Gallant and the rivermen in the other.

The following afternoon, amidst cheers and salutes and rifleshots and with crowds racing along the riverbanks, the two water-stained keelboats appeared, poled up the unruly green river by burly rivermen. The festive moment! Excited squaws flaunting their best finery, proud warriors and hunters in ceremonial skins and furs, dun dogs. Neighing ponies crowded and roiled along the muddy levee fifty yards from Benton's portal. From above the mud walls, Culbertson, his fat nose red, peered down on the swirling uproar, his arm around his quiet, slender Natawista. The fort's engagés slapped backs and traded jests with the weary cordelliers and then began hefting mountains of goods out of the holds and down wobbling planks to the shore. The Piegans and Bloods, Assiniboin and Cree watched eagerly as bolts of scarlet and blue and golden trade cloth vanished into the fort. Candy-striped blankets, heavy black pots and skillets, copper kettles, gleaming muskets, barrels of powder, heavy pigs of silvery lead, boxes of beads, bags of tobacco, aromatic in the June sun, hoop iron, fat sacks of sugar and coffee beans, dried fruits. Mirrors and geegaws, ribbons of every rainbow hue, felt hats, conchos, buttons and hooks . . .

Gallant watched it all paraded in on the soaked backs of laborers, hoping Culbertson wouldn't spot him and put him to work. Not Gallant, the senior man. He watched the fort's men wrestle certain dark casks straight to the Culbertsons' house and knew the spirits had arrived, somehow smuggled, as always, past the confiscating military at Leavenworth. Gallant eyed the *capitaine* lounging at the gate, who looked for all the world like an Indian in his fine skins, with his coarse black hair touching his shoulders. But for the beard, Owen might have been Blackfoot. Tonight the engagés' barracks would rock and roister. Tomorrow, bleary-eyed, he and the *capitaine* and the woman and the boatmen would head down the great river. Gallant peered around for a glimpse of Susannah. He'd scarcely seen the pinched white face of the young mademoiselle the last day or two. He saw nothing. She'd taken to her chamber, at least until the morning. Ah, love! How sad the ways of young lovers! He wished they could be like himself, like Gallant. But he had a cure, *oui*. As *capitaine* of the keelboats, he had a cure.

Chapter Eighteen

The keelboats drifted past fantastic bluffs with white spires and mina-
rets, grotesque fantasies carved from chalky rock; past forbidding
brush-choked coulees and dark shores that hid the high plains above.
The whirling green water sucked the little shiplapped hulls ever eastward, the waters of the great river gurgling and throbbing, wooing and
alarming as the boats swept past white water and boulders, rooted
snares and shallows behind secretive black islands.

Susannah noticed little of it from within her low shadowed cabin
amidships. Oddly, that rogue Gallant had tried to put Jed on her boat,
but he'd refused all entreaties. So they swept down the river separately.
She glimpsed him often as he sat brooding on the deck of the forward
ship, a strange, bearded, long-haired figure unlike the Jed Owen she'd
known. Gallant said he'd talked Jed into a sweat. She could scarcely
imagine what an Indian sweat lodge might do, but Jed had emerged with

glossy hair and the scent of fresh sagebrush about him, and a look in his eye that seemed less stony.

Not that it mattered, she thought. He remained a stranger. This sojourn in the wilderness, over a year out here, had transformed him into a person she no longer knew or understood, a person who savagely shut her out of his life.

She understood least of all his sensitivities about the letters and mementos he'd written and collected from his dying command. Wherever he had walked around Fort Benton, he clutched his blue haversack to him as if it contained the secret of life. Even now, as he scowled on the foredeck of the keelboat ahead, he hugged the haversack to him as if the whole world were trying to rip it away.

It puzzled her. That bag signified whatever it was that separated them now. What did it mean to him? She could scarcely fathom his thoughts about it. He'd promised dying men he'd deliver these letters to loved ones. The other things too, the locks of hair and tintypes. Was that simply loyalty? Yes, but it was more: faithfulness, love, caring. And honor. Mr. Culbertson had told her Jed had wrestled Kootenai and Blackfeet for that bag, fought like a man demented, if the Piegans' stories were true. Faced death for that bag, refused to die of scurvy for that bag. Somehow, some way, those letters and mementos of dying men had become his reason to live, replacing her. He'd lived to fulfill a promise, a bond between captain and command. Over the months of hardship the letters remained real, things he could read, things he could fight for, while the memory of her had evanesced . . . .

No wonder, she thought. Jed Owen had been consumed by his mission, his own strange honor, growing rigid of mind through the wilderness ordeal. What a shock she must have been to him! Out here, where his only thought turned on tattered letters and trinkets—and Elwood's journal. He couldn't fathom her being here, couldn't understand her coming, scarcely even remembered her nature from their few months of courtship. And he couldn't love her. Couldn't get around that heavy lump of a haversack that owned his soul. He found her a stranger, even as she found him utterly unlike the man she'd loved once.

She sighed, glancing out the small square window at the sliding shore, and felt Gallant steer the boat into the swifter current of the channel. She hated even to climb out on the rough plank deck, for then they'd have to confront each other across the running river. She heard the slap of waves on the hull and felt the boat quarter around something.

"Don't give up," Natawista had said, hugging her when they'd said farewell. "He is a good man. The symbols my people worked on his shirt say he is a son of Sun, the greatest god of the Blackfeet. He has the power of Sun."

Susannah wasn't sure she wanted him anymore. The man she loved had vanished. It desolated her. And yet, there he sat. Perhaps she could learn to accept everything. Perhaps when he returned to Leavenworth he'd be her Jed again, maybe even finer and stronger and more loving.

She clambered stiffly up the small companionway and out into the glare. The sun hurt her eyes, needling and stabbing off the river in this high July afternoon. She squinted at Jed ahead. He seemed not to notice her.

"Gallant," she said. "Next time we land, I'd like to move to his boat."

Gallant bowed silently, arms on the tiller. "Mademoiselle, you are not only beautiful, but wise. It is up to you."

She eyed him skeptically. "Why do you try to reconcile us? I'd think—knowing you . . ." She faltered.

"Ah, you don't know the French!" he exclaimed. "I am not happy until lovers are making babies."

She reddened. Gallant had boomed his words across the water, into the ears of the rivermen on the other boat—and the black-bearded man sulking on its prow.

Her chance didn't come until evening. They'd made good time that day, letting the river shoulder them mile after mile across a sunny wild. She had rehearsed the moment, but when it came she found it almost impossible, harsh. Yet she padded along the soft riverbank and climbed the plank into Jed's keelboat, settling herself silently on the deck beside him. He glanced stonily at her but said nothing, staring into a lavender twilight and a magic lemon evening star.

"I miss you," she ventured.

He didn't answer, and she felt resentment oozing from him, hot in the fragrant night. Well if he couldn't bend, she would. If pride blinded him, she had none and needed none to sustain her.

"I shouldn't have come here. I'm sorry, Jed," she said softly.

"No, you shouldn't."

"I don't need to know about the letters or what happened. I don't want them to be a barrier between us. If all that happened—the death of your men, their messages, and the mission you took upon yourself—is something you don't want to share with me, Jed, that is acceptable to me. I saw it as a barrier between us—that you were shutting me out—but I don't anymore. I only see someone I love. I want you just as you are. Whatever you wish to share with me, I'll receive joyously. Whatever is private to you, or is Army, or a thing too personal, I don't want to know. I won't ever pry into your secrets again, Jed."

He peered at her in the dusk, his gray marble eyes alert to her mood.

"I'll think about it," he said shortly. "I don't want to deal with it now. Not until Leavenworth, where you should be."

The curtness disheartened her, and yet she had him talking a little. She knew she was shaming herself, humbling herself in bits and pieces, but it didn't matter. One of them had to bend, to surrender, and Jed would always be too proud to.

"I'm happy just to sit here in this quiet place beside you and listen to the crickets and the river," she said. She wasn't quite sure of that. She wasn't quite sure she cared much for this new, obsessed, curt Jed Owen whose self-imposed mission had enslaved his mind and soul. Nonetheless, she sat silently, inches away from Captain Owen, feeling his presence in a hundred strange ways, sensing in turn his hot irritation, his irked calm, and finally as the skies deepened into indigo, a gentleness.

"We'll settle matters down the river, not here. I may not even be a captain then."

His voice startled her. They'd slid through a half hour of quiet, she with her solemn thoughts and awareness of the man she loved—perhaps—sitting beside her on the uncomfortable hard deck, listening to water thumping softly on the hull.

"Whatever you are, you're the one I love," she responded softly.

"We'll see. I have things to do first. As you know."

The army always had things to do first, she thought, remembering the hours, the days and nights and years her mother had waited at windows, in rocking chairs. Women waited. Some bond tied man to man in the army, and no officer's wife ever stood ahead of that bond, no matter how much she was loved. Susannah wished it might be otherwise, but that would never be.

"I will wait for you."

"You didn't wait. You came up the river."

She fell silent. Her ultimate gift to him—risking everything to find him, come to him, take him into her arms, give herself, body and soul, to him—had become an offense. It hurt.

"I still love you, Jed."

He twitched, discomforted. "It might succeed," he replied.

Might succeed. Love songs whispered sweetly in her ear. *Might succeed.* Jed Owen's own love song.

She wanted to yell at him, scream, hit him. Instead she leaned across in the blackness and kissed his cheek, recoiling from the coarse curly beard that rasped her lips. He flinched.

"It might succeed, Susannah."

He'd addressed her by name.

Around them, rivermen rolled themselves into blankets against the northern night. Gallant lounged silently on the other keelboat, within earshot, absorbing it all. She felt restless with Jed Owen now and stood stiffly.

"Good night, Jed. Whatever you are, you possess me."

She trembled clumsily down the plank and along the grassy riverbank to her own boat.

"Idiote!" Gallant muttered. *"Mon Dieu!"*

She slipped into the inky cabin, feeling her way toward the narrow bunk, as saddened and empty as if she'd found his grave.

Jed worried about the letters. They'd frayed and worn in spite of his best efforts to preserve them, and some were in tatters, falling apart along the creases, bent and twisted. Over a year had passed since he'd penned them on his field desk, dipping his steel nib into his inkpot and scratching out the last words of dying men.

Somehow they'd survived, though they'd chafed each other with his every step, been imperiled by rain and snow and storm, been torn from him and thrown to the earth, fought over. He'd finally packed them in dry moss to stop the chafing and battering, and that had helped, immobilizing them, together with the other things, the tintypes and rosaries and locks of hair, and making the faded blue bag stiff and fat. Still, the letters died a little each day, for he could not bear to leave the bag unattended, and it went everywhere with him, bouncing at his side. They died a little every time he pulled them out to read them, carefully unfolding the weakening rag paper to relive once again those terrible moments of agony.

At first it had been simply a matter of duty and honor, an understanding between an officer and his dying men. He'd deliver each letter if he lived, and comfort widows and sons and daughters and parents if he could. But it soon became more than that, and as time passed he remembered the death of each man more and more vividly, and the need grew larger in him to deliver those last words. Those letters had made death bearable.

Day by day as they skidded down the glinting milky river, Jed Owen relived the death of his command there on a nameless creek cutting through lonely windswept steppes. Down in the grimy cabin amidst bales of pungent buffalo robes, he opened his haversack and pulled out each battered letter gently and read it once again. Coppola's lay before him now, addressed to his priest. A confession, small sins, written in Jed's heavy tight hand. Nothing so grand as to offend the universe much, Jed thought. He had read it back to the private and then felt the peace that crept over the sweating, gasping man, almost as if Jed had been the man's priest, absolving him and sending him off to God cleansed and ready. Coppola had died a few moments later, slipping peacefully into eternal death with all things done as properly as life permitted, his burden lifted and transferred somehow to the letter in Jed's hands.

Jed sighed. He gently replaced the letter among the others, strapped down the cover of the haversack, and clambered out upon the bright deck. How could he share that moment, the peace he saw in the dying man's face when the letter was done, with anyone? Such things as that lay deeper than words, vivid images he would carry always in his soul. Things beyond sharing.

He found Susannah sitting solemnly on the foredeck, where she'd started to come each sunny day. He didn't mind her being there now, though at first it had irked him. She'd never again asked about his year in the wilderness or the contents of the haversack, and that made her tolerable to him. If she'd probed and demanded, he'd have dismissed her. He had no plans to tell her what could not be expressed in words. He could barely live with the idea of any army inquiry at Fort Union, having to describe such moments to the likes of mocking Jay Constable. The letters had become private things, and he would remain as silent about their contents as a priest about confessions.

"I wonder how we'll go downriver from Fort Union," she was saying softly. He pulled himself out of his reverie, faintly annoyed by her intrusion. "The boats have gone. *Mary Blane* and *El Paso*. I wonder who owns the *El Paso* now. He was a fine man, the master. Ricardo Sandoval. A man of great dignity. What a terrible fight."

"You shouldn't have come. I can't understand why Nathan let you," he replied. "This isn't woman's country. Just a couple years ago Indians massacred that mission woman Narcissa Whitman and her husband. Missionaries."

Colonel St. George must have gone soft, letting his daughter come up the river, he thought tartly. Either that or Susannah hadn't told the story quite accurately. Maybe she came against his will, came in her own willful unruly way. He'd noticed that about her. Susannah lacked a proper submissiveness.

She said nothing, not retorting as he'd expected but letting it ride. Maybe she was learning. They drifted past a band of wary elk, watering cautiously as the keelboats slid by. From the rear boat a rifle cracked sharply, ripping apart the morning peace, and Jed saw Gallant set down his weapon and steer the boat shoreward to where the elk slumped at water's edge, leaking red blood into the brown river. Odd how the river changed color from hour to hour, day by day. Elk meat tonight. Unconsciously he gazed sharply at the horizons on both sides of the river to see whether the shot had attracted hostiles. Nothing.

Jed had no weapon and it bothered him. He had the new burden of protecting Nathan St. George's daughter and no means to do it. He'd seen only four muskets, old muzzle-loaders, among the eight engagés who'd drag the keelboats back up the endless river to Benton, probably supplemented by others from Fort Union. Four muskets plus Gallant's breechloader. Still, the wide Missouri itself could be a defense and bastion.

By midday the July sun hammered down mercilessly and the day had become still and oppressive. He peered at Susannah's reddened and blistered face, dismayed.

"We'd better take cover before we get the sun sickness," he said.

She nodded but didn't move.

The boatmen had wide felt slouch hats to protect their dark faces, but their bodies dripped sweat even while they languished on the decks with nothing to do.

They slid by the mouth of a large river debouching from the north and watched the two currents mingle in strands of different color, aquamarine and tan.

"Milk River," called Gallant from the rear boat. "Tomorrow we are at Fort Union."

Susannah stood, dusting off her worn jade dress, which had mends in it. "You're right. We've had too much sun," she said. She started for the cabin, his cabin. Hers was on the rear boat. He followed, faintly annoyed.

She settled herself on a bale of dark robes while he lounged back on the narrow bunk. The air lay pungent and quiet and stifling, but it was better than the harsh glitter of the river.

"Tomorrow they'll know. You'll face Jay," she said, again opening gentle conversation.

He wished she'd be silent or return to her own boat, but she couldn't do that unless they asked the rivermen at the tillers to arrange it.

"I don't know why they sent him. I suppose because he's not competent to do anything else."

"He took command. On the *El Paso*. He saved me and put his six men to good use. Even the clerks, Jed."

"It's his attitude."

She stared out the small porthole at the blinding glare of the river, avoiding the argument that Jed sought.

"Is it just an inquiry? Are they going through the motions to keep Washington City happy? Do you know his orders?"

"Yes, I know his orders. My father told me. They're upset in Washington. It's not just army missing—no one cares much about soldiers, I'm afraid. Two commissioners from the new Indian Bureau. Politics. They sent Jay up here with plenary powers."

Jed groaned. Jay Constable might be a lieutenant, but in the matter of the inquiry he'd be commanding general, able to compel sworn testimony, seize evidence, act like some petty tyrant, lord it over Jed Owen . . .

"We'll see what Jay's made of, then. And I'll see what I'm made of," Jed muttered.

"I think Jay'll be happy to see you, Jed. His inquiry will be a success.

Thank God you're alive. The whole mystery solved. A clear picture of what happened. There's nothing the army hates more than mystery, disappearance, questions."

"Thank God I'm alive and eleven others dead," Jed mocked. "It doesn't matter that they all died, just so I'm alive to tell about it."

"Jed—"

She looked crestfallen, but he didn't care. More important things troubled him, namely the letters. And Elwood's journal. He'd turn over the journal to Constable, but not the letters. Those were private correspondence between dying men and their loved ones, and he'd be damned if he'd turn them over to that smirking lieutenant.

All afternoon they rounded the pearly oxbows of the Missouri, watching the shadows and beams of light in the tiny cabin swing as the keelboat took the curves. She watched him silently from her perch on the bale of robes, venturing nothing, a puzzled desolation plain upon her face.

They anchored that night in a steep-sided gorge, unable to see the stretching plains far above. The heat lay heavy, and small flies and gnats plagued them mercilessly. As soon as the keelboats slid to the brushy shore Susannah slipped off Jed's boat, wincing as the burning deck scorched through her thin shoes. He watched her go, relieved. All the while she'd been there in his cabin he'd felt trapped and restless. She'd been a burden. He and the rivermen would have splashed in the river to cool off now and then but for her.

Tomorrow, then. Tomorrow he'd tell the world what had happened. Tomorrow he'd turn over Elwood's journal. Let them make of it what they wanted. He would tell them about the lies, but whether anyone believed him didn't matter to him. In fact, the attitudes Elwood ascribed to him would only make him popular in some quarters.

But the letters and trinkets would be another matter.

Chapter Nineteen

Drunken Indians. An amusing mystery. Vast boozy numbers of them staggering to the trading window, and nary a drop to drink. Lieutenant Jay Constable found it an engaging conundrum. In the vast brassy flats beyond Fort Union hundreds of lodges forested the sky, and bedlam reigned. A polyglot crowd of Assiniboin, Cree, Sioux, Crow, Gros Ventre, and God knew what else, all enjoying a temporary truce in the neutral ground of the old stockaded fur post during the peak of the trading season.

Most assuredly drunk, he concluded, wandering among them while coppery squaws with squalling babies and lithe bronze men with black braids eyed him warily. Magic! He wandered back to the trading window again, watched the small portal swallow fine black buffalo robes, mostly splits sewn down the center but sometimes whole skins, and belch out an amazing variety of kettles, blankets, muzzle-loaders, powder, lead, sugar—how they all liked sugar!—geegaws, ribbons for m'lady's hair, dresses, tin looking glasses for the warriors to admire themselves in.

But not a drop to drink.

Constable cornered the desperately busy, sweating James Kipp.

"Drunken Indians."

Kipp paused, set down the four-point blanket he was carting, and stared. "I can't imagine where they got it. Must have brought it down from Canada."

"Of course," mocked Constable.

Spirits had always been the lubricant of the fur trade, totally illegal by several acts of Congress. All the Missouri packets stopped at Fort Leavenworth for inspection, and the army had been diligent about it, confiscating everything except small boatmen's allowances.

"It's bad for the tribes. Makes them trade poorly, squander their robes on a drunk," said Kipp.

"You're so right," said Constable. "I imagine the presence of the army at your post this year cools trading."

The weary chief trader sighed. "Not really, Lieutenant."

Constable had the run of the place. He had loitered in the trading rooms, poked around the fur warehouse, probed the magazine and the various barracks, peeked into Kipp's great house, snooped around in every corner of the great American Fur post, and come up with nothing. It amused him, being outfoxed. He had nothing to do anyway but wait.

The maidenly colonel's daughter had wandered off with an aging rogue of a trader, one Gallant—the name delighted Jay Constable. Wandered off, duly arriving at Fort Benton, where Culbertson had waylaid them and sent a runner on down to Union. The young lady would be back with the keelboats, and so would Captain Jedediah Owen, who'd appeared gaunt but otherwise in decent condition with a long story of cholera and captivity in the hands of the Kootenai, a tribe Jay Constable had never heard of.

A fine romance that would send the hearts of army officers' wives afluttering, he thought. When Susannah had bolted, and Gallant showed up missing, Kipp had headed off pursuit.

"Jean Gallant's a man of the wilds, Lieutenant. He'd run circles around your clerks and green privates, laughing all the way. No. She's as safe with him—ah, in most ways—as with the army."

"In most ways," the lieutenant had replied, his eyes bright. "Still,

I'm her chaperone. I'll think of something appropriate. You didn't need Gallant anyway."

"Best man I've got," Kipp had retorted sharply. "Broken no law, hiring on as a guide."

"The army makes the laws here, Kipp. And can invent them after the fact." He'd laughed easily, leaving the trader fuming.

And any time now they'd all wander back, even the illustrious dragoon captain. Constable's luck again. Now if he could just find where those spirits were being dispensed—no doubt the usual Indian whiskey, straight alcohol plus a few twists of tobacco for taste and color and large dollops of river water—he'd really make Kipp sweat. What an entertainment, to threaten the trading license of the great American Fur empire!

It didn't take long. A few blistering days later some Assiniboin boys announced to Kipp that two keelboats had reached the Milk. The next evening they'd be anchoring on the levee below Fort Union, Kipp explained. "The *Wyandotte*'s headed for Fort Berthold. I've sent a runner asking it to call here. We've bales enough, and you'll no doubt want to catch it back."

"I'm sure you're sad to see us depart," Constable mocked.

The trader eyed him dourly and returned to the business of grading buffalo robes.

In an apricot twilight the following day the battered keelboats slid up to the levee at Fort Union, almost unnoticed by the whooping tribesmen parading their new finery and howling raucously.

But Lieutenant Jay Constable watched with bright fascination as stout engagés dragged the prows of the boats up and tied them as well. That rascal Gallant seemed to be in charge. Wearily the colonel's maiden clambered down a plank and stood forlornly, somehow alone. How odd, he thought. He didn't recognize Owen at first, thinking the gaunt man with a wild head of black hair and golden buckskins gaudily dyed belonged to the fur company. But he spotted that blue army haversack clutched under his elbow, and he had that army look about him. Of course. Owen would have long since worn out army duds. He'd make an amusing sensation walking into Leavenworth like that.

Separate boats. Propriety for now. A proper show; the respectable lady and her officer. Still, they carried it a bit far, not even talking to each other. Ah well. Maybe their honeymoon was over.

"Miss St. George," Constable said as she climbed wearily past him.

"Returned to her chaperone after a little lark. Here I thought I'd have to explain sad, scandalous things to the colonel, and he'd—well, you know."

"Don't, Jay."

"Perhaps I should lock you up going down the river. Unless, of course, you have a husband? One way or another. Did Gallant perform the ceremony? Maybe Culbertson?"

She glared.

"Somebody has to govern the wards," he added as she swept by him.

Jed Owen approached dourly, alive and well.

"What a fine new uniform, Jed. You always knew how to dress. Just the thing for the ladies."

"Jay Constable. I hear you're investigating my command."

"Nothing much to investigate until now, Captain. Cholera took them all—except for you, of course. Officers and enlisted men have different rules and different luck. Whoever heard of cholera killing a dragoon captain?"

Some wild menace flared across Owen's face, so violent that Jay Constable stepped back a pace. But it passed. "We'll discuss it tomorrow, lieutenant. You convene your hearing and get your clerks."

"Eight in the morning in the engagés' dining hall," Jay replied. "You can tell us the whole sad tale, right down to how a lovelorn colonel's daughter fetched you out of the wilderness and brought you home."

Constable ducked the fist that exploded in his direction, laughing. "That's called conduct unbecoming to an officer, Jed. I'm a specialist in that."

He watched Owen climb toward the fur post, aware that the captain had been transformed somehow by his ordeal. So that was it. Miss St. George had found it in him, not liked it, and ditched him. Maidenhood intact. Ah, the colonel would be relieved, and the army would be delighted. Daft Owen. He'd dig into that tomorrow. Might be a national sensation.

A phosphorescent light lingered on as the boatmen toted bales of robes up to the dusty post. Gallant supervised.

"Ah, Gallant," said Jay. "All's well that ends well, eh?"

The French trader eyed the lieutenant amiably.

"Did you seduce her?"

"Mon Dieu! I tried, but it is impossible! Night after night I make the grand effort, I woo, I say sweet things, I tell her how strong Gallant is, yes? I peek and make her blush. I tell her she needs experience so she can please her *capitaine*. I tell her she's divine, too beautiful to waste on virtue. I tell her she's got too much virtue for her soul. I tell her to seek new things. But no. She has none of me. She keeps her lovely legs tight together for her *capitaine*, yes? Day by day, she make me sad."

"True love, Gallant. True love," said Constable.

"Ah! That is how the world goes, yes? I love her, she loves the *capitaine*. I sigh and groan all night long, yes?"

"What did she pay you?"

"A hundred dollar. But the *bourgeois*, Culbertson, he take away twenty in company pay. Not bad, eh?"

"Terrible, Gallant. Did you know that I was and am her lawful chaperone, by right of habeas corpus, dereliction and hocus-pocus?"

"No, I don't know that."

"I fear you've broken a dozen laws of the Army of the United States, Gallant."

"Mon Dieu! I never have heard of such laws."

"Ignorance is no excuse. You are a material witness. Tomorrow morning, you'll testify. You'll tell us everything, Gallant, right down to your seductions. And then, my friend, we'll just take you with us down to Leavenworth."

"Down the river?"

"I'm afraid so, Gallant. You should be back in a few years."

"But my wife? My child? Who cares for her?"

Constable laughed. "Which one, Gallant?"

Jean Gallant laughed too, uproariously. *"Au revoir,"* he said as Jay clambered toward the yawning black gate of Fort Union.

Susannah found her way to the engagés' mess hall, a rough grimy place with plank tables and benches, and a way of echoing every word spoken in its wooden confines.

Jay Constable had swung a table around as a dais. Four of his enlisted men stood smartly behind, at parade rest. His clerks sat ahead of him, with large blue record books spread out, along with inkpots, blotters, and an array of nibs.

No spectators. The fur post was engulfed in a frenzy of trading now.

Kipp sat on one bench, glaring. Jed entered, his beaded and quilled buckskin clothes brilliant in contrast with the somber blues of the soldiers. His vast beard and gaudy clothing made him seem somehow twice as large as they were. He avoided glancing at Susannah.

"I believe we're all here—except for Gallant. Where's Gallant?"

"Gone," snapped Kipp.

"Flew the coop?"

"Gone. Forget him. Ten regiments of your army couldn't snatch him from this wilderness. Now if you'll excuse me—"

"No, Mr. Kipp. I may need you to translate."

"But the trading season—"

"Drunken Indians," said Jay, leering.

Kipp subsided sourly onto the bench.

"We'll begin then. This is a hearing into the disappearance of a treaty command under Dragoon Captain Jedediah Owen. The clerks will record that last evening, the twenty-sixth day of July, eighteen fifty, Captain Owen appeared here after an absence of over a year, on a keelboat from Benton, accompanied by Miss St. George and a fur company employee named Jean Gallant. Now then, we'll begin immediately with the testimony of Captain Owen. Let me say, Captain, that we are pleased to discover that you've survived. Under my commission I may compel testimony, swear in witnesses if I choose, collect evidence either voluntarily offered or through confiscation. And so on. I'm sure you're familiar with all this. Now, Captain, if you will begin at your departure last summer from Fort Benton . . ."

Susannah listened quietly as the man she'd once loved, a stranger now, described in clipped tones the departure from Benton, the sickness that swept down on them suddenly near the Sun River, his halting the command in the only shade in sight, and the shocking swiftness of cholera morbus. Jed seemed impatient, snapping through it all out of duty, eager to stay free of army discipline a little while more.

She sat on the backless bench, feeling its wood bite her tailbone, trying to fathom the soul of that extraordinary man she'd loved and still might love. Changed, yes. But forever? What would he be like once he fulfilled his mission, after he'd delivered his letters? After he'd talked to the survivors—those he could reach, anyway—after the obsession that consumed him had fallen away and his life returned to the quiet routine of army duty? She'd wait and see, she thought. She would not surrender yet but would wait and see if her beloved Jed would come home to her. She'd waited this long; a few months more wouldn't matter. She could love him again no matter what trouble he got into, what rank he held, military or civilian. The thought of waiting, of Jed restored to her, warmed her as she sat in the dun mess hall high upon the Missouri and listened dreamily. *Wait.*

". . . Harrison seemed to be slipping fast. So I got my field desk and told him I'd get a message to his kin in Ireland. He—gasped it out . . ."

Jed mumbled now, and Susannah strained to hear him.

"Please speak up, Captain," said Constable.

But something had happened inside of Jed. He paused, mumbled a small dribble of words, and paused again, reluctant to go on.

"Louder, Captain."

"Sorry. Hard to—describe it. It was something . . . felt. Talking about it doesn't work . . . I can't describe . . ."

"These letters. Have you the letters?"

Jed looked up at Constable sharply. "Yes," he admitted.

"We'll want them."

"They're private correspondence, Lieutenant, privileged. One's a confession to a priest. Intimate letters to wives. You can't—"

"Evidence, Captain. We'll have them. Are they in that haversack you've got in hand?"

Jed Owen stared woodenly and then nodded.

"Is it true, what I've heard, that you've fought several times to keep these letters?"

Jed nodded.

"The clerks will record that Captain Owen nodded his affirmation."

It struck Susannah that Jed acted liked a cornered animal.

"That's a fine thing, preserving them, Captain. Now you'll surrender them to the inquiry for safekeeping. They're evidence—the best evidence we have, of course."

"Lieutenant—forgive me; I'd rather not. I gave my promise, my oath as a man, as an officer. I promised them I'd personally see to it—"

"Yes, of course. But they're evidence. You know that. Is there anything else in that haversack?"

"Some tintypes. Rings, each labeled. Locks of hair, labeled. Rosaries."

"Evidence. Excellent. A great service to the army, Captain Owen."

"No . . . *no*. Not for the army. For the men. For my men, my men. My promise, sir. I've made a promise, given my word. My word of honor. Don't you understand? My promise. If breath was in me, I told them."

"You are refusing to surrender evidence, is that correct?"

"Let me read the letters. Then you'll have the text. I'll read them slowly, and the clerks will have an exact copy, and your commission will be satisfied."

"The original evidence is what counts, Captain Owen."

"Then we can make exact duplicates, certified by the clerks, or yourself. You'll have duplicates. And I'll be able to give these letters—"

"Sorry, Captain."

"You keep the original letters and I'll deliver the copies," Jed cried hoarsely. "They're in my hand, most of them, anyway. I'll deliver copies, plus the personal items of the men."

Jay Constable paused. Jed seemed distraught. "Captain," Constable said lightly. "It's a fine instinct to want to take your sad messages to the next of kin. But nothing stops you from doing so. When we reach Leavenworth, you'll be able to pen letters to each of the kinfolk, visit some of them there on the post. Nothing stops you. But what you have there, the things in that sack, are vital evidence. The army needs it all to explain matters properly in Washington City. You know that. They have knives sharpened against us back there. The Indian commissioners' own letters in particular . . ."

Jed didn't reply but he would not surrender the bag. Susannah had never seen him that way, wild-eyed and gaunt, fanatical.

"Perhaps there is something else in that bag you haven't told us about, Captain Owen?"

"A journal, Elwood's journal. The Indian commissioner. He kept a daily journal. You can have that. I don't care about that. He attacks me in it, but I don't care. The army. Some men bend facts—lie outright—to serve their own purposes." He dug into the haversack. "Here!" he cried. He pulled out a buckram-bound blue book. "Take it!" He stood suddenly, marched as jerkily as a windup toy, Susannah thought, and slapped the book down before Jay. Some terrible foreboding filled her. Was Jed mad?

"Not enough, Captain Owen. The rest now."

"No!"

"You are resisting a lawful request from this commission. Shall I have my soldiers wrest it from you?"

"Not the way, Jay. You don't send privates to scuffle with an officer in this army. Not now. Not ever."

Something mocking lit Constable's eyes. He's enjoying this! Susannah thought. She could barely stand the drama unfolding before her. Her Jed half crazed and wrong, and right. The relentless cruel army grinding its way over everything.

"Confine me to quarters, Jay. Do it the right way. Confine me and bring charges back at Fort Leavenworth, as officers do. The army way. I won't resist. I'll go on down the river peaceably. I am on my honor."

"Your honor. Always Captain Owen's honor."

Jed stood and glared, defying everyone about him like some feral animal. His gaze raked Susannah, who shuddered under it.

Lieutenant Jay Constable stood behind his table, head cocked, weighing things, observing with bright knowing eyes. "Defying a lawful order," he said.

"Yes!" Jed snapped. He wheeled about and proudly marched toward the open plank door, where canary sunlight brightened the floor.

"Stop him," snapped Constable.

Two soldiers hesitated, unwilling to tangle with an officer. The two clerks gaped and failed to record the order. Finally one soldier set down his carbine and lumbered after Jed. The remaining young soldier, jerking spastically, snapped his carbine up, aimed at the buckskin-clad back, and pulled the trigger.

Chapter Twenty

She looked up from her reading to find him staring at her from the bunk, his gray eyes focused in the shadows. She returned the stare, saying nothing.

"Susannah. Where am I?"

"On the *Wyandotte*. In eastern Dakota."

"How long?"

"Eleven days out."

She watched him without feeling. Any feelings she once possessed had been crushed out of her. He stirred.

"When I was almost dead of scurvy, the thought of you, the image of you, kept me alive, Susannah."

"I'm flattered."

"Is the blue bag here?"

"No. Jay Constable has it."

He weighed that slowly. "I did all that I could," he whispered.

"Yes."

"Have you been caring for me? Have you been sitting there all this time?"

"Two weeks, except for naps."

"I love you, Susannah."

"Please don't talk like that."

The words lanced through her painfully. She hadn't heard those words in well over a year.

She busied herself then, spooning buffalo broth into him. They insisted it would be good for him; the fur men said buffalo was a powerful meat that would make him strong. She really didn't care, but she did it anyway, the daily feeding.

He'd barely clung to life at first, back at Fort Union, his breath irregular, with alarming pauses. And blood; they didn't know how to stop it from oozing out of the hole above his heart. Once he stopped breathing, and she shook him and waited, and then, slowly, air rasped into his lungs. After that, sweating, tossing, and moments when his fevered eyes opened and she saw madness.

They'd carried him gently down to the *Wyandotte* soon after it arrived. Its white-bearded master refused to stay a minute after the bales had been wrestled aboard.

"River's dropping. Far too late in the season to be here," he muttered. "We'll be fighting sandbars all the way."

It had been an accurate prophecy.

Jay Constable and his soldiers looked in on her frequently and relieved her when she accepted relief. But mostly she'd sat in the shadowed ivory room, wondering why. She didn't love Jedediah Owen and probably never would.

The Captain dozed again, so she did too, lulled by the familiar throb of the steam pistons and the churn of the paddles.

She had not cried. A scream froze in her throat when the carbine exploded violently in those echoing quarters. She saw Jed stagger and then topple like a great tree, landing heavily on his face, the blue haversack crushed beneath him. She edged toward the brilliantly white doorframe as they reached Jed and turned him over. Dead. Surely dead. The Blackfoot Sun dyed on the chest of his elk skin shirt blossomed red, and only its rays remained lemon. They carried him off expecting him to die.

"I said stop him, not shoot him," Constable had snarled at the blond private. "If he dies, so do you."

She had felt nothing and still didn't. None of the horror of it touched her. A distant sadness, yes, an abstract pity for one who'd fought so hard, so long, just to live. But he'd murdered the thing between them, strangled sweet springtime, and drained away her hope of a shared life of joy, of a hearth and home and children.

Now he dozed, a bit of broth wetting his chin, his chest clumsily bandaged in blood-browned sheeting.

"Damn you, Jed Owen," she muttered. Tears threatened. She wouldn't give in to them now. He'd been beside himself. Out of his head. Delirious. And now he'd awakened and said those words, said the one thing that could tear her heart to ribbons. *Love.*

She sat back savagely in the hard wooden chair and waited, refusing the weep.

She never came to see him at the hospital, and he told himself he wasn't sure he wanted her to. For weeks he lay in the grimy sheets of his cot, batting away green-bellied flies and staring out upon the back of the enlisted men's barracks where the latrines sat stinking in the August heat.

Colonel McGonigle arrived one morning and perched himself daintily on a bentwood chair, a stern silver-haired presence beside him.

"Jed," he began. "I'm glad you're healing. Up and about soon, they tell me. Lucky thing the wounds didn't mortify."

Jed nodded, feeling dirty and unkempt in the colonel's presence. The commanding officer's blue tunic seemed immaculate, and every brass button gleamed.

"I want you to know, Jed, that we've copied all the documents you brought back to us at such cost, and I've sent the letters and mementos off to the next of kin with my personal condolences. Damn fine thing you did, Jed. My staff and I are talking about some sort of decoration for you. But I do want you to know that all the things you preserved were sent to kin. They'll all bless you. When you're up and around, maybe you'll visit a few widows, write a few folks on your own. But that can wait."

Delivered, then. All done. He'd kept his promises. And yet the news left him hollow and without feeling. He'd long since forgotten that his news meant grief and tears to many people. There'd been only the one obsession: fulfill his promise to dying men.

He nodded as McGonigle watched intently.

"You have nothing to say?"

"I'm glad," Jed said, feeling somehow distant from it all.

"Perhaps you're wondering about the rest."

Jed nodded, waiting passively.

"Elwood's journal doesn't mean a thing in Washington City. They know the rascal and understand his designs. They honor you back there for what you did. You've nothing to fear, son. People in high places—I'm talking about the president and his cabinet—admire you. And you've got the whole United States Army behind you. We're proud, son. You're the sterling kind we want for our corps."

Jed nodded. That touched him more. He hadn't failed.

The commanding officer eyed him sharply. "You get your rest," he said, rising. "The doctors say you're—a bit off balance. That's how they put it, 'the man's ordeal unbalanced him.' You get yourself healed up and balanced up, Captain Owen."

"I had a duty to do," Jed said dourly.

The colonel nodded and patted him on his good shoulder. The other one, swathed in grimy bandages, ached endlessly.

Jed lay back against his cotton-filled creamy muslin tick, smelling his own rank body odor. Did no one in this gray pesthole ever wash, or think of bringing him a basin and soap?

His next visitor, three days and four hours later by Jed's weary reckoning, was Colonel Nathan St. George.

"Jed," he said heartily, grasping Jed's hand. The aging colonel sat down solemnly, making a deliberate act of it, sitting the way men do when a visit might take unexpected twists and the paths of conversation might drop off cliffs.

"By damn, you're looking better," he began heartily.

"How's Susannah?"

Nathan St. George stared out the dirty window with rheumy, troubled eyes and then back at Jed. "The truth is, I don't know. She keeps to herself. She sits at her window and watches the river, and blessed if I can fathom what she's thinking. But I worry, Jed. Oh, no, she's not right. Not right at all. I'm helpless. She walks in darkness. I try to cheer her up each morning and evening, but what can an old army buck do?"

Some wetness misted the colonel's eyes. He sniffed and stared bleakly out upon the dun August day.

"She hasn't come."

"No, and she won't," Nathan retorted sharply. "I get the sense that somehow you drove her off."

Jed slid back in his memory to the surprised and hostile feelings that flooded through him at Fort Benton, and later on the keelboat. "I wasn't expecting—I wasn't ready. I had other things on my mind."

"Other things! You're damn right you had other things on your mind. Too much on your mind. You're a sterling man, Jed Owen, but it's ruined by pride."

Nathan St. George had nettled Jed. "I did what was right!"

"Right! Right! Always so right? Aren't you ever wrong, Captain? You're crazy with virtue and I damn well call it vanity. Or pride—worse than pride. You hurt my girl. Hurt her! She came clear up that river bringing . . . a beautiful bouquet. And when she reached you, you tossed her posies into the mud! I could strangle you." St. George glared at him.

"I did what I had to," Jed retorted sullenly.

"Did what you had to! Yes, indeed—and didn't do what you should have done. Why, if you loved her you should have welcomed her! Embraced her! Will you ever find another woman like Susannah, who would come up the river to find you and give herself to you as she did? Have you ever heard of such love? Such caring? Risking everything, life and reputation, for you? But you broke my girl's heart. Broke it in two, and her with it! She's a broken mortal, Owen! Stabbed by a weapon as deadly as a steel blade. You thought of virtue and duty and all that, and you didn't think of love." He stood, creaking upward with the carefulness of middle age. "You're one of the best, Captain Owen," he said at the door. "Army doesn't get a man of your integrity very often. Wanted you badly for a son-in-law. You'll have a perfect career. Those records will shine; not a blemish or a blot. But you don't deserve my Susannah."

Jed still stared at the empty doorway long after St. George had gone.

In September Jed returned to his officer's quarters, had new uniforms made to fit his thin frame, and began light duty. In October the golden leaves slid to the frosted grass, piling up against brick buildings and scattering along gravel walkways. Jed avoided Susannah and she avoided him. Once or twice he saw her tall erect form at a distance, or she saw him, and both fled.

Unbalanced. Pride. An excess of virtue. It all fermented in Jed Owen, creating sadness and wonder and finally wisdom. Could there be such a thing as an excess of virtue? The pleasure he'd once taken in his honor slowly dimmed and he saw himself differently, as a strange, cold fish who'd thrown away his one chance at love. He thought of resigning. Her presence there at the post became unbearable to him. So near, and forever distant. Often he passed St. George's comfortable quarters, walking with eyes forward, not wanting to see what lay behind those windows, and not wanting to be seen. Sometimes in the course of his duties he dealt with the quartermaster himself. The colonel always addressed him in curt monosyllables, his old eyes alert.

November came. The river turned silver under pewter skies, and frost nipped his paths. Jed ran into Colonel St. George, and they exchanged brusque greetings.

"How is Susannah?"

The quartermaster colonel stared off into the cold skies. "Come have tea at four and find out," he said hoarsely. "I live in a darkened house."

Jed Owen stood stock still, feeling the icy wind pluck at his greatcoat. "I am honored."

"She may not like it. If she excuses herself, you'll understand."

At four, Jed found it hard to make his boots walk toward the St. George home, but he forced his feet in that direction, although they wanted to turn and run. He'd bathed and shaved and brushed and slipped on an unworn uniform, blue and brass and gold, and still he felt naked. She would not see his uniform.

Susannah answered his soft knock herself. She stood unsmiling, tall, the low sun honeying her hair and making her face glow oddly with anticipation. Her grace staggered him. She surveyed him thoughtfully, searching his gray eyes for something known only to herself, and then she smiled slightly.

"I'm glad you could come, Jed."

"I've missed you so much," he began.

She beckoned him in. Colonel St. George was nowhere in sight. They sat on rose settees and stared at each other over Haviland tea cups.

"I'm an army brat. I'm headstrong and do what I want and sometimes, Jed, I cuss."

"Susannah?"

"The army always comes between a woman and her man. It came between my father and mother; the army hurt them both. The army came between you and me. Men who endure mortal danger together form bonds that are larger than the love of man and woman." She smiled, and her soft eyes caught his.

"I hadn't thought of it that way."

"That's why I brought it up."

"Where's the colonel?"

"Floating around trying to shoot love arrows into you and me." She grinned nervously.

"He told me I don't deserve you, and I agree, Susannah."

"He told me you love me."

"He told you that?"

"He did. He's kept an eye on you. He says you're a better catch now than before a bullet started you thinking. You've learned something. Is he right?"

"Why . . . why, yes!"

"Damn it, Jed, why do I always have to help you propose?"

She tried to laugh, but she was weeping, and he leapt up to kiss the tears away.

0-595-32888-1

Schulz

13101144R00108

Made in the USA
Lexington, KY
14 January 2012